SAVE
STEVE

SAVE STEVE

JENNI HENDRIKS
& TED CAPLAN

HARPER TEEN

An Imprint of HarperCollinsPublishers

HarperTeen is an imprint of HarperCollins Publishers.

Save Steve

Library of Congress Control Number: 2020938934
ISBN 978-0-06-287627-0

Typography by Joel Tippie
20 21 22 23 24 PC/LSCH 10 9 8 7 6 5 4 3 2 1

First Edition

For Chuck

I

Today was the day I would finally ask Kaia Gonzales out.

I watched as she decorated her freshly painted locker with a sticker to "Save the Wetlands." It was the first day of our junior year. And that was our sticker.

Saving the Santa Clara wetlands had been our thing this summer. Along with a bunch of other local activists (most of them much older), we had held vigil on the edge of the nature preserve where a new condominium complex was going to be built. Kaia was always a little late, but she usually brought us Popsicles or spray bottles and was by far the loudest chanter. Watching her scream into a bullhorn at passing traffic was one of the most beautiful things I had ever seen. Together we had endured the blazing sun, melted peanut butter and jelly sandwiches, and a whole lot of indifference. But we never got much of a chance to talk until that one night. We were chosen along with a small group of adults to squat at the site, in order to prevent a bulldozer from sneaking in while the protest rested. Under the shimmering night sky, mosquitoes ate us alive while we tried to keep each other awake reading *The Uninhabitable Earth: Life After Warming*. One by one, everyone drifted off to sleep. By midnight, it was just Kaia and me. We finished the book together. Side by side we watched the sun rise over the marsh, wondering how many more humankind would see. I should have asked her out right then. It would have been the perfect moment. But the police showed up and we were all arrested. After, I'd had a bad reaction from all the mosquito bites and had to stay home for a week. By then the courts had stepped in and the condominium project was stopped. Which was great, except that I hadn't seen Kaia since.

Until right now. As I'd walked down the hall searching for my new locker, she had spotted me first and run over, her long brown hair brushing the tips of the words on her "March for Our Lives" T-shirt. I'd managed a mumbled "Hi" and she not only returned the greeting but had given me a high five. A freakin' high five!

And now our sticker was the first thing Kaia was putting up on her brand-spanking-new locker door. It was proof that it meant as much to her as it had to me. Right? The problem was, she was so active in everything. Another cause might soon eclipse ours. Today was the perfect day to ask her out. And now all I had to do was find the perfect moment.

2

Today was the day I would finally ask Kaia Gonzales out.

She stood at the front of Ms. Hahn's government classroom, leading the first meeting of the Diversity Alliance. It had been a month since I first chickened out by her locker. The right moment never came.

I had thought about doing it at the Gay-Straight Alliance meeting, but it felt too heterocentric.

Then I'd almost asked her at the School Safety Committee, but all that talk about school shootings was hardly romantic.

I shouldn't have been surprised when she arrived at the diversity meeting, but still, watching her stride up to the front of the room and call everyone to order sent shivers through me. She saw me in the back (I hadn't wanted to assert too much privilege) and she gave me a thumbs-up and told me she liked my

"White People for Black Lives" shirt. Now she was railing the group about its own lack of inclusion. I could feel the radiant heat of her anger wash over me like a warm Santa Ana breeze.

That was it. After the meeting, I would tell her how much she inspired me. Then I would find out if she'd seen that new Ava DuVernay documentary. And then I would ask her out. It would be the right moment. The perfect moment.

3

Today was the day I would finally ask Kaia Gonzales out.

I opened a box of posters and taped one to the cinder-block wall in the junior quad. Taking a step back, I admired my design and slogan for a Straw-Free San Buenaventura High—a guilty-looking kid drinking a milkshake through a big plastic straw with the words "Don't Suck!" It had been selected by the Committee to Reduce Plastics after a grueling competition and would finally be posted all over the school. I set one aside and signed it (ironically, of course). After I gave it to Kaia, she would appreciate my mix of humor and environmentalism and then I would definitely ask her out. All those other times hadn't quite been right. But winter break was coming, and what could be better than getting to know each other over tamales and eggnog?

4

Today was the day I would finally ask Kaia Gonzales out.

I stood behind her in line at the Earth First Coffee Company. I couldn't believe my luck running into her over the holiday. We'd just had a three-minute conversation about shade-grown, fair-trade coffee. Once I ordered my iced-blended mochaccino, I would definitely ask her out. It was the perfect moment.

Though this place was kind of loud. And she seemed like she might be in a little bit of a rush, and . . .

5

Today was the day I would finally ask Kaia Gonzales out.
It was Wednesday. We both liked Wednesdays.

6

Today was the day I would finally ask Kaia Gonzales out.

We were marching in lazy circles to protest the new great white shark exhibit at the Channel Islands Aqua Park. It was like Ventura's local version of SeaWorld, except smaller and with a worse reputation.

I watched Kaia's ponytail swing back and forth hypnotically each time she screamed "Save! The! Shark!" I didn't think she could get any more beautiful, but the ocean breeze had pulled her curls loose and the sweat from our three-hour-plus protest made her skin glisten. We'd started three chants together ("Liberty, not captivity," "Hey hey, ho ho, this shark jail has got to go!" "What do we want? Free the shark! When do we want it? Before it gets dark!"). She'd clearly seen the protest sign I had spent all night crafting and I was pretty sure she was impressed. She kept looking at it and then giving me a grin. Was she flirting with me?

She passed by me again. Wait. Had she just winked? Maybe it was allergies? Did allergies make people close just one eye? No. She winked. She totally winked at me. That had to be a sign that she wanted me to ask her out. Oh god. What if she'd been waiting for me to say something for months? Was it getting weird between us because now there was this huge unsaid thing that, for some reason, I just could not seem to say? I would definitely ask her today. She obviously wanted me to.

"Hey, Cam, keep moving!" said a voice, and I realized that I had become lost in thought and had forgotten to walk. The group collapsed behind me like an accordion. Todd Moon, a ponytailed aging surfer guy and leader of the Non-Human Rights Group that had organized this event, kindly motioned for me to continue. He was always extra nice to any high schoolers who showed up. He said we gave the protest "an edgy vibe." No one has ever described me as "edgy," but I still appreciated it.

"Sorry," I apologized, and hurried forward, this time not daring to look up at Kaia. I clearly needed to just focus on marching. "Save! The! Shark!" I sang, and let the winter air cool me down.

"Dude. Go for it." Todd gestured to Kaia. "You've been checking out that chick for hours. Nothing like protest tail."

"'Tail,' Todd?" chided Patrice, flipping her braids over her shoulder and glaring. "Really? You're still using 'tail'?" Patrice

9

Woodson was the co-chair of the group and put up with zero shit from Todd, or anyone actually.

The repeated use of the word *tail* stoked my anxiety and I tried to clarify. "She is not— I'm not trying to—that's . . . I just want to ask her out." Todd shrugged, disappointed at my explanation.

"Hey!" Kaia's impassioned voice rang out near the park entrance. I turned to find her scolding a middle-aged couple in Disneyland shirts as they walked past her. "That ticket you're buying is supporting the slow death of a complex and intelligent life-form! You have blood on your hands!" They ignored her and Kaia jousted her sign in their direction for emphasis.

Oh my god. She was so perfect.

"You know what? Let's call it," Todd announced to the group. They must have been relieved because the marching immediately dispersed.

Crap. I wasn't ready. I mean, I had been preparing all day. Actually, the whole school year. But . . . I wasn't ready. Luckily, Kaia was still scowling at the middle-aged couple as they bought their tickets so I had, at least, another moment. I steadied myself, trying to catch a full breath before she turned around.

"Well, what are you waiting for? The world's not getting any colder." Todd nudged me toward her.

I took a few tentative steps. Was this the right moment? I examined the setting. Sure, there was a bird-poop-covered giant clam fountain, but the aqua park backed onto a wide bay and the soft crashing waves and seagulls' cries that filled the air were as smooth and sweet as a Bon Iver song. The sun had nearly disappeared into the sea, deepening the sky to a royal blue with wisps of pink contrails. And Kaia was standing near a planter of flowers whose names I didn't really know, but they smelled amazing. It was kind of magical. And she had liked my sign. And she had probably winked at me. And we were saving something together again, just like the wetlands.

But the more I urged myself forward, the more my body tightened as one huge, unanswerable question loomed, the same question that had crashed over me like a tidal wave every other time I'd almost asked her out: What if she said no? I tried to imagine a life after that, but all I came up with was a black endless void. Complete annihilation.

My stomach clenched. My legs braced. My chest seized. Breathing was going offline. I gritted my teeth. Sunset, flowers, seagulls—I wasn't going to lose this moment. I would ask her. As soon as I remembered how to move my tongue.

Then she turned around.

"Oh, hey, Cam."

Words. Say words. "Hey . . ." Okay, not the strongest start, but not unrecoverable.

"You know, your sign . . . I've been wanting to tell you all day . . ."

"Oh yeah?" That was two words. An improvement!

". . . it has a misspelling." Kaia smiled and motioned up. My eyes followed her gaze until I saw, for the first time, that the words "Save the Shark" had a smudge on them that made it appear to proclaim, "Save the Shart." What was worse, the shark I had painstakingly drawn to look as harmless and sympathetic as possible now had a stain that, combined with the modified phrase, evoked a billowing, poopy fart!

Kaia stifled a laugh. "I don't think anyone else noticed, but it was distracting me all day!" I pulled down the sign, wanting to hide it, destroy it, make it disappear. "It's kinda funny."

"Yeah. So funny." I tried to play along as I furiously wiped at the smudge. I hoped it was some airborne pollutant that had landed during the march and not a freakin' typo I had completely missed. But the more I scrubbed, the smudgier it got. And the smudgier it got, the further the moment I had waited for all day . . . all year . . . slipped away.

Kaia took a big chug from her water bottle and then sighed. "Well, I think I'm screamed out for the day."

She was wrapping up the conversation. I had to redeem myself before she left. "Yeah, probably gonna need some honey tea tonight. For your throat." Great one, Cam. Now you sound like her mom.

"Not sure they'll have that at Steve Stevenson's party. But you never know. Are you going?" she asked as she spun the cap closed on her water bottle.

"To Steve Stevenson's? The guy who is incapable of passing a locker without drawing a penis on it? Yeah. I'm not super into alcohol poisoning and date rape." I laughed and was sure she would, too.

But she didn't.

Instead she just picked up her bag and continued, "Yeah. I know. Not your scene. But, um, you should come? It will give me someone to talk to."

Hold on. Was she going to Steve Stevenson's party? And was she . . . ? Did she . . . want me to go?

"Your sign . . ." Kaia warned. I looked down and saw that I'd absently let my sign go and a breeze had taken it into the air and right toward the bay.

"Oh my god. No. Stop!" I pleaded with the sign. But it was too late. It wafted into the chilly water, landing like a toxic shart-covered surfboard.

"Litterer!" a fellow protestor howled.

"You should go get that. That bay is already super polluted from runoff." Kaia winced, clearly embarrassed for me.

Torn in two directions, I reassured her, "I know! I— Um— I'm going, but yes! I'll be there . . ." And as I ran toward the bay, I clarified, "At the party! I'll be at the party . . ."

On any other day, the thought of going to a party at Steve Stevenson's house probably would have been as appealing as going to an NRA meeting at a strip club. While his parties were "legendary," I was pretty certain they were just the usual mix of boring teenage rebellion and horny drunkenness. But with Kaia there, it might actually be the perfect spot for us to bond over feeling out of place and detached from normal high school stupidity. So I laid all my best T-shirt options on my bed and searched for the one that said just the right thing. One that might start a conversation or that she'd tease me about. Or maybe we would even be wearing the same one!

The obvious choice would be the "Save the Wetlands" shirt. It was our biggest success. We had camped out together. How could she forget? But when I saw that the shirt had a permanent sweat stain from the last time I'd almost asked Kaia out, I thought I should take a different tack.

I held up my Princess Leia "A Woman's Place Is in the Resistance" shirt, but since I had never actually seen *Star Wars*, it might come off as a bit superficial. (My mom wasn't really a fan of fantasy and sci-fi and steered me toward stories about kids with disabilities or minority voices.)

"Destroy the Patriarchy, Not the Planet" didn't feel right for a party. I didn't imagine we were going to dance on top of any tables, but I also didn't want to seem like I was there to purposely bum everyone out.

"Books Not Guns" and my women's World Cup soccer jersey didn't feel quite right either.

I seriously considered my "No Human Is Illegal" shirt, but because Kaia was Latinx, I didn't want to seem like I was pandering to her.

Finally, I held up the forest-green shirt with the graphic of a tree and the word "Hugger" underneath. That seemed like the right mix of fun and thoughtful I was looking for. And it also said "Hugger," which couldn't hurt.

Tonight was the night I would finally ask Kaia Gonzales out.

* * *

I'd seen a lot of horrible things in my life—oil spills, riverbeds choked with garbage, baby sea turtles trapped in nets—and I knew all those things were more upsetting than what I was seeing right now, but somehow I couldn't make my brain accept it. This had to be worse.

Steve Stevenson stood on the edge of a diving board wearing an American flag Speedo, sunglasses, and a plastic lei, gripping a mic and "rapping" along with . . . was that Cardi B? Through the bass shaking my bones, I heard something about a little bitch and shoes and making money move. Yes. It was definitely Cardi B. In his other hand, a red Solo cup sloshed beer into the steaming turquoise water below. The rest of the pool was packed with people hanging from various animal-themed floaties, gripping their own Solo cups, whooping and cheering him on. God, he was everything I spent my life trying not to be. What was he adding to the world other than lame SpongeBob memes and a certainty that the beer industry stayed solvent? But everyone loved him. Why?

"Steve Stevenson is fucking hilarious," the girl next to me said. I turned. She had a flamingo inner tube hanging off her waist and a lei wrapped around her head.

"Um, I think you mean vaguely racist."

"Huh?" She blinked, confused.

I gestured to the atrocity bouncing at the end of the diving board as Steve dropped into a half squat and shook his ass at the crowd. "Sure, he's skipping over certain words but, I mean, this is the embodiment of appropriation. What connection does a rich white boy from Ventura have to the culture of hip-hop?"

"Maybe he just likes Cardi. She's my girrrrrl!" She swiveled her hips in the inner tube, knocking the flamingo's head into me.

"Really? A former stripper is your role model?" The girl, who I'd had Spanish with sophomore year, just looked confused again. "I mean, have you ever listened to her lyrics? What sort of message is she sending to young women?" Steve was a lost cause, obviously, but maybe I could get through to her. But the girl just rolled her eyes, hitched up her inner tube, and walked away. I sighed. Kaia would understand what I was getting at. I needed to find her. She was probably having a miserable time, too.

I scanned the crowd. It seemed like most of our class was here. People kept bumping into me, shoving past on their way to the keg. The only illumination was coming from the pool or the twinkle lights wrapped around the palm trees, making it hard to see anyone's face clearly. Warm water splashed onto my feet and seeped through my shoes as I inched forward. I saw Conner from PE and asked, "Have you seen Kaia?" But he just shrugged, yelled, "Timber!" and fell like a chopped tree into the pool. I continued, creeping along the slick edge of the concrete. Ahead was an empty area where I might have a better view. Still hugging the side of the pool, I pushed my way through the last few bodies. "Kaia?"

On the diving board, Steve stopped rapping. He tossed the

microphone to one of his bros, chugged the last of his beer, and chucked the cup into a bush. He pulled something over his shoulder. I hadn't noticed the black strap crossing his torso earlier. I did now. Because it was attached to a gun.

A big gun. The sort I'd only seen in movies or video games. Was it an assault rifle? What the hell was he doing . . . ? Why wasn't anyone screaming? Running? Resting the butt on his shoulder, Steve squinted one eye and aimed it.

At me.

He pulled the trigger. I screamed and dropped, automatically covering the back of my neck and rolling into a ball.

Splat. Splat. Splat. Something burst over my head. Specks of wetness hit my hands. For a minute the only thing I could hear was the blood pounding through my ears. When it stopped, it was replaced by a different sound: laughter. I uncurled. Looking up, I saw people doubled over all around me, their Solo cups spilling as they struggled to breathe. Then I saw it. Behind me, an enormous sheet was stretched between two palm trees with a target spray-painted on it. The whole thing was splattered with neon-colored paint. The same paint that now speckled my hands. I'd walked right in front of it.

Steve tossed the paintball gun aside and cannonballed into the pool. People screeched as they were smacked with the wave. Before I knew it, he was climbing out of the deep end and onto the deck next to me, water streaming off his body. He'd lost the sunglasses, but the lei still hung limp and bedraggled around his neck. I hurried to my feet, only to discover the front of my pants was soaked from crouching on the wet concrete. Steve grinned, huge and delighted.

"Oh man, that was fucking hilarious."

Of course. Of course there would be no apology. "Oh yeah. Ha ha. So funny. I had a perfectly normal reaction to getting shot at." I tugged at my pants, feeling the fabric cling to my shins.

"I didn't know a dude's voice could go that high."

And cue the misogyny. "Um, 'dudes' have a wide range of vocal registers." I glared at him. I wasn't going to give him a pass. No one else would call him out, but I would. "And the assumption that something coded female automatically equals bad or less than is not—"

Steve cocked his head, fully taking me in for the first time. "Do I . . . know you?"

My stomach flipped. Technically, I didn't have an invitation. But I'd assumed this was one of those parties where people just showed up. That's how these things were supposed to work, right? I mean, no one was at the door. Well, aside from the guy in a unicorn onesie and fairy wings, who was passed out with a half-eaten pizza next to him. But it wasn't like there was anyone taking names or checking a list. Or any parents.

Steve was still staring at me, waiting. I stuck my hand out. "I'm Cam. Cam Webber. Kaia invited me." It came out all in one breath, which sucked because it made me sound nervous. I wasn't. Very. I tried not to think of old movies where the nerd with taped glasses was unceremoniously thrown out the front door by the big popular guy with cool hair. I swallowed. Why was my mouth suddenly dry?

Steve took my hand, shaking it, looking even more confused, if possible. "Kaia?" Steve seemed to be searching his memory.

"Yeah. Kaia Gonzales. Have you seen her?"

"Kaia . . . Kaia . . ." He put his hand to his chin in a fake "I'm thinking" pose. "What does she look like?"

I tried not to roll my eyes. He clearly had no idea who she was. This guy probably had the entire girls' volleyball team in his phone, but I doubted a girl like Kaia would register. On the other hand, there were two hundred people here, it was dark, and it was his house. I didn't have much of a chance of finding her on my own and maybe he had seen her. "Uh, dark, curly hair? Brown eyes? This high?" I held my hand out to a level slightly below my eyebrows.

Steve shook his head. "You gotta be more specific. Am I looking for a Kardashian or a Swift? What's she working with?"

"I don't feel comfortable answering that on any level."

Steve gave a short bark of surprised laughter, then threw his arm around me. I flinched. Up close I could smell chlorine and beer. I felt my T-shirt getting damp. Suddenly, his face was inches from mine. His eyes were bright and a touch manic. He grinned. "I like you. You're funny. Let's go look for her."

Before I could answer, he started walking, his arm still over my shoulder. I was forced to stumble along beside him. Naturally, the crowd parted in front of us, with no effort on Steve's part. People just automatically made way for him.

Seemingly on a mission, Steve crossed his yard with vigor. "I don't know if you know this, Cam, but I'm a pretty popular guy. People from everywhere showing up. Some I don't even know. Like you! Still, let's ask around." Reaching the pool house, he yanked open the sliding glass door and shoved me inside.

It was even darker than outside, the music was even louder, and the room was humid from all the wet bodies. There were a lot of wet bodies. Holy shit, what was happening back here? My eyes darted around the room, but all I could see were limbs. Tangled together. Half hanging off couches. Pressed up in corners. Thank god the music was so loud because who knew what I would hear if it wasn't. There was literally nowhere to look that didn't feel like I was violating someone's right to privacy.

Steve walked into the middle of the room, stepping over legs and arms with ease, dragging me along behind. I mumbled sorry to the hands and toes I squashed, but no one seemed to notice. "Any of these body parts look familiar?" he shouted into my ear.

"Oh, um . . ." I stared at the poster of a parrot and a margarita on the back wall, too afraid of what I would see if I looked any lower.

"Cam, Cam, Cam. You are not making this easy." He put one hand up to his mouth and shouted, "Yo! Any of you people getting on Kaia?" There was a smattering of laughter from the room. "Is this Kaia?" some guy asked, and the redhead he was making out with smacked him and laughed, "Shuttt uppp." More laughter. Steve looked at me and gave an exaggerated shrug. "Guess not." Then, grabbing my arm, he pulled me back toward the sliding glass doors.

"This is a consent nightmare, Steve!" I shouted over the music as my foot kicked an empty plastic cup. "Everyone's drinking!"

Steve stopped. His eyes widened in surprise. "Oh, thanks, Cam. I missed that!" He turned back toward the room. "Hey! Is everyone getting consensually laid here? Cam is very concerned!"

There was an answering "Wooooooooooooo!" from the pile of bodies, followed by more laughter. A few fists pumped in the air. Steve slung his arm around me again, smiling brightly.

"Well, I feel better now! The search continues. . . ."

He dragged me out onto the pool deck. The cool night air hit me in the face, a shock after the sticky warmth of the pool house. My cheeks were hot. I knew they must be bright red. It was annoying. I had no reason to be embarrassed. I'd done the right thing by saying something. But my cheeks stayed red. And Steve noticed. Of course he did. His smile got even bigger. Sliding his arm from my shoulders, he grabbed a cup off the top of the nearby keg and expertly poured a beer.

"You want? You look a little warm." His eyes glittered with amusement.

"No."

With a shrug, Steve drank the beer. Alcoholic peer pressure didn't seem to be in his repertoire. He wiped the foam from his lip and then leaned against the keg, ready to settle in for a conversation. "So, you and Kaia close?"

"Oh, um, we're friends."

"But you want to get on that, right? Rub that scrawny little body of yours all over her."

"No!" I objected both to the scrawny and to the rubbing. Not that I hadn't had a thought or two . . . but it wasn't . . . and I always . . . "It's not like that," I mumbled.

"Please. You wanna ride Kaia like Aquaman rides a dolphin." Steve started thrusting his hips suggestively. I looked away, but he just thrust his way closer to me. "Kaia . . ." He closed his eyes and let his mouth go slack. I stepped back. He thrust closer. "Mmmmmm. Kaia . . ." Steve started moaning. People turned and snickered.

"It's not just about sex, okay! Kaia's amazing!"

Steve's eyes snapped open. He stopped thrusting. "Let's try inside," he suggested, suddenly all business.

We ended up in what I guess people would say was a den. Or a man cave. I wasn't sure, since my place had a living room and that was basically it for the "hanging out" areas. And even that space had a dining room table tucked into it. You could probably fit two of my living rooms in the space we were in now. A huge squishy L-shaped leather couch filled the room. There were jerseys under glass hanging on the walls—Lakers, Dodgers, Rams. All signed. A popcorn machine sat forgotten and unused in the corner.

A bunch of guys were scattered on the couch, hunched over

the controllers clutched in their hands. I tried to guess what game they were playing but I didn't recognize it. Something with lasers and aliens. Suddenly my vision went black.

"Cease fire! Cease fire! This is a safe space for Cam! He's afraid of guns!" Steve had covered my eyes with his hands. I struggled to get away, but Steve just gripped tighter.

"Stop it! Let go!" Finally, I yanked his hands down only to be faced with everyone in the room staring at me. The game was paused and its silence underscored the players' annoyed glares. Awesome.

Steve nudged me. "Maybe these guys know," he faux whispered.

"Uh . . ." I quickly ran through my options on how to get out of this with minimal embarrassment. Sadly, giving in seemed like the fastest way. "Have any of you seen Kaia Gonzales?"

Blank stares. A few uninterested grunts. Steve clapped me on the shoulder. "Sorry, buddy. No luck." He gestured grandly to the room. "Resume the bloodshed!" Someone unpaused the game and there was a blare of laser fire and explosions. Some sort of tentacled creature splattered into a million pixelated pieces and then my vision went black again as Steve covered my eyes and dragged me from the room.

I ducked out of his grip as we entered a wide tiled hallway. It was big enough and long enough to have those weird half tables pushed up against the walls every few feet. Steve was stroking my back.

"Shhhhh. It's okay now. The bad bang-bang sticks are gone."

I jerked away. "Dude, I'm not embarrassed by my natural fear response. It's totally okay to be afraid."

Steve shrugged. "Being scared is boring."

"Don't pretend that you aren't afraid of anything."

Steve thought for a moment. "You're right. I'm afraid you're ruining my party." He opened one of the many doors lining the hall and disappeared.

I followed him in and immediately started coughing. The room was filled with smoke so dense it was impossible to see anything but silhouettes. The stench of weed was overwhelming. I could vaguely make out a pool table with an assortment of bongs scattered on top. Clearly, Steve's friends were old school. "I hate you," I finally managed after a few more wheezing coughs.

Steve turned to me. He was close enough that I could see the fake look of hurt on his face. "Dude, that's harsh. After all this work I'm doing to help you find your girl?" He spun around and stepped farther into the smoke. "Attention, stoners! Has anyone seen Kaia? Cam here won't tell me what we're working with on the booty and titty front so I can't give you a description." Seeing my chance to escape, I crouched below the weed cloud and made my way back toward the door. I'd find Kaia on my own. Steve continued, "Also, does anyone know Cam? Anyone? Because I'm starting to think this guy's a ghost."

Waving away the smoke, I found the door and stumbled back into the hallway.

And right into a pair of khaki pants.

24

An adult.

Shit.

I straightened, knowing the weed still clung to my clothes, and hoped my eyes weren't bloodshot.

He was tall and broad, with pumped-up pecs that strained the too-tight polo shirt he was wearing. Close-cropped gray hair and a super erect posture that screamed ex-military completed the look. There was no question who this guy was: Steve's dad.

"Uh, sorry, Mr.—"

"Have you been drinking?" he asked before I could finish, his eyes narrowing.

"No!" I'd never been so glad I didn't drink. I had a feeling this guy was a human lie detector.

"Where are your keys?" He continued to eye me with suspicion.

"In the bowl by the front. Where the sign said to drop them." I gulped.

Mr. Stevenson's face split into a broad smile. "Then why aren't you drinking?" He pounded me on the back and slapped a beer he'd pulled seemingly out of nowhere into my hand. I stared at it, too stunned for a moment to do anything but feel the chill of condensation on my palm. Mr. Stevenson strode to a window at the end of the hallway and looked out, cracking open his own beer. "Look at that."

I hung back, but he gestured at me to come closer, so I inched forward. Looking through the window, I could see the full chaos of the party displayed. People chased each other across the lawn in swimsuits, pushed each other into the pool, made out against the palm trees, and danced with cups in the air to music that I could barely hear. Mr. Stevenson sighed and took a swig of his beer.

"Now that is what a high school party should be, right? Those are fucking memories." He clinked his beer to the one I had in my hand, then resumed staring out at the party, a proud expression on his face. It was my chance to back away. I needed to find Kaia in the next few minutes, and if I didn't, I was ready to grab my keys and bail. I took a careful step backward. Steve's dad turned away from the window and glared at me, his eyes flicking to my can. "You're not drinking."

"Uh . . . I . . ."

A door opened and a wave of smoke poured out, followed by Steve. Spotting me and his dad at the end of the hall, he sauntered over. "Hey, Dad. That Granddaddy Purple is the shit. Thanks. Gotta steal Cam, though. We're on a secret mission." He swung his arm over me.

Mr. Stevenson beamed at his son, his pride evident. "Have fun, boys. Don't do anything I wouldn't do." He chortled. Gross.

Steve steered me away, plucking the beer from my hand and leaving it on a table. "We wouldn't want to sully that temple of righteousness." I'd been momentarily grateful for being rescued from his dad, but as Steve dragged me down the hall, my irritation returned. I shrugged out of his grasp.

"You know what? I'm good, Steve. You can go back to your

karaoke or target practice or whatever."

Steve gasped, offended. "What? No way! What sort of host would I be? I mean, it's obvious you don't have any friends. Like, no one knows you. I checked."

"It's not like the whole class is here."

"Um, they kinda are."

"I have friends outside of school," I said, thinking of Todd and Patrice.

Steve clapped his hands to his cheeks. "Ohhh. Are they from Canada?"

I crossed my arms. "Kaia's my friend."

"Right. The amazing Kaia. You told me. So let's go find her! I don't want you to be lonely, Cam." Steve's tone was heavy with concern. I was a pacifist, but he was making me seriously reconsider.

We turned down a hallway.

"How big is this place?" I'd been wondering but now I had to ask. At this point, I had lost all sense of direction. It was one beige tiled hall after another.

"Hmmmm, five thousand seven hundred square feet plus the pool house?" Steve ventured. "My dad's a contractor. Does a lot of shit in Calabasas. This place is basically a write-off."

He pulled us down another hall while I contemplated what it must be like to live in a palace. "Running out of rooms . . ." Steve singsonged. "Where could amazing Kaia be?" I didn't bother to answer.

As we turned a corner, music that had been distantly

thumping suddenly got louder. A wide archway revealed a dining room with a table so big it had two chandeliers hanging over it. It must have looked super impressive and formal most days, but tonight it was being used as a dance floor. Girls were standing on top of the shining wood, swaying along with the music, the drinks held high in their hands occasionally spilling onto the table.

"Lots of medium-sized brown-haired girls up there, Cam," Steve observed. "Any of them yours?"

"Kaia's not mine."

"I hope not, because you're doing a terrible job keeping track of her." He crossed over to the table, helped a few girls to climb off in order to make space, and patted it. "Hop up there, buddy. Ask away!"

I crossed my arms. "Don't tell me what to do."

Steve just cocked an eyebrow and waited. I sighed and climbed up on the table.

"Hi. I'm looking for Kaia."

A girl dancing on the floor squinted up at me. "Who are you?"

"I'm Cam, Sadie. We have AP Bio together."

She scrunched up her nose. "I don't think so."

"He's the one who hates Cardi B!" I turned. Stumbling from the corner where she'd been dancing next to (or possibility with) an oversized vase filled with artistically arranged sticks, the girl from earlier weaved her way toward me.

Steve whirled around to face me, aghast. "What? A Cardi

hater? How did you get in?"

"He said she was a bad role model for me," the girl whined.

Steve gasped and clutched his chest. "No!"

"She glorifies being a stripper! How is that good?" I sounded defensive, but come on.

Steve nodded. "Ahhhh! Now I get it! You're here to rescue Kaia from my corrupting influence!"

"What? No—"

"With the beer. And the Cardi. And the fun. I mean, look at all this." He gestured to the debauchery around us. "Poor Kaia. She must be so frightened."

"That is not at all— Kaia can take care of—"

Steve cupped his hands around his mouth. "Does anyone know where this Kaia is so Cam can save her?"

"I'm not here to rescue anyone!" I wasn't. Kaia was obviously the last person on earth who would need rescuing. Not that Steve would be able to wrap his mind around the idea that there were girls out there who were as strong and independent as her. The only person who needed rescuing right now was me. From Steve. I just needed to get off this table and go home. At this point I was pretty sure Kaia wasn't here. It was obviously not her scene. We could laugh about it at the next Save the Shark meeting.

"Kaia's in the kitchen!" A girl ran into the room through another archway, waving her arms in drunken excitement. Behind her, I could see the glow of overhead lights and the corner of a granite countertop. My heart stopped. "I found her!"

she continued excitedly. "She's in the—" The girl vomited on the floor in front of the table. People leaped out of the way, shrieking.

"Oh my god! This is so exciting!" Steve squealed. "Our long journey is finally at an end. Just one more obstacle to surmount. The lake of vomit!" He said this last bit in a low booming voice and then gave me a shove, pushing me toward the edge of the table. "Go get her, big guy."

Holy shit. Kaia was here.

I didn't need Steve to push me. I jumped off the edge of the table and over the vomit and stepped through the archway.

Kaia. It took me a second to process that she was really there. But she was. Kaia was bent over a trash can, pulling out recycling and stuffing it into a bag, and I was pretty sure my heart was going to pound out of my chest.

Okay, this was it. I was here. The reason I came to this party was happening right now. All I had to do was walk up and say hi. She'd smile at me like she always did. I'd try not to explode with happiness. We'd talk about the party and the protest today and then I could mention how we first met at the wetlands. She'd remember that and laugh. And then I'd just . . . ask her out. And she'd say yes. Right? Of course she would. And if she didn't— Nope. I definitely wasn't going to imagine that endless black void. Not this time. Because everything was going to work out. It was. There were no misspellings. No stains on my shirt. Nothing that would make Kaia think less of me. I was ready. It was simple. Hi. Party.

Protest. Wetlands. Date. Hi. Party. Protest. Wetlands. Date. Now walk.

But my stomach clenched. My legs braced. My chest seized. And for some reason breathing was no longer a thing I knew how to do. Shit. It was happening again.

I just needed to walk to Kaia.

I put one foot forward. Toward the void.

My shoe squeaked on the shiny tile floor. Kaia looked up.

"Cam?" She dropped the bag of recycling with a clatter. "You came!" The smile on her face was so wide and real it hurt. And, oh my god, her shirt had a tree on it. My shirt had a tree on it! I'd picked the right one. So why did my body hurt so much? I'd finally found the moment. The perfect moment. We were both wearing tree shirts. At this disaster of a party. Alone together. And still I gasped for air as she approached.

Hi. Party. Protest. Wetlands. Void.

No!

Hi. Party. Protest. Wetlands. Date.

"Hi, Kaia." Even speaking was painful. But I urged out a few more words. "This party is awful, isn't—"

There was a whoosh of air as something swooped past me.

Kaia's eyes swung from mine. Her smile grew . . . brighter. And she extended her arms toward . . .

Steve.

And then he was there, lifting her up off the ground. Swinging her around. I heard laughter. Clear and happy. Was it hers? It had to be. It wasn't mine. Then she was wrapping her legs

31

around his waist. Her arms around his neck.

No.

No no no no no no no no no.

She tilted her face down toward Steve's, her smile softening. Steve answered her with his own, gazing into her eyes. She leaned down and . . . kissed him.

Kaia was kissing Steve Stevenson.

She was kissing him. And I was standing there in Steve's kitchen with empty cans rolling around my feet, not kissing her. Because she was kissing Steve. Why was she kissing Steve?

"There you are!" Steve said to her when they finally broke apart. "I've been looking all over for you!"

That. Asshole.

Kaia laughed. "Oh, sorry. I just saw that people weren't separating their trash and I got distracted."

Steve shook his head, smiling, and gently twirled a piece of her hair around his finger. "God. You are *amazing.*"

That. Fucking. Asshole.

Kaia giggled. And then she leaned forward and kissed him. Again. Steve pulled her more tightly against him and deepened the kiss. Oh god. They were using tongues. Kaia was touching her tongue to Steve Stevenson's tongue. I thought I was dying before but this was worse. This was so much worse. Because there was a giant hole inside me now. And it was filled with tongues.

As they kissed, Steve turned them so Kaia's back was facing me. He peeled one arm away and raised his hand. And then

32

slowly, ever so slowly, he uncurled his middle finger.

I made a sound. A sad, pathetic sound. And then I left.

Propelled by rage, I stomped across Steve's front lawn. He had played me. From the moment I'd asked about Kaia, he had played me. Steve must have been laughing the whole time. Every single room I'd entered, every time he'd coax me to ask where Kaia was, he'd been laughing. And he'd gotten the whole class to laugh with him. Because everyone must have known she was dating him. Of course they did. He was Steve Stevenson. The most popular guy in school. God, I was such a colossal idiot.

But worse than the rage was the other feeling. The one that threatened to overwhelm me every time the white-hot anger started to fade. Because once I stopped thinking about Steve, I started thinking about Kaia. Playing through my mind on repeat was every single moment I'd almost asked her out. By the lockers. In a meeting. At the coffee shop. At the protest. On that Wednesday. It had never been the right moment. I'd wanted it to be perfect. I'd waited for it to be perfect, but now . . . she was with Steve. When? How? Why? The questions tumbled through my head.

I squeezed my way through cars parked practically on top of one another, some even pulled onto the grass, searching for my faded blue Prius.

Tongues.

The image of Kaia and Steve kissing flashed through my

mind and I wanted to die. Dammit. Where was my car? I had to get home. I was losing it.

Tongues.

No. I wasn't thinking about that. I had to think of something else. An oil slick. A forest fire. Glaciers melting. Steve exploding like one of those aliens in the video game. Anything but Kaia's face pressed against his. Finally, I spotted my car, miraculously not boxed in.

"Giddyup!" a distant voice slurred. Across the street a guy with a towel slung around his waist and no shoes was yanking on his car door. "Giddyup. Gotta ride . . ."

Oh shit. He was going to try to drive. I dashed across the street. "Hey!" I waved my hands, trying to get his attention. "Hey!" The guy turned. I stopped, out of breath. "You're too drunk to drive. Get in. I'll give you a ride home."

Five minutes later, Giddyup was plastered against the passenger window, singing a country song I didn't recognize as we coasted along the nearly empty streets. Except for a few pockets near Main Street, the town was pretty quiet past nine p.m.

Tongues.

"Fuck!" I slammed my hands against the steering wheel.

Giddyup lurched forward, startled. "Dude! Not cool. My head's not doing so great." He belched. "Or my stomach."

"Sorry." I waited to see if he'd vomit. But once he slumped back against the window, we seemed to be in the clear. I had to ask him. "How long has Steve been with Kaia Gonzales?"

"I don't know. A couple of weeks?"

Well, it wasn't months. It was a new relationship. That was good, right? She couldn't be in love with him. Not after two weeks. Of course, I wasn't sure how anyone could fall in love with Steve, especially Kaia. He wore an American flag Speedo, for fuck's sake. But did that mean I'd missed my chance? If I'd asked her out earlier, would it have been me in the kitchen kissing her instead of Steve? Would that have been my tongue?

"She's lucky. Steve's the best." The guy gave a weak thumbs-up.

My head spun so fast I almost sprained it. "The best? Seriously?" All I could see was Steve's stupid smiling face as he asked me if Kaia was a Kardashian or a Swift.

"Yeah." Giddyup smiled and gave two thumbs-up. "Such . . . the best." It was too much.

"NO!" I slammed my hands on the steering wheel again. The guy jumped. "He is not the BEST!" I kept going. "You know who's the best? Me." I thrust my finger at my chest. "I'm the one driving you home. I'm the one keeping you from getting killed. Would Steve do this? Hell no! He's probably doing Jell-O shots off a pool floatie right now! I'm saving your life!"

There was a beat of silence. For a moment, the only sound in the car was my panting. The guy's face scrunched up. "Who are you?"

Enraged, I shoved all my stupid T-shirts off the bed.

"Gaaaaah!!!!" I stood in the middle of the rainbow of fabric and a terrible realization flickered to life. Steve had probably told Kaia everything. Why wouldn't he? It was too easy to imagine him leaning over with his stupid smirk, telling her how I was obsessed with her. That I was some sort of stalker who'd wandered around the whole party looking for her. I was so stupid. So fucking stupid! I deserved it. I'd waited so long. Why had I waited so long? I crashed onto the bed and screamed into my pillow.

I had to get back at Steve. Somehow.

I chucked my pillow across the room and brainstormed the worst thing I could do to him. Get a nationwide ban on Solo cups? Crash the *Grand Theft Auto* server? Block all porn?

"End his party." The idea was so good I'd said it out loud. I sat up, inspired. "I should call the police. There's underage drinking, weed . . . They would shut down his stupid party in a second! Even with his dad there."

I grabbed my phone and pulled up Ventura PD.

"Not afraid of anything, huh? I bet you're afraid of the cops showing up at your door."

But as I was about to hit call, my signed photo of Michelle Obama caught my eye. On the top she'd written the words, *When they go low, we go high, Cam.* Her warm, smiling visage stared back at me, asking if this was who I really was. Was I going to be just like Steve? Petty? Cruel? Selfish?

Was this where I went low?

"Goddamn it, Michelle!" I clicked off the phone and flopped back on my bed. I could only imagine Steve's giddy laughter if he ever saw her photo on my dresser. But screw him.

This wasn't the first time Michelle had stopped me from doing something stupid. That photo had watched over me since the day my mother and I had waited four hours to get it. That day I was one of the only teenage boys in the entire line, which was pretty common for us. I was also one of the only teenage boys at the Ventura Women's March and the local Planned Parenthood fundraiser. My mom and I always joked about it. Actually, I was pretty proud of it, even if my mom would always find a time to proclaim to the crowd, "I've got the best boy in the whole damn world!" I shouldn't have been surprised that when we finally reached Mrs. Obama, she had clearly heard my mother's unsubtle brag. "So, this is the best boy in the whole damn world?" she asked with a mischievous smile. I blushed and made a lame joke. And she laughed. Michelle Obama freakin' laughed at my joke! Then she signed my photo and told us how heartened she was to see me. When Michelle Obama looks at you with those deep thoughtful eyes and tells you she is heartened to see you, that shit stays with you.

"Okay, I can rise above it. I can go high," I assured Michelle.

Though now I felt even worse because I saw how weak I was. How quickly I was willing to ignore my own values because of some moronic proto frat boy with a shit-eating grin.

"I'm so stuuuuppiiidd! I'm the worst!" I screamed.

Knock. Knock.

I shouldn't have screamed.

"Cam?" My mom, her worry evident even through the closed door.

"Sorry, Mom."

"You okay?"

"I'm fine."

But she opened the door anyway and peeked in. "You sure?"

"I'm fine."

She tilted her head, confused, and motioned to the crumpled pillow on the floor. "Oh, okay. Because your pillow called and wanted to file an assault charge."

"Very funny."

She smiled and walked over to my bed. "What's wrong?" she asked, looking down on me like I was a wounded baby bird.

The last thing I wanted to do was tell my mom I went to some generic high school drinking party. It's not like she would have any sympathy for that. She'd tell me it served me right for even wasting my time on something so pointless. Instead, I covered with a different truth. One she could get behind.

"The protest didn't go as well as I hoped. People have a hard time understanding that Channel Islands Aqua Park isn't an aquarium. It's a theme park. They don't care about conservation. Sure, they may say the shark's living in an open water sea pen. But it's really a cage. Sharks need to swim forty-five miles a day."

"Hey, Superman, you can't change the world in a day, okay?"

"I know. I think we raised awareness, though. The organizers are planning to get a petition started to ban the shark tank. Realistically, the city council's our best option, even though it may take a while. I signed up for a couple signature shifts."

My mom sat on the side of my bed. "Hey, did you hear the news?"

"What?" I knew the answer, but didn't want to rob her of saying it.

"I've got the best boy in the whole damn world." She mussed my hair.

"Thanks," I muttered.

"And I don't have to share credit with any other dickwad, because I did it all by myself. I get full credit, right?"

"Sort of."

She frowned. "Hey, your asshole father doesn't get squat for those seven bullshit years he was barely here!"

"I was talking about Michelle." I smiled and motioned to the photo.

My mom laughed. She then took a deep breath, a little embarrassed at her outburst, and leaned next to me. "Fine. Me and Michelle Obama. I can live with that."

God, I hope Michelle never tells her what goes on in here.

7

The first week after the party, I spent most of my time on anxious lookout for Steve. I was certain he was going to burst from behind every corner like a deranged fun-house clown and scream out, "Where's Kaia?" Then he'd cackle, fake punch me, explode into hysterics after I flinched, do a chest bump with one of his friends, pop open a Rockstar, chug it, crush it, and saunter away as cheerleaders danced behind him, chanting, "Steve! Steve! Steve!"

As for Kaia, whenever I saw her, I panic-ducked behind a trophy case or into freshman algebra. I couldn't bear seeing a look on her face that would confirm Steve had blabbed everything to her. My current plan was to stay invisible until next summer. Steve would have broken up with her by then, since his girlfriends never lasted longer than a month or two, and Kaia and I could bond over what a jerk he was. Then maybe

40

I could start to paint over the shitty caricature he'd drawn of me in her mind. I'd have to do something amazing, like save a dozen sharks. But it would be worth it.

The final bell had rung and school was clearing out. I walked with my hoodie up, earbuds in, and eyes down, trying to be as invisible as possible while debating what new cause I could join. Saving the shark would mean running into Kaia, so that had to go. I was pretty sure I would melt into a humiliated puddle if I got within five feet of her. I hoped I could find something on the school's Wall of Service bulletin board that would be a good replacement.

WHAM! Suddenly I was much, much closer than five feet. I wasn't even five inches. I was on top of Kaia. I leaped back.

"Kaia! Sorry, I didn't see you," I mumbled, ready to run for the bathroom and hide in it until morning if necessary, when she spoke.

"It's . . . okay." Something was off. I looked up, alarmed. Had I really injured her?! It wasn't that big of a bump. My elbows were bony, but could they really have done damage? Then I heard a sniff and, from my peripheral vision, saw her wiping her eyes.

"You're crying! Oh god. I'm sorry! Did I really hurt you?" My words tumbled over each other, in a pathetic attempt to soothe her.

"It's not you. It's . . . It's . . ."

There was no need for her to finish the sentence. It could only be one thing. One person.

"Steve."

She nodded and began to cry harder.

The asshole had assholed her even quicker than I thought he would. And while there were so many things he could have done to hurt her, it didn't really matter. I didn't need to know the specifics. But maybe she wanted to talk about it?

"What did he do?" I asked gently.

She shook her head, unable to speak. I wondered how Steve could just cast her aside so easily like all the other girls he'd dated. I mean, this was Kaia. Feeling mostly helpless, I reached out tentatively and put my hand on her shoulder. I could feel it trembling. This seemed to release even more pain, and she suddenly swiveled and threw her arms around me.

Around me!

Her cascading hair was a soft curtain on my face. As I inhaled, its mysterious scent exploded in my brain, muddling my thoughts. The Wall of Service bulletin board spun around us like a disco ball of community engagement. Thankfully, my shoulder could absorb her tears as I tried to regain my bearings. With great focus, I summoned the basic agility to pat her back.

"I'm sorry. Whatever happened, you don't deserve it. You're amazing. Really, really, really amazing . . ." I sucked in another breath. I wanted to say the right thing. The perfect thing. The blood in my heart crested, overflowing with emotion. I searched for the words until finally . . .

"Is that coconut?" Crap. That damn shampoo smelled so freaking good!

"What?" she asked, and I prayed she meant, *What did you say?*

and not, *What are you doing talking about the luscious scent of my hair?*

"Steve!" I sputtered. "That Steve! What an ass—"

"Steve has cancer."

Certain that her intoxicating shampoo must have somehow affected my hearing, I searched for possible homophones— "Steve likes canned pears"? or "Steve has back hair"? or "Steve makes Cam scared"? Accurate. But since none of that made any sense in this situation, I bravely asked her to repeat herself. "What?"

"He hasn't been feeling well, so he went to the doctor. And . . . they felt something. A lump. So they did a bunch of tests. And . . . it's cancer!"

"Steve has . . . cancer? Like, 'cancer' cancer?" I searched for something that would keep those words from being real. "But he just threw that enormous party . . ."

She pulled herself from me and reached into her bag for a tissue as she explained, "I know! His parents let him throw it to cheer him up. He . . . he . . . didn't tell me . . . till yesterday!"

As she blew her nose, I tried to make sense of what had just happened. Steve Stevenson was indestructible. He was The Rock. Literally every year for Halloween. And he looked healthier than anyone else at his party. How could he have cancer? Obviously, I knew anyone could get cancer, but Steve always had a force field around him that made it seem like the whole world just moved out of his way. And now . . . cancer . . . How?

"That's . . . terrible . . ."

"He keeps saying it's no big deal. 'Hodgkin's is the good cancer.' But how can he not be freaked out? His mom's a mess. His dad had to take leave from his business to care for him because his mom's the one with insurance. Which totally sucks. I mean, that house. The payments are so high. And I guess their insurance isn't that great because they've already got like twenty thousand in medical bills. . . ." She stopped herself. "I'm sorry, it's not your problem. . . ." Then she wiped her eyes and tried to regain her composure. For a moment she seemed okay, but then the news hit her all over again. "It's just so messed up!" Another wave of grief washed over her.

She leaned into me and I cautiously put my arm around her. She was right. This was so messed up. I thought about poor Steve. And his family. And Kaia. And how life was so delicate. And how we were all just a moment away from death. And Kaia exhaled and let her full weight rest on me. And the scent of the Hawaiian Islands swam in my head. I wished this moment would never end.

How could I make this never end?

"We should do a fundraiser for him!" I blurted. Wait. What did my mouth just say? But then Kaia pulled back, blinking away her tears, and I just went with it. "Get them the twenty thousand dollars, you know?"

"Oh my god. That's a great idea!" The hopeful light in her eyes was like rocket fuel.

"I mean, you and I, we can fundraise anything! Can't we?"

And then she paused and looked a little confused.

44

Crap! Was that too familiar? I shouldn't have assumed she knew everything I volunteered for. I was just some guy she saw around.

"I mean, saving the shark is just my latest thing. I also did a book drive for the local homeless shelter and I campaigned for bike lanes to be added to Main Street. And didn't we work together on the Straw-Free-Campus campaign and the Santa Clara Wetlands Preservation?"

"Oh, wow . . . I didn't . . . I mean, I knew about the wetlands."

"And we did dune restoration, too, didn't we?" Okay, that sounded desperate.

"I didn't realize we'd worked together so much." But she seemed surprised and not creeped out, so air once again filled my lungs.

"And last year you ran the Fun Run for No Guns and the Love Is Love Valentine's Day Bake Sale, right?" I added, to let her know it wasn't all about me.

"Yeah," she confirmed. "But they were small."

"Well, I think we'd make an amazing team." Was "team" too far? But then she smiled. A big, happy smile, directed right at me. But just like that, it faded.

"Look, you don't have to do this. I mean, you're not really friends with Steve, are you?"

It was true that there was no universe, not even in a multiverse scenario, where I was friends with Steve Stevenson. But I didn't see that as a problem. "Just because Steve and I aren't best friends doesn't mean I don't want to help him. I'm not friends with the shark either, and I'm still trying to save it."

She laughed. Oh my god. I needed to hear that again. Should I go for a joke? I was going to go for a joke. "And the shark doesn't even have cancer!"

She laughed again, and damn, I could listen to that forever.

Kaia breathed a sigh of relief. "God, just the thought of doing something is already making me feel better."

"Right?"

"You really want to do this?"

I wanted to say, *I want to do this more than anything in the whole world.* But I went with, "Yeah. Totally."

"Okay then." She pulled out her phone. "Put your number in." She held it out to me, its purple biodegradable case sparkling in the light. It was just a standard phone, but feeling it in my hand and staring at its unlocked screen seemed suddenly so intimate. Her whole life was in there and she was letting me stare into it. Well, at the blank page of the contact app, but it still rattled me. It took me way too long to get my info right as I debated adding email, social media, home phone, address, birthday . . . Finally, I settled on just my number and handed it back before things got too weird.

She examined it, tapped something quickly on her screen, and then looked up at me.

Buzz. My phone shuddered and I picked it up, gathering that she'd sent me a test message.

On my screen were the words: You're the best.

46

I dropped my phone and the screen cracked into six fissures.

"Oh my god, your phone!" Kaia gasped.

I picked it up quickly and assured her it was no problem. The screen still worked. Her text was still there.

And I would happily look at those cracks until the end of time.

I pulled down my *Dear Evan Hansen* poster and made room for a Save Steve vision board. I darted around my room like a deranged dragonfly as I plotted the biggest fundraiser Ventura had ever seen. Grabbing a pack of blank note cards and a Sharpie, I stared at the empty space in front of me.

Car wash? Bake sale? No! It had to be bigger. Run-a-thon? Dance-a-thon? Too small! This had to be special. Memorable! Impressive! Epic! Or else Kaia would think I was just some mediocre do-gooder.

Kaia.

Our moment by the Wall of Service bulletin board still swam in my head. Mostly the pungent smell of tropical paradise, but also . . . everything. She had let me comfort her. She felt she could trust me. She knew who I was!

You're the best.

I couldn't stand still anymore. I jumped up on my bed and giddily bounced. "You're the best! You're the best!" I banged my head on the ceiling, forgetting that I wasn't seven anymore, but it didn't matter. I continued bouncing (a little more cautiously) and I just kept repeating, "You're the best." Then I flopped on my bed, held up my cracked phone, and gazed at her text to make sure it wasn't accidentally erased.

Kaia: You're the best.

There it was. I had added her name to her number, making her text even more heart-stopping. She was in my phone! I sat up and let that thought linger. We were going to save Steve. Together. Then I felt a presence and knew exactly who it was.

Michelle.

I looked over at her proudly. "I am going so high, Michelle. Did you see who I'm saving? This isn't an orphaned child from Syria with cancer we're talking about. This is Steve fucking Stevenson. I mean, look at this guy!"

I opened Instagram and flipped through his feed. Each photo that came up was more obnoxious than the next. Steve photobombing the science fair. Steve photobombing the Cesar Chavez assembly. Steve photobombing last year's production of *The Crucible*.

"I'm not sure it's as big as you hanging out with Melania during the inauguration, but we are close. We are very close."

"Look, I know he's scary and has a terrible reputation, but if you just give him a chance—" The woman pushed her shopping cart past me without stopping. I was in front of the Ralphs on Victoria Avenue with my fellow activists Todd and Patrice. Armed with clipboards, we had a five-minute spiel about the negative impacts of keeping a shark in captivity, if only anyone would stop long enough to listen. Most people rushed by, refusing to make eye contact, but we'd managed to get a few signatures.

Todd clapped a hand on my shoulder. "Good try, kiddo. Now, about saving this Steve kid . . ." I'd been explaining to Todd and Patrice my plan to help Steve. They'd worked together up and down all of California on various causes— they'd gotten a law passed that forced almond growers to use less water and saved a riverbed in Mendocino from a strip mall development. I figured they'd have some pointers. "Noble shit, man. But he sounds like the biggest asshole," Todd continued.

"But that's a good thing, right? Helping someone who doesn't deserve it?" I'd left out anything about spending more time with Kaia, because I didn't think that was super pertinent. But Patrice suspected something.

"This is a bad idea," she said.

"What?"

"Didn't you ever watch *The Fault in Our Stars*?"

"Is that the doc about corruption in the Pentagon?" Todd asked.

"No. What the fuck rock do you live under? It's the tragic love story about two teens dying from cancer."

"Uh, Kaia doesn't have cancer," I offered.

"Not my point." She waved to a passerby. "Excuse me, do you know that a shark is being kept under sickening conditions for the amusement of humans?" The mom with her two toddlers gave us a horrified look, then scurried toward the safety of the grocery store. "Hey! I know your kids love that 'Baby

Shark' song. How 'bout some love for a real shark?" she called as the double doors snapped closed. She turned back to us. "Okay, how about the movie *Love Story*?"

"Haven't seen it," Todd said.

"*Terms of Endearment*?"

"No."

"Uh-uh."

"*A Walk to Remember*?" We stared blankly at her. She sighed. "Whatever. There are a thousand of these. My point is, a cancer love story is an unstoppable force. You don't get in the middle of something like that."

"I'm not getting in the middle," I protested.

Patrice leveled her gaze at me. "So that was just your passion for rescuing sea creatures that had you all starry-eyed at our last protest and not cute little Kaia."

"Uh . . ."

"I'm gonna bring you my copy of *Before I Die*."

"Stop. You don't understand. Steve's not dying. He has good cancer."

Both of them raised their eyebrows. "Good? Cancer?" Todd asked.

"Pretty sure that's not a thing," Patrice added, crossing her arms.

"No, I know, but it's not like serious, dying cancer. It has a ninety-four percent recovery rate." I looked back and forth between them, seeking assurance.

Patrice put her hand on my shoulder. "Look, I stand by it. You don't mess with a cancer love story."

* * *

Rattled, I got home as the sun was setting, turning the taupe stucco of our town house a vibrant orange. Letting myself inside, I could hear the TV and smell enchiladas.

"You stood by that pussy grabber all those years, and now you're telling me what to do with my body? Fuck you and your patriarchal bullshit!" My mom was watching the news while she cooked. It was one of her favorite activities. She said it made the food spicier. I tried to sneak upstairs, but the screen door banged behind me. "That you, Cam, honey?"

"Yeah. I just—"

My mom came out of the kitchen, wiping her hands on her jeans. "Can you believe those manipulative, conniving dip-shits?" She wrapped me in a tight hug, then let me go. "They'll do anything to get what they want. Oh, sure, they pretend it's for a good, noble reason, but deep down it's evil." Hold on. Was this about me helping Steve? Did she sense I had more than one motive? Was this a not-so-coded message? "Don't ever be like one of those assholes."

But just as I started to explain, her frown switched to a bright smile. "Dinner's in half an hour, okay?" Without waiting for an answer, she walked back to the kitchen, already screaming at the TV again.

Okay, maybe that wasn't about Steve and Kaia after all. Regardless, I stood alone in our entryway with a horrible thought: Was I a manipulative, conniving asshole?

Upstairs in my room, I lay down on my bed and stared at the ceiling. I could feel her eyes on me. Michelle. I rolled over.

She stared at me from her picture frame.

"You think I should back out, don't you?"

Michelle continued to stare, knowing she didn't need to say anything. I already knew the answer.

"But this is my chance!" I pleaded. "In fact, all those moments I missed before, that was probably for the best. Kaia might have said no. But if I do this, she'll know for sure what a great guy I am. And I'm not trying to break them up. Steve will do that on his own. Whatever, Patrice is wrong. This isn't some tragic cancer love story."

But Michelle wasn't having it. I could feel her skepticism radiating through the glass of the picture frame.

"It's a good thing, I swear. You of all people know what a mess health care is in this country, Michelle. His parents need the money. If I back out now, I'm actually taking something away from him."

I was pretty proud of that point. But Michelle still wasn't buying it.

"Fine. You're right. Kaia could totally do it without me. But then she'll probably hate me for saying I'd help and then backing out."

If Michelle could raise her eyebrow, she would have.

"Yes! Okay! I know! She won't hate me. She'd totally be understanding. She'd probably even check on me to make sure everything was okay. That's the problem. She's amazing! And I . . . like her. I really, really like her."

I covered my face with my arm so Michelle wouldn't see the

tears in my eyes. She waited patiently. I took a deep breath and let it out.

"I'm doing a good thing for the wrong reasons and that's not okay." I sat up and grabbed my phone. Michelle watched. I rolled my eyes at her. "Yes, fine. I'm circling Kaia like a horny vulture. You don't need to rub it in." I scrolled to Kaia's last text. "Okay, Michelle. I'm going even higher."

I texted: Hey.

I started to type, About earlier. I'm going to be too busy with the shark . . . but before I could get further, Kaia texted back.

Kaia: I was just about to text you! I've been thinking about what you said all day! Can't wait to get started! We are gonna fundraise the shit out of this!

Then she sent a "making it rain" GIF. But I wasn't focused on the dollar bills falling gently on my screen. I was focused on a single word.

We.

Holy shit. Why were those two little letters doing such crazy things to my insides? I looked at Michelle, lost.

"I . . . I don't know . . ."

My phone buzzed.

"It's gonna be great, Michelle!" I shouted over the music. I'd cranked up my favorite "get to work" playlist. Notebooks and sketch pads were scattered around me on the floor. I had markers out and was working on approximately the fiftieth version of the "Save Steve" logo. My laptop was open with the beginnings of a website.

"By the time we hit twenty thousand, Steve's four months of chemo will be over; he'll be in remission and back to peak bro form."

I ripped off the latest attempt from my notebook and walked over to the wall above my desk. A bunch of stuff was already pinned to the corkboard I kept there: facts on Hodgkin's, a list of ideas to raise awareness, local businesses to contact. In the center was a picture of Steve. I tacked the logo next to him.

"In no time he'll be chugging Natty Ice by his pool again and singing Cardi, and Kaia will be tired of his bullshit. Bro shit?" I chuckled. "Anyway, they'll be broken up. And I'll be that thoughtful guy who helped her now obviously terrible ex-boyfriend through cancer."

The logo wasn't quite right. It needed to be more . . . "Steve." More aggro-in-your-face. I ripped it down and started over.

"And then . . . this time, I'll be ready. The moment will finally be perfect. And I'll ask her out." The marker stilled on the paper as a thought occurred to me. I did some quick math. The timing was too good. "No. I'm not going to ask her out, Michelle." I stood and walked back to the corkboard. Pinning the logo next to Steve's face, I smiled. It was perfect. "I'm going to ask her to prom."

8

As Kaia scrolled through the website I'd built, I tried not to let on that there were, like, a thousand butterflies having a Steve-sized party in my stomach. We were sitting in Ms. Torres's English classroom. First bell was half an hour away and the only sound was the janitor watering the hedges outside the window, the distant hum of the school orchestra practicing, and Kaia's occasional tap on the keyboard. And my nervous, shallow breathing. But I was pretty sure Kaia couldn't hear that.

Every few seconds the corner of her mouth would quirk upward as she came upon some new element and the butterflies would swoop en masse. I'd worked on the Save Steve website all night, and even I had to admit it looked pretty good. It was simple and clean with a big bold logo and a ticker that would show how much money we'd raised. Finally, she looked up.

"Wow. You did all this last night?" She was impressed. I'd impressed Kaia.

Did I say there were a thousand butterflies? Make that a million. And they were doing loop-the-loops. "I was inspired." I couldn't believe I'd managed to say that in a totally normal, almost cool tone of voice and not in the squeak that I was really feeling. This was going even better than I'd hoped.

Kaia looked at the website again and the top goal number on the ticker. A slight frown creased her forehead. "It will be amazing if we can raise that much. Do you really think we can?"

The butterflies stopped their looping. A few might have even died. It's not like I hadn't wondered that myself a hundred times. I'd never raised that much money before.

"Um, of course!" I wasn't going to think about what would happen if this didn't work. Because it had to. We were getting that twenty thousand. I grabbed the rolled-up papers I'd stuffed in my backpack. "Yes, it's a lot of money. But people always underestimate the importance of a good ground game." I took the rubber band off the papers. "Sure, we'll do all the social media stuff to get the word out, but I also made these." I unfurled the papers. They were posters I'd designed last night and printed up in the copy room this morning. They had all the information for the Save Steve campaign on them and in the center was a picture of Steve looking, say, less than perfectly healthy. It was a great poster. Even better than the one I designed for the Straw-Free-Campus campaign. Anyone seeing it would want to help. Kaia examined the top one.

"Where'd you get this picture of Steve?"

"His Instagram feed. I think it was the morning after homecoming." His puffy red eyes and frazzled hair hung over a tired, goofy grin.

She snorted. "Well, he does look sick."

I tried to suppress the quick stab of joy I felt at the less than adoring expression she wore. I rocked back on my heels and tried to sound as casual as possible. "So I was thinking after school we could head over to Main Street and ask businesses if we could post them in their stores. That area gets a lot of tourist traffic as well as locals. I did it when I was volunteering for the Deaf Dog campaign and it got a great response."

I waited for Kaia's reaction.

"Well, I've got a student council meeting after sixth period." The last few butterflies in my stomach dropped. "But can I meet you after?" And they were back! Dancing the floss and the robot and the electro shuffle.

"Yeah. Sounds great."

With a smile, Kaia grabbed her backpack and headed out. I gathered up the posters and my laptop, barely aware of anything but the stupid grin on my face. I couldn't believe it. I was going to spend time with Kaia Gonzales. Alone. Putting up posters to save her terrible boyfriend, but still. Not that I was hoping anything would happen. I wasn't going to even try. Not while she was dating Steve. I wasn't that sort of guy. And yes, I'd felt that moment of doubt over whether doing the fundraiser was wrong, but that's all it had been—doubt. I was helping people. Lots of people. Steve. His parents. Kaia, so she'd feel less helpless. And if I was helping me a little, too, that was okay. I was doing a good thing. I was sure of that now.

I zipped up my backpack as another thought occurred to me. Actually, it was the same thought, just with new, horrible ramifications. I was going to be alone with Kaia. Yes, I'd managed to sound like a relatively cool, normal person just now, but with hours to fill? The butterflies in my stomach swarmed.

"Wow. That kid looks awful. Of course we'll hang it up." The owner of the antique store reached for some tape and walked over to the window of the store to hang the Save Steve poster. I felt a surge of triumph and glanced at Kaia. In the gloom of the cluttered shop, her eyes mirrored the same proud expression.

"Thanks so much, sir," I said as the man fixed the poster next to one advertising an improv night. "You have no idea how much you are helping."

Seconds later, we were back on the sidewalk, awash in the bright, clear sunlight with matching smiles on our faces. Kaia gave me a high five.

"Seventeen for seventeen! How many more posters do we have?" I looked down Main Street, with its mix of antique shops, cafés, and clothing stores. Every window now had a Save Steve poster clearly displayed. We'd been out for hours and the crazy thing was, I hadn't been nervous at all. As soon as we'd met up, we'd just slipped into this rhythm like we'd been

58

working together for ages. I never wondered what to say, we'd had a thousand things to talk about, and when we didn't, any silences we'd had felt comfortable rather than awkward. I'd never felt this in sync with anyone.

I checked my backpack and pulled out the remaining posters. "Just these three—" There was a rip as one caught on the zipper. "Two," I finished with a laugh. Kaia grabbed the top one.

"Okay. Last two. Let's make 'em count."

Kaia handed her poster to the woman draped in turquoise jewelry at the candle and crystal shop. ". . . and he's really great, and funny, and smart," she pleaded. My stomach tightened. I told myself it was the ten thousand scents assaulting my nose right now and not how Kaia's voice softened when she talked about Steve. I examined the Sea Breeze triple-wick candle next to me. It smelled like soap. Honestly, everything in here did. ". . . so if you could just hang up the poster, that would be a real help," Kaia finished.

The lady looked at the poster and recoiled. "Oh my goodness, of course I will, honey. Are you his girlfriend?"

Kaia glanced down. "Yeah."

Nope. I wasn't going to look at how Kaia's cheeks just turned pink. I picked up another candle—Sage and Sunlight—and sniffed. Still soap. There must be something here that didn't smell like laundry detergent.

"And you must be his best friend." I looked up, startled, my nose buried in Moonlight and Magnolias.

"Uh . . ."

"Actually, he's not friends with Steve at all," Kaia answered. "He's just the sort of person who's always willing to help out." She beamed at me. Moonlight and Magnolias slipped a bit in my hands. I shoved it back on the shelf. I didn't trust myself with a fifty-three-dollar piece of soap-scented wax when Kaia was looking at me like that.

It was too bad we only had one poster left, because this day was turning out to be pretty perfect.

The old man glared at us from across the chipped Formica of the liquor store counter. "No. No way. Not that fake ID motherfucker." He slammed the poster down. The dusty glass bottles behind him shook. Kaia took a step closer to me, alarmed. "Do you know how much liquor he and his friends have stolen from me? He's banned."

"Oh . . . I'm sorry. I didn't realize . . . ," Kaia stuttered.

The man wasn't finished. He reached under the counter. "I have a poster of him, too," he said with a scowl, and held up a laminated picture of Steve taken by a security camera. In bold letters it said, "DO NOT SELL." I stifled a snort of laughter. Kaia looked horrified.

"Maybe we should try the thrift store," she said under her breath.

"But this is the busiest corner on the whole street," I muttered.

"Yeah . . . but . . ." Her eyes darted to the angry old man.

"Let me try," I said, and pasted on my best friendly but

respectful smile, which I usually saved for adults who didn't believe in climate change.

"You know, I totally get it," I said, putting my hands up in the universal gesture of surrender. There was a flicker of surprise on the man's face. I continued. "When we tried to raise money for a straw-free campus at my high school, Steve drew penises all over the posters and changed the motto to 'DON'T stop sucking.'"

Kaia's eyes widened in surprise. "That was Steve?"

I shrugged nonchalantly and carried on. "I worked hard on those posters. And Steve ruined them. But I'm here because, well, no one deserves cancer." The owner stared at me, unimpressed. Kaia looked nervous. But I wasn't done. "Look, I'm not saying you have to like him. I'm not saying you have to forgive him. But think of his family. Think of his girlfriend." I motioned to Kaia. She gave him an apologetic smile. "They are good people. And they are hurting, too."

The old man's scowl softened a fraction. "I don't know. . . ."

I pushed the poster toward him. Steve's face looked up at us. "Think of it as being against cancer, not for Steve."

A moment later, we watched from the sidewalk as the old man carefully taped the poster of Steve to his window.

"I can't believe you flipped him!" Kaia cheered. "That was crazy."

"Thanks. Having you there helps." Shit. Did that sound too flirty? It just kind of slipped out. It was true. Working by her side filled me with a crazy confidence I'd never experienced before, but I didn't want her to think I was hitting on her. "Uh, I mean, as a visual reference." Okay, that also wasn't great. I'd just made her sound like a pie chart.

But Kaia didn't seem to notice. "Was Steve really the one who drew all those penises?"

I rubbed the back of my neck. "Um, yeah. But, I mean, that was a while ago. I got over it. I wasn't bringing it up to, you know . . . It's just easier to convince people of stuff when you use something personal. I figured you knew."

"Oh . . . um . . . no."

Maybe that explained why she was with Steve. She didn't really know him. He was one person to people like me and another to people like her. And while I could easily pull out more examples of the Ways of the Steve, I didn't want to push it. We'd been having such a good time. I mean, as good a time as you should have putting up posters for someone with cancer. "I can't believe we got all those stores to agree," I tried.

Kaia's expression brightened. "Right? We make a pretty good team, Webber." She punched me on the shoulder.

Oh my god. Were we a team? I had to extend the moment. "Do you want to get a coffee? We can go to that fair-trade place down the street where I ran into you over Christmas break," I blurted. Oh god, way too much info. Now I sounded like a stalker.

"I have a better idea."

"You do?" My heart began to pound. Did she mean a full meal? There was that 1950s-style diner a few blocks down with the really good milkshakes where you could pick your own songs and . . .

"Let's go tell Steve!" Kaia clapped her hands together with excitement.

Crap.

It was probably insane that I hoped we'd never have to see him at all. "Um, but, should we? He probably just wants to rest, right?"

But Kaia was already walking toward our cars. "No. No. It will totally cheer him up. Seriously. He needs it." I tried to imagine Steve needing any sort of cheering up and utterly failed. But I hadn't seen him since the party. He was probably really hurting. It was cancer, after all. Still, I was pretty sure me showing up on his doorstep wasn't going to lift his spirits.

"Maybe we should wait. Then once we've raised all the money, we can do a big reveal. You know, like those reality shows where they make over someone's house when they aren't home. Boom. Big surprise! Everyone cries."

"No way. It's too good to hold off."

"Maybe you should just go," I tried desperately.

Kaia stopped and put her hands on her hips. "I see what's happening here."

I felt a stab of panic. "You do?"

"You listed off a ton of causes yesterday that you helped on and I'd totally forgotten that you'd been involved with half of them. You are way too modest. I'm not letting you blend into the background on this one."

"But . . ."

"Come on." Kaia grabbed my wrist and tugged me forward. Whatever argument I'd been about to mount was lost to the feel of her fingers wrapping around my wrist.

Even as I stood in Steve's foyer, I searched for a way out of seeing him. Fake a phone call? Sudden allergy attack? Brain fart?

"Steve will be so happy to have some company," Mrs. Stevenson said as she hugged Kaia. "He's in the back resting." Her eyes were puffy and her whole being seemed tired. I think her blouse had a stain. This was awful. We were making her put on a brave face and host us while she should just be curled up on a couch with a cup of tea and a soft blanket. I considered telling her that I had terrible stomach pain (true) and excusing myself, but she was already leading us through the house.

Our footsteps reverberated around the vaulted ceiling. Instead of pounding music, party debris, and swarms of drunk, screaming kids, there was just a bright, cavernous space like a suburban mausoleum. Vases filled with flowers were perfectly placed on every surface. People were sending them flowers. Because this was bad. Because Steve had cancer. Cancer.

"Oh god. Should we have brought something?"

"Relax," Kaia whispered.

Photos of Steve lined the walls. Unlike his Instagram feed, they were loving family shots, and for the first time I saw Steve from his parents' perspective. He was a sunny little kid with a big smile. Their pride. Their firstborn. Shit.

As we walked past the kitchen, Steve's sister, who was maybe twelve or thirteen, did her homework on the white granite countertop. She nibbled absently at a bowl of pretzels and brushed her blond hair out of her face. And then . . . was that a sniff? Had she just sniffed?

What were we doing here? Or really, what was *I* doing here? Kaia said it was "good cancer," but this felt more like hospice. And I was the horny vulture.

Steve's mom slid open the moving glass wall and we followed her out toward the vast flagstone patio. I braced myself for Steve's sickness. My only experience with cancer had been my dog, Hillary, and we had just put her to sleep. What would he look like now? Did he need extra help? A feeding tube? Was he still Steve?

"I am fucking unstoppable!" I heard a voice bellow triumphantly, and I wondered if Steve had another friend over.

Then I saw him.

Drifting on a giant inflatable shark in the middle of his pool, a tanned and toned Steve Stevenson reclined luxuriously with an Xbox controller in his hand and a "Cancer Is for Pussies" baseball hat on his head, his wild brown locks spilling out from underneath. At the edge of the pool was a seventy-five-inch LED TV with a Sonos soundbar blaring Snoop Dogg's "Gin and Juice" as Steve murdered a prostitute in *Grand Theft Auto*.

This guy needed cheering up? I looked sicker than Steve. Kaia was right, this did seem like a "good cancer." Steve sure seemed to be enjoying it.

"Look who's here!" his mom called out.

Steve turned to see Kaia. "Hey, there's my girl!" He patted the spot next to him on the shark. "Come on board and grab a controller!"

"Let me know if you guys need anything," his mom offered, and then headed back into the house, I presumed to cry into her throw blankets.

Steve still hadn't noticed me, and I was thankful. Maybe we could both just pretend I wasn't here. I was pretty good at being invisible.

But then Kaia motioned to me. "This is Cam."

Steve switched his eyes my way, crooked his head sideways, and squinted. "Cam?" Then I could see the memory of that humiliating night light up his evil synapses, and an amused grin blossomed on his face. "Ooooooooh . . . Cam! Cam, my man! You're back! In my house!" His voice lowered to underscore his confusion. "For some reason!"

Kaia slid off her shoes and sat by the side of the pool. "How are you doing, sweetie?"

Steve forgot about me for a moment and maneuvered his floatie over to Kaia. "I'm backed up like a bottle of ketchup and I've got a rash that looks like Gucci Mane, but otherwise I'm doing fine."

His raft in reach, Kaia pulled it close to her. "Well, we have a big surprise for you."

"It's a pretty big surprise that Cam is in my backyard right now." He oversmiled in my direction. "Did I lose a contest? Oh yeah. I did. I have cancer." He looked back to Kaia and said as sweetly as possible, "Is Cam a side effect?"

"Cam had an amazing idea," she gushed. I wished she were less enthusiastic about it, because Steve's eyes became lasers trained in my direction.

"Did he?" he said, elongating each word.

Kaia nodded to me bright and encouraging. "Tell him what we're doing."

"Yes, Cam," Steve agreed, and then articulated each syllable. "Tell. Me. What. You. Are. Doing. I. Am. Really. In. Ter. Es. Ted. In. All. The. De. Tails."

I tried, probably unsuccessfully, to hide the fear in my voice. "Oh, well, Kaia and I are putting a fundraiser together for you." I gave a meek smile and looked to Kaia, hoping she would take over. But she just urged me to continue. Steve's eyes seared deeper into me. "You know, to help you and your family with your cancer."

Kaia unzipped her backpack. "Look! He made you a poster!" and she pulled the ripped one out with a flourish.

Oh no. He didn't need to see his hungover photo being used as a double for cancer. I spazztically sputtered, "You don't . . . It's nothing . . . It's not—"

But my stammering had the opposite effect on Steve. "Oh. I think I need to see this poster." Kaia handed it to him and he unfolded it like a dead fish was inside. He stared at it for a moment and his face found a new level of irritation. "Fuck no."

I thought he might pull his automatic paintball rifle out

from behind him and use me for target practice. But something distracted him—the swoosh of the moving glass wall. Without another word, he crumpled up the poster and threw it into the bushes.

"Steve! Cam worked really hard on that!!" Kaia protested.

Steve's body shifted quickly from enraged to chill. A voice behind me called out, "Heads up!" An orange Nerf football rocketed past my ear and Steve caught it casually with one hand. I turned to find Steve's dad bounding our way. "That's my boy!" he bragged with his chest puffed up. "Did you see this guy? Look at him. Does it look like this kid has cancer? No! It does not. He's crushing cancer like a boss."

His dad marched over to me and slapped me on the back. I stumbled forward just a little. "So, this is where the party is, eh? You want me to turn on the waterslide?" He thrust something into my chest. "Cheryl said you probably didn't bring a suit, Cam." The swim trunks had a series of pineapples wearing sunglasses on them and I knew that they must be Steve's. I took them in the tips of my fingers, not wanting to be rude.

"I think the slide makes Cam nervous," Steve snarked.

"Well, let me at least hit the jets in the hot tub." He then patted Kaia on the shoulder and continued, "Towel warmer is fired up and the mini fridge is stocked. Need anything else? Snacks?"

"Actually, I'm jonesin' for some In-N-Out." Steve rubbed his stomach like a hungry five-year-old.

"Yes! Look at my boy's appetite. Those drugs aren't stopping you." His dad clapped his hands together. "Animal Style Double-Doubles coming up for everyone."

He was already rushing back to the house and then, I don't know why—I certainly wasn't hoping to be here when he got back—but still, like a reflex I couldn't control, I explained, "Oh, I don't eat meat."

I heard an actual "skrtt." Steve's dad spun on his heel and glared at me with as much disdain as he could muster. After a weighty silence, he spat, "My son has cancer and you don't eat meat? What the fuck is wrong with you, kid?"

"Um . . ." I shrank. Why was I so stupid?

He took a few steps until he was too close to me. The muscle in his square jaw flinched and a vein in his neck swelled. "You'll eat the meat."

Before he could deck me and toss me into an incinerator, I nodded and mouthed, "I'll eat the meat."

He pumped his fist and flipped a switch right back to extremely upbeat. "Whoooo! Okay then. The Stevenson boys' cancer-cation continues! Be right back." With a hop in his step, he was gone.

"Cancer-cation"? Did he think this was some sort of vacation for Steve? An excuse for Steve to skip school and have a nonstop pool party? I knew parents who thought kids were under too much pressure these days, but this was ridiculous.

"Where were we?" Steve pushed himself off the edge of the pool and spun on his raft lazily. "Oh yeah. You can shove your sad cancer-boy poster up your meat-free ass, Cam. I don't need it."

This seemed like my cue. "I can just go——"

But Kaia stopped the inflatable shark mid-spin with her foot and glared at Steve. "Stop being a dick." To my shock, he didn't tell her to "calm down" or "have a sense of humor." Instead, he kind of withered as she continued, "Cam worked really hard on that and he didn't have to."

"I——" He tried to stop her, then faltered. He actually seemed a little afraid of her.

"And this isn't all about you. Maybe your dad thinks you're on spring break, but your mom's having a hard time. They need the help. So cut the macho bullshit and accept a little generosity." And while Steve shriveled under Kaia's scolding, I swelled up. If there was a streaming service that only showed Kaia chewing out Steve, I'd be the first subscriber.

"I'm sorry," Steve mewed.

Having decapitated Steve's objections, Kaia softened. "Come on, honey. Nobody's saying you're a sad cancer boy. We just want to help you and your family, okay?" The one-two punch of Kaia's anger and her sweetness left Steve dumbstruck. He just nodded and looked down.

"You won't have to do anything," I assured him, and hoped this would be the last time we'd all have to be together.

But Steve reengaged his laser beams at me and I figured I should just shut up. Kaia was doing a good job all by herself. "I feel so helpless. Just let me do something. Please . . . ," she pleaded sweetly, and flashed her big eyes at him.

And that did it.

"Ugh! Fine. But I don't want a pity party."

She leaned over and hugged him. "No pity party. I promise."

"Make it fun."

"Definitely." She kissed him and I looked away. I was suddenly very aware of my third-wheel status.

He whispered in her ear loud enough so that I could hear, "You left your suit here last time. Wanna join me?"

"Sure, baby," she said, and ran her fingers down his arm.

I had to get out of here.

But then she bounced up and turned to me. "You gonna come in?"

"Wha . . . No . . . I'm good." I was not going to be the weird guy in the pool while Kaia and Steve made out.

"Well, show Steve the website while I get changed," she suggested.

"Oh, there's a website!" Steve sang, a little too excited.

"Uh . . . yeah . . ." I wanted to fling my laptop into the pool rather than show him the stupid website.

"You're gonna love it, Steve," Kaia said, and skipped toward the house. "I'll be right back."

She opened and closed the moving window wall and Steve and I were suddenly left alone.

Avoiding eye contact, I slung my backpack onto the patio table and unzipped it so fast I almost broke the pull. I could hear Steve climbing ominously out of the pool. I yanked out my laptop and flipped it open with shaking hands. The *splat splat splat* of his feet approached. I mistyped my password four

71

times but finally logged in and brought up the Save Steve site. "I could put it up on the TV if you want," I offered. I could feel him at my back. Drip drip dripping.

"Wow, dick move, Cam."

Wham! He slammed my laptop closed.

"Trying to steal a cancer guy's girlfriend?" His breath was hot on the back of my neck.

I had a vision of him strangling me with the hose from the pool sweeper. Quickly, I spun around. "What? No! That's not what this is. Kaia and I are just friends. That thing at the party was just a misundersta—"

"Relax." Steve smiled. Still, I stepped back a safe distance. "You really think I'm worried Kaia's going to dump me for a bottom feeder with a shitty website?"

"You don't like the website?" I asked.

Steve laughed and flashed his teeth. "Look, I'm stuck at home for, like, the rest of the school year and I'm already burned out on *Grand Theft Auto*." He swiveled my laptop toward him and began digging around. A wave of fear crawled up my back. "So, you know what?" Steve's finger slid around my trackpad. "Do your best. Steal Kaia." Then he stood back from my laptop, revealing a crude drawing of what I guess was me having a giant erection with Kaia's name written on it.

I ignored it. Because I went high. "My best is raising money to pay your medical bills. Because that's all this is. I'm just trying to help, Steve. Trust me. I'm a good guy. And you have cancer."

"I do?!" Steve asked, and then assumed a wide-eyed soap

opera startle as if he'd just been given the news. "Oh no . . . not cancer!" He grabbed his chest and then his crotch, gasped, and then collapsed on a lounge chair. The water from the pool lapped in the background as he lay there motionless with his tongue splayed out. I didn't move.

He flicked open his eyes and gave a bored sigh. "It's only a little baby cancer." He sat up, shook water from his ear, and walked back to the pool. "I've had worse colds."

I still couldn't believe how casual he was being. Most people said *cancer* in a whisper, because they were so afraid of the word. Steve just kicked it around like a hacky sack. "Aren't you a little worried?" I asked, hoping to find the human beneath.

"Nope." He popped the *p* and hopped back onto his raft. A Steve-sized wave spread across the pool, smacking the edges. "But I am bored. And crushing you is just the entertainment I need. So, go for it, friend zone." With one hand, he pushed at the water and his raft spun in circles. With his arms spread wide, he pretended he was adrift at sea and called out, "Save me."

The moving glass wall slid open and Kaia sprang out. "I call the Pfister 811!" I hoped that was a car in the game and not a sex position. She closed the wall, ran past me, and jumped into the pool. She climbed onto the shark and slipped next to Steve. He handed her a controller and slung his arm around her. With a sly grin back at me, he said, "This is gonna be fun."

9

Buzz. Buzz. I buried my head under my pillow, not quite ready to face Monday. *Buzz.* With a groan, I rolled over, sliding the pillow off my face and blinking in the hazy morning sunlight. *Buzz.* What the heck? I fumbled for my phone, finally registering that it wasn't my alarm waking me up. Someone was texting me. I blinked a few times, clearing my eyes as I looked at my screen, then sat up. The pillow flumped to the floor.

Fifteen texts from Kaia.

Fifteen. Texts. From. Kaia.

Fifteen.

One. Five.

Holy crap. She'd been thinking about me for fifteen texts. I couldn't stop smiling as I read the last one.

Kaia: You don't have to do this.

She could already see what a selfless, great guy I was. My worries about Steve and his promise faded to nothing. This was worth it. Brushing my hair from my eyes, I quickly thumbed a response.

Me: I know. But when I think of what Steve's going through, I have to do something.

Sent. God, that sounded good. I waited for her response, watching the three little dots on the corner of the screen. Would it be a smiley face? Another heart? I hoped it was a heart.

Kaia: Yeah. But a diaper?

A diaper? What was she . . . ? I scrolled back through the texts, my heart pounding now for a totally different reason. Words flashed by: Wow. Unexpected. Didn't seem like you. Kinda worried. Are you sure?

No. This was not real.

Leaping out of bed, I scrambled to my desk and flipped open my laptop, typing in the Save Steve address as soon as it flickered to life. On the main page there was a new banner.

"To kick off awareness for the Save Steve campaign, I, Cam Webber, will wear an adult diaper to school." I read it out loud just to make sure I was really seeing this. Below the text there was a stock image of Depends with a hand-drawn arrow and the words, *Yep. My butt. In these.* And a smiley face.

I slammed the laptop close. Steve. I paced, running my hands through my hair. How did he . . . ?

Of course. Back at the pool. Steve was leaning over me when

I typed in the password to the site. He must have memorized it. I flipped open the computer again and tried to log in to the administrator site. A line of red text appeared, telling me my password was wrong. I clicked "Forgot Password" and typed in my email.

This email is not recognized.

Fuuuuuuuuuuuuuucccccckkkkkkkkk.

I slammed the laptop closed again. It was fine. No one had seen the site yet. We hadn't officially launched. Maybe some people who had seen the posters had visited the site and seen the banner, but they probably didn't go to the school. I could just ignore it. No way was I going to school in a diaper.

My phone buzzed.

Kaia: TBH I thought it was a little juvenile at first, but then I thought, if you're comfortable with it, it will get people's attention. And Steve will definitely think it's "fun."

He sure would. I had to get out of this. I typed back.

Me: I was

Delete.

Me: But

Delete.

Me: Yeah, I changed my

But Kaia started typing.

Kaia: Thanks so much for this, Cam.

My thumbs hovered above my phone. Two hearts. She'd just sent me two hearts. Which I knew didn't really mean anything. They were just little digital pictures. A bunch of pixels. People used them all the time. They used them to describe their affection for tacos. But also . . . they kinda did mean something. To me. No one had ever sent them to me before. Especially not Kaia. And . . . I didn't want to stop getting those hearts, even if they were meaningless. Even if it only meant I was on the same level as tacos.

How bad was a diaper really? It's not like it was worse than a swimsuit. And yeah, people would laugh at me, but it was for a good cause. We'd been planning on making an announcement at morning assembly, but this would be better, right? And Kaia thought it was a good idea.

Me: Anything for you.

Delete.

Me: Anything for Steve.

Send.

One package of men's Depends and an assortment of rainbow Sharpies later, I strolled into school, my backpack over my bare back, my Nikes and gym socks my only articles of clothing. I'd used the markers to write SaveSteve.org over the front and back sides of the diaper and then drawn little pictures of Steve kicking cancer's butt. The marine layer made the air a bit chilly and I was covered in goose bumps, but I was smiling. Steve may have been trying to embarrass me, but I was going to make sure this worked out for the best.

"Yo. That's hilarious!" A group of guys from the baseball team pointed at me and hurried over. "Man, we heard about

Steve," one of them said. "Sucks. Can we take a picture?"

"Make sure to tag Steve so he sees it," I said. "And hashtag Save Steve." They posed with me. I flexed absurdly and they all laughed. They gave me fist bumps, then hurried off, already tapping their phones.

After the baseball team took selfies with me, it seemed everyone wanted to. Soon I was surrounded by kids who usually never even spoke to me, asking me to take pictures with them. I got into it, coming up with even more ridiculous poses. I was actually enjoying myself. Yes, I looked stupid, but usually when I was working on a cause, people avoided eye contact and walked the other direction. This was a nice change. Though there was one minor point of irritation.

"Poor Steve . . ."

"I cried when I heard."

"Shouldn't have happened to such a good dude."

People would not shut up about Steve and how great he was.

"Oh my god, is he dying? I heard he was dying." A girl had her arm wrapped around my waist as she took a selfie.

"Actually, his cancer is highly curable," I said as she took picture after picture.

"I just think of him wasting away . . ."

I pictured Steve floating in the middle of his turquoise pool.

"He's not . . ." But she'd already run off, phone in hand, posting her pictures. I sighed.

On one hand, I was excited this was working out so well. On the other, it totally sucked. Steve was definitely not my

most worthy cause. Climate change, gun control, the shark . . .
no one seemed to care about those. But now that the King of
Kegs wasn't feeling well, suddenly people were invested.

"Looking good, Mr. Webber. I'm proud of you," Mrs. Cotes,
my ancient and usually perpetually grumpy history teacher,
said as she tottered past.

"Thanks!" I gave her a thumbs-up. My phone buzzed. Kaia.
I hadn't seen her yet, but she must have seen people's posts by
now. I pulled out my phone.

It wasn't a text from Kaia.

It was a picture of a naked lady pressed up against a red-
wood tree.

I fumbled trying to close the window, my suddenly sweaty
fingers sliding over the cracked glass.

Thought this might be your sort of thing.

No name, just a number, but I knew who it was. Steve.
Before I could respond, another photo flashed up.

Or maybe this?

Another naked woman. This time a PETA activist promising not to wear fur.

These?

A barrage of photos followed, one after another of naked
environmental activists. All I could see were breasts. Legs.
Waists. Belly buttons. And lots and lots of skin. So much skin.

Anyway, just wanted to thank you for all your HARD work.

I finally managed to click the window closed, breathing
heavily.

"Oh my god." A burst of giggles rang out a few feet away from me. A couple of sophomores were burying their faces in their hands, shaking with laughter, their cheeks bright red. A few more nervous titters had me spinning around. Everyone I turned to wore an expression of either shock, disgust, or amusement. Sometimes all three.

"Wha . . . ?"

And then I felt it, tugging against the diaper. I looked down, begging it not to be true. But it was. It was so horribly true.

I had a boner.

It was popping a tent up in the middle of my carefully drawn SaveSteve.org. And it wasn't going away. The laughter intensified. Cameras came out. The soft *click click* of pictures being snapped filled the air. My face was on fire. I had to get out of here. And probably out of the school. And the city. And the state. Actually, Canada was looking good, because after today I was pretty sure I'd have to go international to find someone who hadn't heard of my boner. I searched for an escape, but there were too many people. How were there so many people? There couldn't have been this many a second ago. A gnarled hand gripped my bare shoulder. I yelped.

"Sweetie, do you maybe want to take that inside somewhere?" Mrs. Cotes peered at me through her smudged bifocals. She turned to the crowd, waving her frail arms. "Nothing to see here, people!"

Which of course made people completely lose their shit. Clapping my hands over my still inexplicably raging boner, I ran.

The echo of my classmates' laughter bounced down the hallway. Still covering myself with one hand, I used the other to try door after door. None of the classrooms were unlocked yet. Finally, one door pulled open and I threw myself inside.

The door clicked shut behind me, blocking out all sound but my ragged breathing. I looked down.

"You've got to be kidding me!" I still had a boner. "What the hell? Go away!" I waved my hands at it. The only thing that happened was I created a slight breeze. The traitorous boner remained. "Go away! Please!" I closed my eyes. Was it going to stay like this forever? I counted to ten, then peeked, hoping for improvement. Nope. Still bonering. "Fine." I ripped off my backpack and pulled out my clothes. I yanked on a T-shirt. "Just . . . fine. Go. Stay. Who cares? My life is over. So whatever you were hoping was going to happen by popping up and saying hi is never going to happen now. Ever. Good job." I tugged up my pants. It was covered, at least. "Finally. Thank you." And now that it couldn't embarrass me, it was gone.

My phone buzzed. I grabbed it, ready to murder Steve through text.

Kaia: Where are you?

Shit. My fingers trembled but I managed to punch out a response.

Me: I bailed on the diaper. People didn't get it.

That sounded reasonable. She was obviously running late, so there was a chance she hadn't seen the hashtag yet. There was a pause as I waited for her reply.

81

Kaia: Where are you? I heard what happened.

"What? No! Noooo! NOOOOOOOOOOOOOO!!!!" I dropped to my knees, clutching my phone.

The door opened. Kaia poked her head in, smiling a little. "I thought I heard someone in there. I've been looking all over for you."

I jumped to my feet and brushed off my pants, then shoved my hands into my pockets and tried to look like I just hadn't been having a complete mental breakdown. "Oh. Hey. Hi."

Kaia entered the room all the way, gently closing the door behind her. "Are you okay?"

"What? Me? I'm fine. I just wanted to reference the periodic table for a minute." I gestured vaguely to the poster at the front of the room.

"Everyone's talking about the diaper."

"Oh. Wow. They are?" I tried to play it off. Maybe I'd misunderstood her text. I mean, yes, "I heard what happened" sounded pretty damning, but maybe she meant all the social media buzz we were getting from the hashtag. That was a possibility. Maybe. Right?

"I guess you made quite a statement," she said. Her cheeks colored.

Nope. She knew exactly what had happened. She'd probably seen pictures. Pictures of my diapered erection. I sat down on the edge of the desk, my vision suddenly a little dim. Kaia rushed over.

"Hey, Cam. Relax. It's okay. I was just teasing." I couldn't breathe. "It's okay," she repeated.

"It's not okay!" I managed to gasp. Great. I was now melting down in front of her. But I couldn't seem to stop. "I don't know what happened. I was just standing there. And then it . . . it . . . Did people think I meant to do that? Oh god." I tried to breathe. Failed. Tried again. "Do they think it was some weird sex thing? Like I got off on it? Am I a sex offender now? Does that make me a sex offender?" I knew I was being ridiculous, but the thoughts were piling up too fast.

Kaia laughed a little. "Stop. Please."

"You must think I'm a weird, perverted sex offender now."

"Cam, no—"

"But—"

She put her hands on my shoulders and looked me in the eye. "Cam, I promise I do not think you're a weird, perverted sex offender."

Feeling her hands on my shoulders, my breathing began to slow. I dropped my head. After a moment, Kaia stepped away. I chanced a look up. "Are you sure?" I asked, my voice small.

She put her hands on her hips, her eyes flashing. "Is there something I don't know?"

"What? No!" I yelped. Kaia could be straight up terrifying. "Of course not."

Her face broke into a smile. "Then there you have it. Not a sex offender."

I laughed a little, scrubbing my eyes. "This is so embarrassing."

Kaia sat down next to me. "No, it's not."

"Yes, it is."

"Okay, it is." We both chuckled. Kaia smirked. "Apparently Mrs. Cotes had to go to the teachers' lounge to recover."

"Really?"

Kaia threw her head back and cackled. "Wow. You really have a high opinion of the power of your junk." I blushed, embarrassed. But somehow her teasing didn't have any sting. She knocked me on the shoulder and stood. "Come on. We should get to class."

I remained sitting. "Oh. Right. I guess." I wondered if I could hide in the supply closet at the back of the class all day.

As if she could read my mind, Kaia smiled and dragged me to my feet. "Come on. I'll be your bodyguard. Keep all those geriatric teacher ladies from mobbing you."

"Oh my god, shut up." I laughed. Kaia looped her arm in mine and we set out.

Arm in arm, we walked through the halls now packed with people on their way to class. Most everyone ignored us. Once or twice someone shouted "Nothing to see here!" but it was accompanied by high fives and laughter. Somehow with Kaia right there, laughing along with me, it didn't seem that bad.

We got to my first-period class and Kaia stopped at the door. "Good luck," she said, and left. As she disappeared into the crowd, she turned around to smile at me one last time. I watched from the entrance of the classroom until I couldn't see her anymore, a warm glow filling my chest.

That glow completely disappeared when my phone buzzed

halfway through class.

Steve: Saw the pics. Thanks for taking such a FIRM stance against cancer.

Steve: That was SWELL.

Steve: You really ROSE to the occasion.

I typed under my desk.

Me: I could just show Kaia those pictures you sent.

Steve: Go ahead. Tell her everything. I will too.

I started and deleted four different responses.

Steve: Thought so.

Steve: Can't wait to see what you do to save me next . . .

10

I manned the Save Steve donation table at the CIF Girls' Soccer Championship and searched the crowd for the next attack. I had successfully reset my password for the site after hours with customer service and regained control. But I was sure Steve was still plotting away at home. A loud laugh swung my head one way and then a bang swung it back the other. Maybe he'd have one of his bro friends jump out from behind a bush or throw a water-filled condom at me.

Or maybe he had just begged Kaia to come play nurse to him so that I would be stuck raising money by myself. She was supposed to be here thirty minutes ago. Wouldn't she have texted me if she was going to bail? I checked my phone again, but there was nothing new from Kaia.

I texted her: I'm at the game. You?

I didn't want to be too demanding. But still, she seemed excited to see the new Save Steve T-shirts and hats that I had convinced Gary's Customizables to expedite. They looked pretty cool, if I said so myself. And Steve shouldn't be embarrassed, since I got them in Pricedown Black, the *Grand Theft Auto* font.

I checked the website again just to be sure nothing had changed. I still couldn't believe we had already raised almost a thousand dollars off the diaper. At this rate we'd have twenty thousand within a month and then I'd—

SLAM!!

I jerked back in my seat, almost falling over, then ducked and covered, expecting an incoming projectile. But it was just two shaggy seniors who bumped into the table. They were wearing diapers over their shorts in solidarity with Steve. "Nothing to see here!" one of them shouted, and then held up his hand for a high five from me. I gave him one, still a little uncomfortable with the catchphrase I'd apparently inspired. Hopefully if we reached our goal, I'd be remembered for more than that.

"Sorry! Late!" I looked up and there was Kaia hurrying into her seat behind the table. "I got asked to be on the prom committee. Of course the first meeting had to be right after school." She stopped and took in the new Steve merch. "These are awesome, Cam!" She held up a shirt and admired it. I got a little light-headed at the compliment. Then she put on a hat. I needed to take a big drink of water because Hat-Kaia was even cuter than Hair-Kaia. "We'll sell a million of them. Even people who don't know Steve are gonna want one."

"We've sold eight hats already and a couple of shirts." I showed her the spreadsheet where I was keeping track of sales. "I think maybe I'll ask if Gary will make us some hoodies and—"

"Cam Webber?" A short man in a black shirt and baseball hat interrupted.

He didn't look like one of Steve's bro friends, but I still winced. "Uh, yeah . . ."

"Your dinner is here." He lifted up a couple of large red coolers and set them down on our table.

"I didn't order dinner."

"Looks like it was paid for by Steve Stevenson." I froze. Was the cooler gonna explode? Would snakes pop out?

"Really?" Kaia lit up.

"He included a note." The delivery guy handed it to me.

This was going to be the explanation of the joke. Something about meat and how I should man up and eat it. But as the guy unloaded pile after pile of hot veggie burgers, fries, and shakes from the awesome farm-to-table café on Loma Vista, I began to doubt my assumption and read the note. *Dear Kaia and Cam, Dinner's on me. I can't tell you how much I appreciate everything. Don't worry, it's vegetarian. Respect, Steve.*

"Awwww. He's so sweet," Kaia swooned.

I read it again twice, looking for the clue or hidden message. I even turned it upside down. But it was just a nice note. I scanned the massive amount of food he'd ordered for something gross. Was it covered in worms? But the only odd thing was that he ordered enough for ten of us. "Are we expecting anyone else?" I asked Kaia, wondering if she'd invited the prom committee.

"I don't think so. But I'm starving." She grabbed a bag of fries ravenously.

I watched her take a bite and felt a little bad that I was waiting to see if she had any adverse reaction. What was I worried about? He ordered his girlfriend . . . and me . . . dinner. That wasn't weird. We were raising money for him. I should be able to accept a little generosity. From Steve. Maybe my "going high" had shown him a new way. Also, the burgers smelled delicious.

Kaia's phone buzzed to life. "Steve?" I assumed.

"No," she said, a little stressed. "I just have to tell the women's shelter I'll be there for my shift tomorrow." She began replying when another thought hit her. "Oh, shit. I've got academic decathlon this weekend." She flipped through her calendar and then assured herself, "Oh, it's Sunday. I can make it."

The women's shelter. Academic decathlon. The prom committee. She did it all. And now Save Steve. She clearly only gave her time to things that were really important. Which meant I—I mean, Save Steve was really important. I absently ate a fry as her thumbs tip-tapped on the screen. The rhythm of her altruism was entrancing. "Wow. You never stop, do you?"

"There's just so much to do. Anyway, you should talk." She gave me a playful shove.

I dropped a couple of fries and tried to hide my goofy smile. "Not like you. Right now, I'm just doing the Steve stuff and the shark thing—"

"Oh my god! Did you check your email?" she asked. I panicked. What had Steve done? But she continued, "The city council is going to consider a law to ban captive sharks! The petition worked!"

"Wait. Seriously? Holy shit!"

"Right!" The thrill of this small victory rushed through us and then she hugged me.

The rotation of the earth slowed. Flecks of dust from the nearby field glittered around us. And I was again bathed in some sort of amazing coconut infusion.

Then almost as soon as it began, we both became aware that we were hugging in the Save Steve booth at the CIF Girls' Soccer Championship and we separated. I saw her start to awkwardly laugh and I laughed back to make sure she knew that I also thought that was super weird.

Our eyes caught. I froze and searched hers for the answer to the most important question. Was that just a hug? Or was that a *hug*?

She looked at the bag of fries and began picking at them. "Anyway, um . . . Steve was really nice to get us dinner." Guilt seemed to wash over her and the energy between us evaporated.

We were quiet. The crowd roared for what sounded like an amazing goal. I felt bad she was feeling guilty. I'd never caused guilty feelings in anyone before. Actually, I usually carried enough guilty feelings for everyone else.

My phone buzzed, snapping me out of my little moment. It was a text from my mom.

Mom: Your petition worked! My boy kicks ass!

This was followed by a series of emphatic Bitmojis of my mom carrying a trophy, knocking people out, etc. I laughed.

"Blowing up there, are you?" Kaia asked.

"Um, if you consider my mom 'blowing up,'" I joked. "She just saw the news about the shark petition."

"That was quick."

"She, uh, has a Google Alert for any cause I'm involved in." Kaia's eyebrows rose a little. "Yes. I'm aware that is deeply embarrassing."

Kaia held her hands up and shook her head. "No, no. That sounds totally normal. In fact, I need to hear more about this super normal mom of yours." She leaned into me with exaggerated interest.

"There's not much else."

"Nope, don't believe it."

"Really, we're pretty much just a typical family."

Kaia waited.

"Fine. I'm pretty sure she moisturizes my elbows at night when I'm sleeping. I can't prove it, but they are unusually silky."

Kaia snorted. "Ha ha. No, she doesn't. Try again."

"She does," I said with great seriousness.

"Nope. That's not a thing someone would do." Kaia shook her head to doubly emphasize the insanity of it.

"And yet my elbows say otherwise."

"Okay, I need to see these suckers." She grabbed my bare arm.

"What? No! Stop. Those are private," I said, even though, who was I kidding? She could take my elbow wherever she wanted.

As if chalking a pool cue, she rubbed her palm over it. Incredulous, she grabbed the other one and compared it. She even ran my elbow along her arm. Her shock was real. "They are like a toddler's!"

"I told you."

"Cam, your mom is not normal," she said, a little concerned, "but those things are a work of art."

"I'll let her know." Actually, I had never confronted my mom about this. I probably should.

"Does she do it for your dad, too?"

"Oh, no. He left when I was seven." I could feel the "poor Cam" section of the conversation coming on. That's what usually happened when I told people my dad left. They either looked away, embarrassed, like I'd just said I was dying, or they become way too touchy-feely and wanted to show me how much they were concerned about me.

"Oh, wow. Sorry. We were just having a fun conversation and now it's a bummer." She made an "oops" grin and ate a fry in mock awkwardness. I laughed, so relieved she didn't pity me. It made me like her even more. Which really shouldn't have been possible.

"It's actually good he left. My mom is, like, twice the parent he would have been." After throwing my mom under the bus with the whole elbow thing, I wanted Kaia to know that she wasn't a serial killer. It also gave me an excuse to bring up a story I hoped she'd be impressed with. "I mean, there's no way that guy would have waited in line for four hours to get a signed photo of Michelle Obama and a copy of *Becoming*."

"Hold on. You met Michelle?"

"I did."

"Did you let her touch your elbows?!"

"No. But it was the greatest day of my life. I keep the photo of her by my bed. She watches over me while I sleep." Kaia gave me a funny look.

Oh no. She didn't realize I was joking.

"Kaia! Oh my god. How are you holding up?" a girl I think I knew from English class asked Kaia, interrupting us. This was bad. I shouldn't have tried to joke, but Kaia had said the elbow thing and I wanted to keep it going. But now she thought I had some weird thing with Michelle. Shit. I mean, I did talk to her sometimes. But I didn't really believe she could hear me.

"This must be so hard," the English-class girl said to Kaia.

"Um, that was a joke! You know that, right—" I tried to squeeze in, but I didn't think Kaia heard me. The dramatic girl was getting her full attention.

"You are so brave," the girl continued with a sympathetic sigh.

I tried again. "The Michelle thing. It was—"

Kaia shrugged, a little uncomfortable. "Oh, um, thanks. But Steve is really the brave one."

"But it's kind of romantic, right?" The girl seemed to be picturing Kaia dabbing Steve's head with a cool cloth.

"Uh, I don't know . . ." Kaia deflected to me. "Have you

met Cam?" The English-class girl looked at me, trying to place my face and then shaking her head. Kaia continued, "He's got a photo of Michelle Obama by his bed. It watches over him at night."

I froze.

The English-class girl gave me a creeped-out grin and then quickly excused herself.

But then Kaia burst into laughter. "The look on your face!"

"You suck so much." My body temperature plummeted back to normal.

"Come on. That was hilarious." She patted me on the back. I'm sure she felt the moisture on my shirt, but she didn't say anything. Instead, she leaned in, propped her chin on her hand, and said with great interest, "Now tell me everything about Michelle."

An hour later, empty burger and fry wrappers had piled up in the small garbage can under our table. I usually didn't eat much when I was nervous, but our conversation was so effortless and relaxed that I've been absently gorging nonstop. I swallowed a burp as I wondered out loud, "Would it be better if I was pre-law or environmental science? I kind of want to work at the NRDC, but Tesla is also doing amazing stuff."

"Right? I can't decide between the ACLU or Médecins Sans Frontières or Greenpeace. I mean, those are all totally different things. I'm just worried I'll pick one and then I'll find out that someone else needs more help and I'll already have specialized and . . . arggh!"

"Exactly! I—"

Kaia's phone buzzed and I was disappointed when she checked it. "Oh my god! I knew I shouldn't have gotten roped into this. They are still debating between 'Under the Sea' or 'Atlantis' for prom. Can't they figure this out without me? Why do I have to be the deciding vote?" She yelled into her phone, "They are the same, people! It's blue balloons either way!" She let out an exhausted groan.

"Is there a balloon substitute?" I tried to sound helpful. "Like something they could recycle or donate after?"

"I wish! They'd kill it anyway. I tried to get them to include an endangered coral reef display to raise awareness. But they thought that was a 'downer' for prom. Which it probably is."

"If it were you and I planning it, the dance floor would be a floating plastic island." I was only half joking, but she laughed.

"Can you imagine? It's probably good we aren't. Can I tell you a secret?"

"Yes!" I said way too eagerly. Nobody ever sent me notes or told me secrets. It really didn't matter what it was. It was a Kaia secret!

"I actually like the idea of a totally old-school, cheesy, super romantic prom." I could see the vision of it in her eyes as she spoke.

"You do?" Could I live up to that fantasy? My concerned face must have looked to her like judgment.

"Nuh-uh. Don't be one of those people who doesn't think it's possible for a girl to be super into sparkles and saving the world."

I scrambled to recover. "No, I mean, I like prom." She needed to know that I was on board with her super cheesy prom if I was going to make it *our* super cheesy prom. "Who doesn't like prom? It's the one time we get to be cheesy."

"Right?" she agreed emphatically. But then her face fell, and she sat back. "Though I have no idea if Steve will even be well enough to go."

"Oh . . . No . . ." I tried to find sadness in my voice, but it just wasn't there. Was she giving me an opening? Holy crap. Did she want me to take her, just in case?

"And I already bought a dress . . ."

Oh my god, she was. She'd mentioned her dress and not being sure she could go and how much she loved prom. Those were almost all the green lights! Did I really need her to say, *Cam, will you just freakin' ask me to prom already?*

My stomach lurched, but that could just be my digestive system trying to manage the massive sludge of food I'd just eaten.

"Can Cam Webber please come to the field?"

Hold on. Had I just imagined that I was being called onto the soccer field so I could avoid asking Kaia out? That was a fun new twist in my anxiety.

"Did they just call for you?" Kaia asked, at least confirming I wasn't hallucinating.

"I don't think—"

"Cam Webber, please join us on the soccer field," the PA announcer repeated.

Kaia gave me a confused look. "Filling in as goalie?"

96

* * *

Grass crunched under my feet as I stepped onto the field. The stadium lights painted everything a bright, ghostly white. I squinted, waiting for my eyes to adjust. Someone was standing at center line.

"Hello, San Buenaventura High School! Have you missed me?" The voice boomed out over the crowd. There was an immediate answering roar. Beside me, Kaia gave a surprised gasp. My stomach roiled, and I suddenly felt every bite I'd taken of the burgers threatening to return. Steve Stevenson stood on a small platform in the center of the field, wielding a wireless mic as he paced back and forth in front of the crowd. "I know. I know. You're probably like, what? This guy has cancer? No way! He's so sexy!" Steve flexed a bit, showing off. The crowd tittered. "But tonight is not about my abs . . ." He lifted the corner of his shirt. The crowd screamed. ". . . or my guns . . ." He flexed his biceps. More screaming. ". . . or the fact that I can deadlift three hundy." Catcalls and whistles. Steve smiled appreciatively, then grew serious. "No. I'm here for something even more amazing."

Putting the mic back on the stand, Steve hopped off the stage and strode to where Kaia and I stood frozen, probably for very different reasons. She wore an expression of stunned delight. I was fairly certain mine was just stunned. Steve reached us and took Kaia and me by the hands, pulling us toward the platform.

"How are you— Why? Where did— I can't—" Kaia

97

stuttered breathlessly as Steve pulled us along. *Yes*, I thought. *All those questions.* Steve dragged us to the mic.

"I'm not dying," he whispered in Kaia's ear while looking right at me. His eyes glinted with amusement. "I can do fun stuff." Before I could wonder what he considered "fun stuff," Steve threw his arm around me, grabbed the microphone again, and addressed the crowd. "I'm here to support my buddy Cam and his latest insane stunt that he posted on SaveSteve.org tonight!" People reached for their phones, a murmur of interest rising. I turned to Steve.

"But . . . I changed the password!" I whispered.

Steve covered the mic with his hand and leaned in close. "Camdog, you seem to think that just because I am popular and way more attractive than you, I am also a brainless tool-shed. I assure you, I am not." It occurred to me then that Steve was in all my AP classes and even some honors classes I wasn't taking. How had I not realized this? Satisfied with my blank expression, Steve had turned back to the crowd. "Now, as the site says, Cam is inviting you all to come down and, for a small donation, roll him into the goal!"

"What? Roll?" I looked around, frantic.

Steve raised both arms in the air. "Bring out THE HAMSTER BALL!" His words thundered over the crowd. There was an answering cheer. Music played from the loud-speakers, and four smiling cheerleaders appeared, rolling a giant, clear plastic, inflatable ball, at least eight feet high. In the center there was a small circular hole big enough to squeeze through.

Steve leaned close. "How are those burgers sitting, Cam my man?" And with that, Steve's plan became brutally, vividly clear. I grabbed Steve's arm.

"I am not—" Then I belched. And tasted it. Oh god.

Kaia leaned over. "Cam! Why didn't you tell me? I've seen these on YouTube! This is such a great idea!" She was smiling at me. That warm, beautiful smile. Suddenly all I could think of was palm trees and ukuleles. Waves lapping at our bare feet. Paradise.

"I . . . wanted to surprise you?"

I was an idiot.

"Whoa! Look at that!" I wrenched my gaze from Kaia's. Steve was pointing to the crowd of twenty people who were now waiting at the base of the platform. They waved five-dollar bills in the air. "People really want to roll Cam!" Steve turned to Kaia. "Why don't you collect the donations, Kai?"

Kaia walked along the edge of the platform, taking money and getting people to form a line. "Only five bucks, Cam?" Her forehead creased with concern.

"Yeah, I was surprised it was so affordable, too," Steve said, and slapped me on the back.

". . . five?" I echoed. I wanted to cry.

"But I can see the affordability is drumming up more excitement." Steve gestured to the now massive line stretching back to the stands.

Kaia nodded. "True. Right." Her frown disappeared.

With a shove Steve pushed me toward the waiting ball.

"Time to get in, buddy!" I stared at the big plastic sphere, very much not wanting to get in. The field seemed impossibly long and wide, my stomach impossibly full. I forced back another nervous belch, but Steve noticed. His eyes twinkled. "Cam. Cam. Cam. Cam," he began to chant.

The crowd caught on. "Cam. Cam. Cam. Cam."

Kaia joined in, clapping her hands. "Cam. Cam. Cam. Cam."

Not being able to feel my feet, nevertheless I inched to where the ball stood, held in place by the cheerleaders with their matching bright smiles. I leaned forward and gripped the sides of the entrance. The plastic squeaked under my fingers. I slid inside.

Immediately the sound of the crowd dampened and the world outside was reduced to a smudgy blur of colors and faces and lights. I realized that there was a much smaller ball inside the larger ball, and that was where I now crouched, barely able to stand upright. I could hear my breath bouncing off the plastic walls. The air smelled strongly of chemicals and there didn't seem to be enough of it. What would happen now? I couldn't hear anything. Did I just wait for someone to roll me to my doom?

Suddenly, Steve's face filled the entrance hole like some parody of a horror movie and he sang, "In-N-Out! In-N-Out. That's what a Camburger's all about!"

"Steve!" I leaped toward him, ready to beg, but he was already gone. Through the filmy plastic I saw him step back to the center of the platform and make an announcement. I could hear the answering cheer even inside my bubble.

Four blurry figures stepped toward me, replacing those of the cheerleaders. From their hulking size, they had to be football players.

The ball began to roll. I stepped along with it. Okay, this wasn't bad. It really was like I was a hamster. The football players picked up speed. Okay. This was harder. I tilted forward, my hands scrabbling on the slick plastic as I tried to keep up. Then with a heave and a cheer they released me, and suddenly I was bouncing wildly. My feet slipped out from under me. *WHAM*. My face slapped against the plastic and then I was tumbling. Rolling. Head over heels. All I could see was blinding stadium lights, then grass. Then lights again.

My stomach protested. I clenched my jaw, refusing to give in.

THUMP. I jerked to a stop. The ball was wedged into the goal. Inside I was splayed out like a starfish. My hair was plastered to my forehead; the air inside the ball was damp from my sweat, but I hadn't thrown up. Outside, I could hear the crowd cheering wildly. Through the entrance hole I thought I could even see Kaia clapping. Take that, Steve.

"Again! But this time, THE WHOLE FIELD!"

Wait, what?

I saw a pack of figures running toward me. I sat up.

"Hey, guys. Hold on."

Hands thumped on the plastic all around me. It grew dark inside, the light blocked by the crowd of bodies. The ball began to roll.

"Wait. Give me a sec."

But no one heard. Outside, they were laughing and yelling, "Cam. Cam. Cam." The ball picked up speed. Again, I scrambled, trying to keep my balance. I pressed my hands to the walls. My feet slipped and slid. My stomach rolled. The sharp scent of chemicals mixed with my frightened sweat.

Faster. They were pushing me so much faster.

"One. Two. Three." It was like a wave hit me. I didn't even have a chance. The ball bounced hugely. My legs flew out from under me. *BAM*. I slammed into the floor. *BAM*. I was on the ceiling. I somersaulted inside the ball. Over and over. Feet over head. Lights. Grass. Lights. Grass. It blurred together too fast.

A cold, slick sweat coated me. My mouth suddenly filled with a gallon of saliva. It was coming. Oh god, it was coming and I couldn't stop it. I tried to swallow but couldn't. My throat tightened. My stomach pushed up. *Give in.* The thought rose, unbidden. *Give in and you'll feel so much better.* No. No. I couldn't. Kaia was watching. I gritted my teeth and closed my eyes.

That was a mistake.

With a heave, vomit spewed from my mouth, splattering the inside of the ball. I felt bits fleck my face. Which naturally made me heave again, bigger, longer. I couldn't stop. It just kept coming. Vomit coated the inside of the ball as I rolled over and over. It was on my face, my arms, my pants, inside my shoes. The entire inside of the ball filled with the stench of veggie burger and lactose-free chocolate shakes.

Outside, the crowd reacted. But I kept rolling, no one able to stop me. Over and over in my own personal ocean of puke.

Finally, the ball rolled gently to a stop. I lay with my eyes closed, feeling the vomit coating my eyelashes, a warm dampness soaking the back of my neck and hair. I heard the thunder of footsteps as people approached and then their horrified reactions as they got close enough to see and smell the disaster that was me.

"Cam? Cam? Are you okay?" It was Kaia.

"Don't come any closer . . . ," I begged, my voice a rasp. But I knew she couldn't hear me outside the thick plastic. And I knew what she must be looking at: a giant hamster ball completely coated with the insides of my stomach, with the dinner we'd just eaten together. I could hear the splat of it as it slowly dripped from the ceiling.

"Get a stretcher!" someone called.

Footsteps. Someone approached. There was a squeak of plastic as they put their hand on the ball to peer inside. The whole thing shifted slightly and I tamped down another wave of nausea. "Wow. How much did that guy eat?" Steve. Fucking Steve. "I feel bad I sent those burgers now." The voice receded as he stepped away. "But, I mean, he knew he had this planned. . . ."

The spray of icy water pounded into my back.

"Over there, by his ear. I think I still see a chunk," Steve said. Kaia aimed the hose a little higher and the water hit my ear, momentarily deafening me. After I'd been carried off the field to the sidelines, Kaia insisted that she help me clean up.

The medics decided there wasn't really anything that required their expertise and handed her the hose. Steve followed, and had been resting on a bench, meticulously pointing out every part of my body that was covered in vomit.

"I think I'm good," I said. I was completely soaked, but it was a huge improvement over my previous state. Kaia turned off the hose.

"Are you okay?" she asked as she stepped closer. I stared at her shoes, unable to meet her eyes.

"Yeah."

She must have sensed she wasn't going to get anything more out of me. Her feet shifted from side to side. "Um, I think I'm going to go, then. Steve needs to get home. This was a lot for him. For all of us, really." I nodded. I'd want to get as far away from me, too, which was obviously Steve's whole plan. And it had worked.

"Okay, then. Bye."

"Bye."

Kaia's and Steve's footsteps crunched the gravel as they walked away. Steve murmured something. Kaia responded in a low whisper, "I know. I don't think I'm ever going to get that smell out of my nose."

II

I woke up with a slight taste of vomit in my mouth. And terror in my heart. Steve still had control of the website.

I snatched my phone from the side table. Last night I had attempted to reset the password for hours, but I was totally locked out now. How did he do it?

"Nothing new. Nothing new," I prayed.

I opened the site. I stopped praying.

On-screen, SaveSteve.org now promised, *If we reach $1,300 in donations, I will wear a beard of bees!*

I threw my phone across the room and earned three more cracks in my screen.

An hour later, I was standing at the door to Steve's house, again. I had to put an end to this before he killed me. I rehearsed in different tones, "We both want the same thing, Steve. We both want the same thing." Not convinced I had found it, I still knocked.

Maybe his parents would answer. Preferably his mom. She liked me. Maybe I could use her goodwill against Steve. Somehow.

The handle clunked and the door swung open.

Steve. In a hot-pink bathrobe. Eating a bowl of ice cream. Unfazed by my presence. "Oh, hey, Camburger. I'm so sorry. There must be some mistake. The Vomiters' Anonymous meeting was last week. Why don't you come back maybe . . . never?"

And he slammed the door as hard as he could.

I should just tell Kaia that Steve hacked the site. But what was my proof? That I didn't have the password? I had gone along with the diaper and the hamster ball. What kind of crazy person would do that?

I knocked on the door again. Nothing. I leaned in closer and tried to shout through the heavy oak. "Steve, I just want to—"

The door jerked open and Steve smiled like it was the first time he'd seen me today. "Oh, hey, Cam. Wow. Thanks for stopping by, but I'm just hanging with people who don't have a boner for my girlfriend today. Maybe tomorrow . . ." He reached to close the door.

"Can we talk about the website?" I blurted.

Steve feigned confusion. "Website? What website?"

"You know, the website you hacked," I demanded.

"How could I hack a website, Cam? Do I look like some

computer nerd? I'm just a dumb bro-ham with cancer. And it is really debilitating, as you can see." He then shoved a massive scoop of cookies and cream into his mouth, the excess spilling over the edges of his lips baby-style.

"I'm just trying to help you. Can't we get along?"

"Get along? That sounds boring."

"Steve . . . just give me the password back. How did you even get it again?"

"You know, you're pretty stupid for a nice guy, Cam. I just added my email to the main contact and made myself administrator. Which means I can remove any old contact emails from some bot named Cam. Now I'm the only one who can reset the password." Steve took another bite of ice cream. "Though I could be persuaded to give you back the website if you say one simple thing."

"Sure. What?" I tried to sound accommodating.

He spoke in a voice that I guess was supposed to sound like me, but sounded more like a little old lady. "Steve, you're right. I'm just doing this to get in Kaia's panties."

"Steve, I'm not—"

"Say it."

"I can't. It's not true."

"Using Kaia's name as your new password says otherwise."

"That's only because we were working on it together."

"You didn't want to just use 'Steve'?"

"You can't use the name of your website as a password."

"Say it, Cam."

"Seriously, I'm not doing this to—"

"Get in Kaia's panties?"

"Stop! I hate that word."

"You can say undergarments if it suits your Victorian sensibilities."

"I'm not going to say anything."

"Then you're going to look so nice with a face full of bees." Steve actually seemed happier. "Do you think they will crawl up your nose? What if one gets stuck?"

I crossed my arms. "I'm not going to show up, okay. How about that? You can post whatever crazy stunt on there you want, but it doesn't mean I'm going to do it."

"Cam? What are you doing here?" Kaia appeared behind Steve. Had she been there the whole time? And we'd been talking about her panties!

"Uh. I just . . . I wanted to check on Steve."

"I thought you wanted to talk about the website, Cam?" Steve's smile could cut glass.

"Oh, um, yeah. I . . ."

"Oh my god. I saw the bee thing," Kaia said, horrified.

"Yeah, it's a stupid idea, right?" I should just tell her it was Steve's idea.

"So stupid," Steve agreed, sounding concerned. "I told Cam he shouldn't do it. Sounds kind of dangerous and it might hurt a fuckload if they accidentally swarm." His expression was serious, but his eyes were dancing.

"That's what I thought," Kaia said. Thank god. I relaxed

until she continued, "But you have to come see this!" She motioned for us to follow her back into the house, and her enthusiasm scared the shit out of me.

Steve raised an eyebrow, excited for whatever it was.

I gulped.

Back in Steve's den, Kaia picked up her laptop and presented it to us. "Look!" On-screen was the Save Steve website. "You set a goal of thirteen hundred and we are already at five thousand!" Oh shit. Shit. Shit. Shit. Shit. Shit. "That hamster ball stunt was disgusting, and I don't think I've ever seen that much vomit come out of one person, but it really caught people's attention."

Speaking of vomit, I tried to hide a wave of nausea now churning inside of me. "Oh wow. That's . . . great." I could already feel the bees on my face.

Steve relished this new level of torture. His voice was almost falsetto. "But you're not still going to do the bee beard, right? I'm worried for you, Cam. I don't want you to get hurt."

He had me trapped. If I relented, Steve would win and look concerned and thoughtful at the same time. If I agreed to do it . . . bees. Why couldn't I find another girl to like? I mean, I had liked other girls. There must be a different one I could fall for. Kimberly Longacre was kind of cute. But Kimberly Longacre hadn't spent all night with me in the wetlands reading about the end of the world. Kimberly Longacre didn't volunteer for fourteen different causes. Kimberly Longacre didn't comfort me after my diaper erection. Kimberly Longacre didn't smell like coconut.

Arrgggh!

Kaia had picked up on Steve's new maternal instinct. "I know. I know. You're right, Steve. Cam, it's crazy. You can't do it." She put the laptop down and closed it with a sigh.

Oh god, I'd disappointed Kaia.

"Agreed." Steve grinned and plopped down on the couch, victorious.

Were bees really that scary?

"We can just give people their money back," Kaia said, now completely deflating. "I'm sorry, I got excited because that put us a quarter of the way to our goal." She could taste the twenty thousand, too. *Our* twenty thousand. "But it's not worth it if you get hurt." She patted my arm gently. The crush of her disillusionment bore down on me like a collapsing glacier.

They were just tiny little bees. Right?

"No, I can do it."

"Cam!" Kaia sounded scared. "You can't."

"Yeah. Cam. Please. It's too dangerous," Steve deadpanned. Damn, he was enjoying this.

I focused on Kaia. "It will be fine. I'll be fine. Those people at the bee sanctuary must know what they're doing, right?"

"Maybe. Seemed a little low rent when I looked at their site." Steve crossed his ankles and put his arms behind his head.

But Kaia's eyes were on me. "Are you sure?" There was a flicker of hope in her eyes.

"Totally." Our eyes held for a moment as she drank in my bravery (or insanity, it was hard to tell).

Steve sat up. "Welp. Glad that's sorted. Kaia, Netflix is waiting. . . ." He flicked on the TV.

"Do you want to stay?" Kaia asked, like she kind of wanted me to.

Steve leaned back and spread his arms across the back of the sectional. "Yeah, Cam. It's just going to be me and Kaia cuddling, but you can sit on the couch and make it awkward."

"Steve! Don't be an asshole!" Steve shrank into the pillows. I really needed to record his reaction the next time that happened.

"Sorry," he whined. "I was just excited to spend time with you."

Kaia turned back to me with an apologetic sigh. "Sorry, I've just been pulled in a thousand directions lately. We haven't had any time together. You know?"

I nodded, happy for a way out of here. "Sure. Yeah. Of course. I guess I'll see you at the bees."

She hugged me. "You're amazing, Cam." Having her arms wrapped around me in front of Steve almost made me forget about the hive of bees waiting for me. Almost.

Anxious to escape before Steve found another way to torment me, I hurried to the front door. But before I reached it, I heard Steve's dad. "I'm not taking charity, Cheryl!" I froze, unsure what to do.

"It's just his friends. They want to help," Steve's mom pleaded. "You saw those co-pays. We need the money."

I didn't want to hear this. I tried to open the front door silently.

"Oh, did you want me to take those jobs?" Mr. Stevenson's voice dripped with acid. "I turned down three already. But then who is going to take care of Steve, huh?"

"I would have stayed home—"

"But you have the health insurance. I know. We've been over this. That doesn't mean we're taking charity like lazy fucking moochers."

I didn't really remember exactly what my parents' arguments were about, but this one sure sounded familiar. I felt terrible for Steve's mom. Unlike my mom, she still had to deal with Steve's dad's toxic male posturing.

I shut the front door gently just as I heard him laugh, "Though I am kind of excited to see that weird kid wear a face full of bees."

Bees.

Watching every bee-beard video I could find on YouTube was actually helping a little bit. Sure, the people squirmed and winced, but they all survived. It probably wasn't as scary as I'd imagined it to be. It turned out, bee bearding was something bees did naturally. They even did it outside their own hives, clustering together to get a whiff of their queen. I assumed the queen bee smelled like coconut.

And who knew, maybe we could get to ten thousand? A few stings were worth it, right?

On the edge of the screen, YouTube recommended a similar video titled: "Bee Beard Gone Wrong!" What? Why would the algorithm recommend that? Whatever. I didn't have to click on it. Why would I? I was trying to calm myself, right? I wouldn't click it. Nope, not gonna click.

Click.

Twelve thousand bees swarmed and attacked a chubby guy on-screen. He shrieked and ran into a nearby field while the angry mob of insects followed. Even the camera guy was fleeing, screaming, "We're all gonna die!"

I began hyperventilating.

Buzzzzzzzzzzzz. That sound wasn't on my laptop. That was in my room. Oh shit! They were in my room! Shit! Shit! Shit!

But it was just my phone vibrating. It was Kaia.

Kaia: I got the afternoon off so I could record it.

I should tell her not to come. I didn't want her last memory of me to be me spazzing out in an orchard, being stung to death.

My bedroom door opened. I quickly closed my laptop.

"Did you see?" My mom held up her phone. "The bee sanctuary has the cutest little café that does a high tea!" She scrolled down the page. "Actually, they call it a 'High Bee.' Adorable, right? You should bring me back something." A cute café? That was her takeaway.

"You're not worried about me doing this?"

She put down her phone and sat down heavily on my bed. "Sweetie, I am terrified, of course. I *was* going to forbid you because, frankly, it's insane. But I realized, you're just doing what I taught you. To make a difference, you have to risk something. So, while I was at work having a small panic attack, I reminded myself that you don't have a bee allergy. And the place seems very professional. They did twelve bee beards last year."

"That makes me number thirteen . . ."

"Also, when you think about it, you're bringing attention to two great causes—Steve *and* endangered bees." Her expression darkened. "Did you hear that report on NPR about Monsanto? Goddamn agribusiness oligarchs! Their Roundup weed killer is basically causing colony collapse. If they called it 'bee poison,' do you think people would still buy it just to get rid of some dandelions? It's all about profit margins for them." She pointed a finger at me. "Don't be like those assholes." Then she scooped me into a hug. "Dinner's in ten minutes." As quick as she'd come, she left.

Buzz!

Another text from Kaia.

Kaia: It's gonna BEE amazing. 🐝 🎉

Steve's puns irritated the crap out of me, but when Kaia did it, I melted. I couldn't tell her to stay away. Then my mom's words echoed in my head: "cutest little café." I pulled up the bee sanctuary website on my phone and sure enough, there was a bee-themed café. *The most romantic lunch spot in Ojai*, the site boasted. Romantic? Lunch?

I texted her back: Glad you'll BEE there. That'll take the sting out of it! 😜

This might be perfect. If I survived.

Vaseline was slathered under my eyes and on my lips. Cotton balls bloomed from my ears and nostrils. My sleeves were taped tight. But I was still terrified of the caged hive that buzzed nearby. Kaia wasn't here yet and I was kind of glad. I wasn't certain I wanted her to see me this way.

But we had reservations at the café and it was obvious why it was voted the most romantic lunch in Ojai. The surrounding fields glowed and waved in the always-gentle breeze. The air was so fragrant that I was in a constant state of almost sneezing out my cotton balls. It was a living Monet painting. Or was it Manet? Art history was one of my worst grades.

The formerly welcoming beekeepers Jesse and Paula were getting impatient. I knew we were running late, but at least they had hats with veils and white bodysuits protecting them. I was basically naked. Regardless, they kept checking the watches they couldn't even see.

"Just five more minutes," I pleaded.

I scanned past the beds of bergamot, primrose, and wild lilac (I had been given the full farm tour earlier) toward the rustic wooden farmhouse. Only hummingbirds and insects arrived and departed. Their buzzing and tweeting sounded impatient, too.

"We better get started, Cam. We've got to do rounds in about half an hour." It shouldn't surprise me. Kaia was always late. Maybe she'd still come mid-beard.

"Oh, okay. But, um, can one of you record it? I need proof."

Paula pulled her phone out of her bodysuit and Jesse carried the cage with the queen bee toward me. Did they have to move so fast?

"I usually offer a Xanax or some CBD beforehand but, being as you're a minor, I guess you're gonna have to do some deep breathing and just think of a happy place. Like I said, first thing we're gonna do is tie this little wooden box with the queen around your neck," Jesse's gruff voice explained even though he was already tying it on. I couldn't see the queen, but I could hear her agitated buzzing.

Paula held her phone up to record me and I tried to smile. But then I heard Jesse bringing the hive over. "So, what I'm going to do is just start scoopin' 'em up on you. We'll start on your chest and then they'll gradually crawl up."

A flying bee strafed me, and I flinched. Just one bee! He was about to dump twelve thousand bees on me. Oh god. Thousands of zuzzing, crawling bees! I was definitely the stupidest person in the history of Ventura County. Goddamn Steve!

I remembered Jesse's advice. Deep breathing. A happy place. What *was* my happy place?

Jesse took a scoop of bees out of the hive and they clung to his hand. He was gonna put them on me. I wanted to run, but that would cause worse problems with the queen around my neck. He tossed and shook the cluster onto the words "Save Steve" emblazoned on my T-shirt. I felt all my organs recoil. Bees clung to my shirt. Even with cotton in my ears it was getting loud. I didn't dare look down. I stared ahead, hoping Kaia would still come. Then we could have lunch. A romantic lunch. With Kaia. That was my happy place.

The café. Late afternoon. The light is soft and Kaia looks radiant. She laughs at something I say. She licks some honey and smiles. She says I have to taste the honey, too, and holds up her spoon so I can lick it. It is soooo good. . . . Zazzz!

A bee riot was pushing and pulsing all over my chest. A few started crawling on my neck. I could feel every tiny little claw as it pulled at my skin. More followed. Bees on top of bees on top of bees! Tiny bee hands grasping at my pores. Each bee was holding on to a bee that was holding on to a bee that was holding on to my neck skin! It was stretching!

Honey tea slides down my throat as Kaia brushes her hair behind her ear. She tells me honey is an aphrodisiac. (Really, I would have told her that because I just read about it online, but it seemed creepier for me to suggest.) *I take a flirty bite of honeycomb. Crunch. Crunch . . .*

The first bee just pulled itself onto my face. The Vaseline was supposed to protect my skin, but I could feel him digging away at it. He was interested in my lips. Now more bees were joining him. They were looking for moisture in my mouth. Their minuscule bee claws were trying to pry open my mouth. They were strong. So damn strong. I clenched my mouth closed.

"Might want to close your eyes, too, at this point," Jesse suggested. "They like to drink tears."

I slammed my eyes shut. In the darkness, the scratch of bees scaling my face was even more visceral. I could feel the bees scraping my face with their stingers to intimidate me. I didn't know if I had a bee beard yet, but I might have a heart attack if it wasn't over soon.

"Oh, hey, your friend's here!" I heard Paula say.

And just like that, everything was okay. The buzzing turned into a soft Tibetan chant. The scratches became a playful, warm tickle. I wanted to say hello to Kaia, but I couldn't open my mouth. Instead, I hummed, "'Ello."

I wanted to see her and bravely squinted one of my eyes open. All I could make out was her bee-suit silhouette, but she waved and I, very cautiously, wiggled my fingers back. She looked good even in that suit. I could taste the café honey now. She was going to love it. I wasn't going to bring up the aphrodisiac thing, though. Unless she did first.

"Okay, that's it!" Jesse announced.

I couldn't believe it. I'd made it. I was a bee beard veteran. All I had to do now was get them off me. But with Kaia here, I felt more confident than ever. Bees were friendly, after all. Jesse just had to suck 'em off, back into their hive.

"So, you're gonna jump up and land hard," Jesse explained. "You want them to fall off." What?! He wanted me to jump around? With bees on me? "Then we're gonna blast the leaf blower at them. You got it?"

At least there was a leaf blower.

"One." Jesse counted off. "Two."

I went to my happy place one last time.

We feed each other honey-covered ice cream with little chocolate bee candies.
"Three!"

118

I jumped. I could feel the bees fall off. But they didn't just drop to the ground and take a nap. They began flying around in chaotic patterns. They seemed angry. And the queen was still on my neck! "Get her off. Get her off!" Then the leaf blower chugged to life and I was blasted by a massive gust. My jowls warbled. *Wwabababab.* I stumbled back in a buzzing wind tunnel. Bees smacked my face like fuzzy bullets. Ouch! One just stung me in the ear! This was not how it was supposed to go. Once one stung you, that was like a signal for the rest to attack. That's what Google said! Fuck! Fuckity fuck! "We're all gonna die!" I screamed. "AHHHHHHHHH!"

"Relax. You're all clear, buddy," Jesse said as he unhooked the queen from my neck.

All clear?

The buzzing died down. Now I could hear laughter. Familiar laughter. Maniacal laughter. Not Kaia's laughter.

I opened my eyes.

Steve.

In the beekeeper outfit.

FML.

"Buddy!" he sang, relishing my disappointment. "Sorry, Kaia was buzzzzzzy. She got wrapped up in another angry righteous thing. She asked me to come instead. I promised to send her a pic."

He held up his phone, said, "Smile!" and snapped a picture of me that I'm sure looked like a cross between Einstein and a three-year-old who'd just dropped his ice cream.

This was not my happy place.

I speed-walked toward my car along the flowered path. The sting on my ear was the least of my pain.

"I think they do a full-body bee blanket if you want to go bigger, buddy." Steve trotted after me like a smug golden retriever.

I charged ahead and swatted a bee away. "Glad you think this is hilarious. I don't see anyone else doing all this for you." I had just worn a freakin' bee beard to raise money for his family and he couldn't even say thank you.

"Cam Webber?" A woman in a bright yellow bee-themed dress appeared. "We have the table ready for you and your guest."

Steve's ears pricked up and he skidded to a stop. "Table?"

"For high tea. We call it High Bee," the hostess explained.

"High Bee! Oh, Cam?" Steve squealed, giddy. "For me?"

"Actually, that's okay. I think . . ."

But Steve had a bone and he was not giving it up. "What? No, it sounds romantic. Almost like . . . a date. Is this a date, Cam?" he asked with just the tiniest threat in his voice. "And you didn't even know I was coming."

"It—"

"Any chance we can get a table by the window? I just looooove the view here." Steve batted his eyelashes at the hostess.

"Of course," she chirped. "Right this way."

Steve locked his arm in mine. "Let's go, honey!" And he pulled me toward the most romantic lunch in Ojai.

There were bees dressed as cooks and bees dressed as farmers. Bees with fairy wings and mer-bees with long fins instead of stingers. There was a section of famous bees—Buzz Aldrin, the Bee Gees, and Sting. Mobiles of bees chasing flowers dangled from the ceiling. I was sure whatever concerto was playing in the background was in B-flat.

And there were lace doilies. On the table. On the chairs. On the walls. On the ceiling! So many doilies.

"Well, this is just delightful." Steve glowed as he poured himself some tea from the bumblebee-shaped teapot. A plate of teeny tiny sandwiches were stacked high between us (cucumber, watercress, arugula). Next to them was a pyramid of honey jars (blueberry, coffee, alfalfa, orange blossom, and BBQ sauce).

The only other people in the restaurant were older women in festive hats. They smiled at us. I could have sworn one of them even checked Steve out.

Steve picked up a sandwich ever so delicately. "I am overcome with cuteness. I think . . . I think this petite sandwich is making me fall in love with you, Cam." He popped it into his mouth and played footsie with me under the table.

"It's not a date, Steve. It was the only place to eat around here." I refused to admit my fantasy even if it was blindingly obvious.

The waitress arrived with another tray, this one piled high with bee-adorned desserts. "Everything okay?" she asked.

"Delectable," Steve crooned.

She smiled and walked away.

"Cam, this is an itty-bitty little cake with a bee on it. This cake definitely says, 'May I stick my penis inside you?'"

"It's dessert, Steve. There isn't a hidden message."

"And this tea! So aromatic! Will I suddenly find your gawky ass more attractive if I drink it?" He took a long slurpy sip and then stopped. His eyes went wide as he sloshed the tea in his mouth and then swallowed. "Goddamn! This tea is the shit." I rolled my eyes at him. "Dude, I'm not lying," he insisted, and poured me a spot.

Certain he was just mocking me, I took an unenthusiastic sip and put the cup down. But then it hit me. "Whoa!"

"Right?"

It was like an eruption of syrupy goodness in my mouth. "It's the honey. It's the fresh honey."

"It's not the tea?" Frenzied, Steve grabbed the top honey jar from the pyramid, popped it open, and thrust his finger inside.

"I don't think— You're not supposed to—"

But he shoved the honey-covered finger into his mouth anyway. Again, his eyes burst wide. "It's not just honey. There's something in it."

He handed me the jar he had just penetrated with his finger. I grabbed a tiny teaspoon, scooped some out, and tasted it. Wham! Pleasure spread through my body. "It's orange. You can taste the orange blossoms!"

Steve took the jar back. "Holy shit. You're right. That's crazy. You can taste what they ate." The older women were craning to see us and shaking their heads.

"Yeah," I said, and savored the remaining sweetness.

"So we're eating bee shit."

"No. It's not like that. It's an excretion."

"So it's bee jizz?"

"Staaaahhhpp."

"Bee jizz is delicious." He drizzled the jar directly into his mouth.

The waitress appeared. Embarrassed, I sat back and kicked Steve to stop drizzling. She had clearly overheard our idiotic conversation and felt the need to clarify. "Actually, honey is stored in the part of a bee's stomach called the ingluvies. When the forager bee returns to the hive, they regurgitate the nectar and begin the process of trophallaxis, where they transfer it via mouth to the house bee." Pleased with her speech, she filled our teacups and left.

Steve and I sat for a moment as we pieced together what she'd said. Then Steve slowly put down the jar.

"So . . . it's vomit?" I stared at my full cup of tea.

"No. Worse. They vomit into each other's mouths and then vomit it out. It's double vomit."

I pushed my teacup away.

But the syrupiness still coated my mouth. Was it any more gross than yogurt? I mean, that was just bacteria. "It is delicious," I tossed out there to see if Steve could also look past the barf factor.

Steve sighed. "Fuck it. Pass me one of those bee vomit cookies."

I laughed and took one before handing them off to Steve.

The crunchy biscuits crumbled in my mouth like an avalanche of honey bliss. Before we knew it, we'd dusted off the entire tray. While we basked in our golden glory, I wondered if this wasn't a good turn of events. Maybe I'd just needed some time with Steve, so he could see that I actually cared?

"So, how's your treatment going? You've had two rounds of chemo, right?"

But Steve groaned. "Wow. Talk about a buzzkill, Cam."

"Seriously, this must be more difficult than you're letting on."

"It's fine," he answered, and scooped up crumbs from his plate. "If I knew a little cancer would get me out of school so quickly, I'd have gotten my lymph nodes to tumor up long ago."

I thought about leaving it there, but then I remembered his parents arguing at his house. I'd lived through something like that. "Well, your mom is pretty upset."

But instead of softening, he became rigid and put down his plate. "What do you know about my mom?"

"It's just. I heard them arguing. . . . That must be stressful for you." I tried to sound sympathetic but could see him bristling.

"Oh, it's not enough to try to steal my girlfriend. Now you're going to sit there and judge my family?" What was happening? We'd just been drizzling honey moments ago. How had we ended up here with just a few words?

"I'm not trying to— I'm just being friendly—"

Steve shoved his plate my way and the rest of the flatware shuddered. "Look, just stay out of my life, okay? We all know why you're here. And it's not because of me." He was sincerely pissed. "I don't need you to suddenly start pretending to be my bro because you spied on my parents and overheard something you don't understand. We are fine. Nobody wants you hanging around, Cam. Nobody wants *you*." My stomach clenched. My legs braced. "So just go back to sniffing around Kaia and stay out of my family's shit." He stood up and threw down his napkin. "We aren't friends."

The old ladies in their hats watched on.

"We could be . . ." I tried desperately to calm him down.

"Really?" He smiled but his eyes were hard. "We'll see about that." And he left.

I was motionless, stunned at the sudden turn.

A moment later the waitress walked up to me with the bill. It was on a doily that had the inscription: *Bee the Change You Want to See in the World* —*Ghan-bee*.

12

Because he's my very best friend in the whole world, if we raise $15,000, I'll get Steve Stevenson's name tattooed on my ass, read Steve's latest challenge.

I glared at the posting through the cracked glass of my phone. What a dick. I'd already raised $8,000 for this guy and he just kept coming. We could be friends. But instead of seeing an opportunity to talk about his family, he was going to take out his stunted emotions on me. Well, whatever, Steve. I'd almost gotten stung by twelve thousand angry bees. Did he really think I was worried about a little tattoo? You could get those removed. I scrolled back through all of Kaia's amazed texts about the bees.

Kaia: Mind blown!
Kaia: Video's got 3,000 views! 🎉

Kaia: So much buzz! 😊

Kaia: Just had a dream about your bee beard! Guess I still feel guilty I missed it. I suck. You're the best! Hero!

She was dreaming about me! I could taste the $20,000. And Steve's tattoo might just take us over the top.

Bring the pain!

"You're going to regret this," my mom said as she scrawled her name on the permission slip, "but that's okay. Mistakes are part of growing up. Actually, you still make mistakes when you're a grown-up, too. Anyway, I already talked to Mario about cover-ups. He's the one who put the roses over your dad's name."

It had taken a lot of convincing to get my mom to agree to this, but I was determined. Steve wasn't going to beat me. Not that I'd told my mom that. I'd just showed her how much people had already donated, then reminded her that she'd gotten her first tattoo in her friend's garage when she was fifteen. Sometimes my mom's chronic oversharing came in handy. "Have you considered henna?" my mom asked. "It'd still make a statement. A less permanent one."

Barely listening, I scanned the room. Steve was in the back, chatting with Mario. Of course, Steve had insisted on recording the whole thing himself. He caught my eye and gave me an excited thumbs-up. After our bee lunch, we hadn't spoken more than a few sentences to each other. But today, Steve seemed to have decided to pretend nothing had happened.

My mom glanced at her phone. "I have an open house I got

to get to. Good luck, bud." She straightened her blazer and kissed me on the cheek. "It's your butt. It's your choice. Even though I don't approve, I'm proud of you."

Five minutes later, I lay on my chest with my pants pulled down while Mario, who kept talking about my mom and how great she was, carefully placed the paper with the design of the "Save Steve" tattoo onto my body. I focused on the giant demon mural painted on the back wall. I was glad I hadn't invited Kaia. She did not need to be staring at my bare butt. Neither did Steve, but apparently that couldn't be helped.

"That looks beautiful. Cam, you are *such* a good friend." He pushed his phone closer to my ass. "Show him, Mario."

Mario pulled out a mirror and tilted it so I could see his handiwork. It was bigger than I'd hoped it would be. And in Comic Sans. Steve had run a poll on the site and of course everyone had chosen the goofiest font. Out of my peripheral vision I could see Steve's giant stupid grin.

"So?" he said, clearly relishing this. "You like?"

I held his gaze, not giving him any hint of regret. "Looks great."

He matched my stare. "I love that wacky font. Such a great choice for something that will permanently mark your body."

"For you, Steve, anything." I gave him as sincere a smile as I could muster.

"All right. Buckle up. Should just take a few minutes," Mario announced, and grabbed his needle. He flicked it on and it zapped to life. It sounded like a couple of harmless bees.

I took a deep, confident breath. Steve leaned forward with his phone, right up to my face.

I smiled and spoke into the camera. "Save Steve.org, every-one!"

Mario coached, "It should feel like a pinch . . ."

ZIZAZT!

A shock of searing pain jabbed me. It flashed up my spine and arced through my body. I was like Homer Simpson getting electrocuted, his body flashing between flesh and skeleton. "Yeooooowwwww!"

I bolted up, jumped off the table, jerked up my pants, and ran. Fast. Away. From Mario. And his death pen.

As I slammed through the front door to the tattoo parlor, Steve's voice trailed behind me. "Come back, best buddy. Come back!" And then, through tears of laughter, "You're my best frieeeeeennnndddd!!!"

"You've been hacked like the Democrats were in 2016 and you can't let that prick get away with it. You need to tell Kaia the website isn't under your control anymore, my man." Todd paced, reusable coffee cup in hand. We probably should stop holding our city council planning meetings at Earth First Coffee because everyone just ends up agitated from the caffeine. I was jacked up on a double mochaccino, which was why I'd even started blabbering about Steve.

Patrice chimed in, "I told you, Cam. You can't mess with a cancer love story. Watch a classic, *Here on Earth*."

"Here we go . . . ," Todd huffed.

Patrice ignored him and leaned in, excited. "I know it's way before your time, but I really think it's the most relevant. A cancer-ridden girl has to choose between a nice boy and an asshole jock. Guess which one she chooses . . . ?"

"Kaia doesn't have cancer," I tried to clarify.

"The asshole," Patrice declared. She took a sip from her turmeric latte like a mic drop.

"I'm not sure what I'm supposed to take away from that." Clearly Patrice didn't understand the dynamics at play here.

Todd nudged me and motioned to the entrance. Kaia had just walked in, wearing her Save the Shark hoodie. The other protestors greeted her, and I hopped up. It was the first time I'd seen her since the tattoo debacle and I needed to assure her that we would still reach our goal. I had the start of an S on my ass but nothing more. It looked like a weirdly shaped birthmark and definitely didn't fulfill the requirements of the pledge.

Squeezing through the tightly packed tables, I finally reached her.

"Hey," I said, with my hands in my pockets.

She looked flustered. "Sorry I'm late. I had a thing with mock trial I couldn't get out of. How's it going? Did we pick a speaker for the city council meeting yet?"

"Not yet." I looked down at my shoes, more nervous around her than I'd been recently.

"Oh, good," Kaia said, and waved at Todd. He gave me a prodding smile.

"I'm sorry I couldn't go through with the tattoo. It turns out I have an unusually low threshold for pain—"

"Hey, I don't blame you. Did you really want every girl to think of Steve when they saw you naked?" She laughed. Why hadn't I thought of that? And why were we talking about other girls? And me naked? "It's a bummer we might have to give the money back." She sighed.

Once I'd bailed on the stunt, there had been an onslaught of complaints. "I know, who knew HelpSomeone.org has such a convenient refund policy?"

"People are such assholes. Like the more important thing isn't saving Steve."

"Right. . . . Well, I have a couple of ideas that could get us back . . . ," I began, ready to inspire her confidence.

"I think it's gonna be pretty hard to top the bees, really." Kaia stopped me before I could even get going. "And if you keep on having to top yourself and then can't follow through, I think people will get annoyed and we'll have burned up all our goodwill."

"Right, but—" I rushed to stem the tide of her withdrawal.

"Maybe we should stay with social media and email and stuff. It's easier schedule-wise anyway." She gave me an apologetic smile. I could feel my pedestal being pulled out from under me. I was going down. Fast.

"I still want to get the twenty thousand." I sounded desperate.

"I know. But it was crazy to think we could." The dream was vanishing. She was ready to move on and let Save Steve be

131

one of the things we did together that one time. A memory.

"Look. Just give me one more shot. I have a great idea."

"You do? What?" There was doubt, but also a glimmer of interest. She was still in. Barely. And even though I had absolutely no idea what this brilliant idea was, I could keep the dream alive for a little bit longer until I figured out something more amazing than a beard of bees.

I summoned my best carnival barker smile and trumpeted, "It's a surprise."

I pressed the doorbell to Steve's house and waited. The various bags and buckets I was carrying dug into my shoulders and palms. There was a crackle of static. "What?" Steve's voice sounded small and tinny over the intercom. I fumbled, switching the bags to one hand, and pressed the button to respond.

"I came up with our next fundraiser! You're going to love it." There was no answer from Steve. Just as I started to wonder if he had gone back to shooting things on his Xbox, the door opened.

"Aren't you done? I assumed that scream of pain was your final surrender." Steve glared down at me. He was wrapped in a fuzzy bathrobe with unicorn slippers on his feet. But the ridiculous footwear wasn't what I noticed first.

"You're bald." The words slipped from my mouth, unbidden.

Steve's expression flickered, but then he rolled his eyes. "I have cancer, dweebnuts." He opened the door wider. "Well, let's see what you got."

Standing in Steve's backyard in a swimsuit, my phone mounted on a tripod nearby, I lifted a pitcher over my head. Steve watched, nonplussed, still wearing his robe and slippers. At his feet were the various buckets I'd brought.

"Is this a sex kink?" he asked.

"Just start filming." With a shrug, Steve clicked on the phone. I tipped the pitcher and a golden river of honey poured out, coating my hair, then eyes, then body.

"This is definitely a sex kink."

"It's called the Honey Stick Challenge. You know, like those viral stunts people do for various causes? I do this, then people copy me, and we'll raise tons of money."

"I don't know. I'm getting weirdly turned on."

"It's not a sex kink!" Actually, it came out as, "Bits naw a se kinf," because a big glob of honey rolled over my nose and into my mouth. I choked it down (it still tasted deliciously of orange blossoms) and continued, "It's honey. That's, like, our thing, right?" I needed to make sure Steve would approve of the stunt, but also wanted to see if we could pave over our rough patch at the café. Show him I had no hard feelings. Go higher.

"I'm sorry. We have a 'thing'?"

I ignored Steve and gestured to the containers. "Now open the buckets and you'll see stuff to throw at me. Get it? Honey—"

Wumph! I was hit in the face with a handful of flour.

"Stick!" Steve finished, delighted. "Yeah. I think I got this." After that, it was five solid minutes of flour, Froot Loops, glitter, feathers, Legos, and rainbow pom-poms being either thrown at or dumped on me. Steve practically skipped as he decorated me like a Christmas tree, tossing glitter into the air and letting it rain down. Every time a pom-pom or a Lego came close to hitting me in the nuts, he let out a happy giggle. Finally satisfied with his work, he sat down, a bit out of breath, and turned off the camera. We were both smiling. "Oh my god," he panted. "That was actually fun!"

"Right?" I wiped a Froot Loop off my eyebrow. "People will love it."

"I'm impressed, Cam."

"So you're in? We can upload it?"

Steve nodded. "Definitely."

I stepped out of Steve's bathroom, toweling my hair dry. I'd managed to wash all the honey off. It hadn't taken long, because Steve had, like, twelve shower heads in his enormous glass-enclosed shower. As I'd dried off, I couldn't help but notice all the bottles of pills lining the sink. There was even one of those rainbow pill cases with the days of the week on them that I thought only old people used. It had felt wrong to stare at them, like when I looked at Steve's bald head too long.

When I stepped into his bedroom, Steve looked up from his computer.

"Cam, my sticky friend, I just posted your new idea!" He spun the laptop around for me to see.

"Wait . . . that doesn't look like the Honey Stick Challenge."

There was no video on the website, just a box of text.

Steve leaned back in his chair, resting his arms behind his head. "Did you actually think I was going to post that lame-ass honey stunt? Something that was clearly engineered to be painless and only mildly humiliating, but would still let you raise money to impress my girlfriend? Oh, sweet, stupid Cam." He gave a short, fake laugh. "But it did give me a great idea."

I leaned in closer to read. "Sorry I totally failed Steve as a friend and bailed on the tattoo thing. To make it up to him and everyone, I'm taking over Steve's spot in the lip sync contest next week. I will be performing his—and my—favorite song ever, 'Money,' by the goddess of music, Cardi B. And if you want to see me do it in this costume, donate now."

I scrolled down to reveal a picture of Cardi B in a very bright . . . very minimal . . . piece of clothing, then looked up in horror, but Steve wasn't at his desk any longer. He was rummaging through his closet. He emerged seconds later with the costume from the picture. It was very, very small. The only part that really covered anything were the thigh-high boots.

"I already bought the outfit before I got cancer. I've ruled the lip sync battle for two years. I have the confidence and charisma to pull off a scrap of spandex. But not you, Cam. Not with your fifth-grade pecs and your sad partially S-marked ass. Whenever Kaia thinks of you after this, she's not going to see Cam, the nice do-gooder activist with a heart of gold. No, she's going to think of Cardi Cam with his droopy package slapping all over the stage." He leaned closer to me and whispered in my ear. "Oh yeah. That's happening. I tried it on, Cam. It leaves zero to the imagination. There is—no—support." He pulled back. "But that doesn't matter, right? Because it's all for me." He practically sang the last word.

My phone buzzed.

Kaia: Cam, I'm not so sure this is a great idea . . .

Steve leaned over and looked at the message on my phone. He smiled. It wasn't the delighted smile he'd worn when he'd been decorating me with glitter. It was cold, triumphant, and evil. "I can't wait to see you twerk." I gripped the phone in my hand and tried not to react. But Steve knew he had me. He knew I hated Cardi. He knew I'd look ridiculous in that outfit. He knew Kaia would never look at me the same way again. There was only one thing he didn't know . . .

13

. . . I'd had seven years of dance lessons.

"Thank you, Abby Rosendale, for that medley from *Cats*," the announcer, our drama teacher, Mrs. Buyikian, boomed. I waited in a dark corner of the auditorium. The lip sync contest was a highlight of the year and pretty much everyone showed up. The room was packed. "Before we get to our next routine," Mrs. Buyikian continued, "I'd like to welcome back, for one night, Steve Stevenson!" There was a huge roar from the crowd.

In the front row next to Kaia, Steve stood, bowing to the audience. I could see his smug smile all the way from where I stood, hidden in the shadows. He'd been texting me the whole week about how he couldn't wait for this moment. Neither could I. For once, Steve had no idea what was coming.

"Next up. Cam Webber performing Cardi B's *radio-safe* version of 'Money'!"

The lights dimmed. There was a rustle of anticipation from the audience. I could see Steve's silhouette as he leaned over to whisper something in Kaia's ear. The soft hiss of a fog machine caused everyone to still. Steve cocked his head, confused.

Nine years ago, my newly divorced mom was determined that I would be a well-rounded young man with an expansive and progressive sense of masculinity. It translated into lessons at Ms. Bea's Dance Academy three times a week. I studied ballet, hip-hop, jazz, modern, and tap. All of it. I performed in the Ventura County *Nutcracker* for six Christmases. So when Steve shook that flimsy costume at me, it took every ounce of self-control I had not to grin. Like I hadn't worn a leotard before.

The first thumping beats of the song shook the room. Onstage, four lights snapped on, illuminating four dancers in matching patent leather corsets, tight buns, and black lace thigh-highs, chins tucked and eyes on the ground. Fog swirled around their ankles. As one, their arms shot into the air. The intake of breath from the audience was practically audible. In the front, I saw Steve stiffen.

The first thing I'd done after Steve posted the challenge was to return to Ms. Bea's and ask a favor. Soon, I had four of my old classmates and studio space. Other than for school, we hadn't left that room for a week. Yes, I objected to Cardi's music, but the idea of a white guy performing a woman of color's art for laughs was far, far more offensive. So I made certain no one would laugh at *this* routine. I was going to use every ounce of my dance training to fucking nail it.

I did my research. I posted to r/thatsracist to make sure I wasn't crossing any lines. My mom and I made some modifications to Steve's costume. I'd watched every performance of Cardi's I could find. I became even more motivated when I discovered that she and Michelle Obama had teamed up to get young people to vote. I worked my ass off. All for this moment.

"Who are these dancers? I want to see my man Cam," Steve called from the front row. From the back of the auditorium, I smiled and mentally counted . . . *five, six, seven, eight.*

The spotlight hit me. There was a wave of creaks as everyone in the audience turned to look. I flung my arms high, letting the satin of the dress my mom had sewn catch the light. It was a riff off the Thierry Mugler one Cardi had worn to the Emmys, where architectural folds sprang up in a semicircle from just below her hips all the way to her neckline and made her look like a pearl in the center of an oyster. I strode forward, the center aisle of the auditorium my runway, a swivel to my hips, the dress swaying around me like a peacock's tail.

Cardi started to rap, her voice echoing through the auditorium. I lip-synched along about fat checks, big bills, and tall heels. And I *was* wearing heels, the platform thigh-high boots Steve had given me. They flashed through the slit in the front of my dress with every step.

The audience was dead quiet. My heart stuttered and I felt a film of sweat break out on my back. But I had to keep going.

Stopping now would be worse. I kept my chin up, refusing to let the doubt show on my face. I was doing this. I stomped toward the risers leading up to the stage. Two of my backup dancers hurried down them in unison.

As we crossed each other on the stairs, the girls reached out, gripped the edges of my dress, and tugged. With a rip of Velcro, the dress tore away and billowed to the ground, revealing the leotard Steve had given me. I'd covered it in a mosaic of diamonds. The lights bounced off my body in blinding flashes, sending rainbows dancing around the auditorium. I stepped onto the stage. Finally, the audience found their voice. They screamed.

But I was just getting started. On the word *cartwheels*, I thrust out my launching leg, took a small hop with my back foot, pushed my front leg into the ground and, keeping my arms wide, flung myself into an aerial cartwheel. My head perpendicular to the floor, I swore I could see Steve mouth "HOOOOLY SHIIIIIITTT" in slow motion. My heels slammed into the ground, landing me perfectly so I was facing the crowd. The roar from the audience was so loud it temporarily blocked the music, but I didn't stop. I crouched down, the patent leather boots creaking, looked into Steve's stupid, stunned face, and kept going.

Behind me my backup dancers twisted, contorting their bodies, and beat out a counter rhythm to the song with their sharp, precise steps. I reached the chorus.

"Diamonds on my neck. . ." I dropped my hands behind me, pointed my chest to the ceiling, and bent one leg. I sliiiiiiiiiiid

the other one forward, pointing it, and began to thrust my hips.

Pandemonium.

"*. . . But nothing in this world . . .*" I flipped over again and writhed along the floor, feeling the grit of the stage cut into my hands and thighs. Steve's mouth hung open. Kaia's eyes were wide and unblinking. I didn't allow myself a smile, keeping my expression fierce as the song picked up.

"*. . . That I like more than checks.*" I spun to my feet, falling back into formation with my dancers. Together we splayed our thighs open and closed. We rolled our heads. Popped our shoulders. Swiveled our asses. All in perfect synchronization. I couldn't even hear the crowd or the music now. I was just dancing.

Steve was the furthest thought from my mind.

Finally, the girls ran to the back of the stage, leaving me alone as my routine reached its crescendo. This was the part that had given me trouble all week, but not tonight. Faster and faster I pounded out the steps, twisting, dipping, and spinning, the crowd screaming, then with a final burst of speed, I dropped to my knees and slid to the edge of the stage, turning as I did so I landed with my ass facing the crowd. Arching my back, and looking over my shoulder with coy tilt of my lips, I reached behind me and yanked the edge of the leotard up to reveal . . .

. . . a completed "Save Steve" tattoo. I'd gone back to Mario last week, determined to fight through my low pain threshold and redeem myself. As the audience took it in, a giant banner with SaveSteve.org on it unfurled at the back of the stage and fake one-hundred-dollar bills rained down around me, the word *money* echoing over the last beats of the song.

The entire room completely lost their minds. Everyone leaped to their feet, hugging, screaming, fists pumping the air. I panted, sweat dripping into my eyes, making my vision sparkle as applause crashed over me. It kept coming. Wave after wave, never seeming to end. There was only one person in the whole place who wasn't standing: Steve.

I locked eyes with him and grinned.

Backstage, I changed into sweats and an old T-shirt, carefully hanging my costume back on its hanger. I scrubbed at my face with a washcloth, trying to remove my makeup, though I'd forgotten how hard it was to get off and was probably just smearing around eyeliner and glitter. The one thing that definitely wasn't coming off was my smile. I was pretty sure it was stuck there permanently. I was flying. I could do anything right now. I could walk into Channel Islands Aqua Park and free that shark myself. Giving up on the eyeliner as a lost cause, I tossed the washcloth aside and stepped out of the makeshift dressing room they'd set up for the performers.

I was immediately mobbed. Every theater tech kid in the vicinity dropped what they were doing and for a moment all I could do was high-five, fist-bump, and hug my way through the crowd. Then, through the press of black-clad bodies, I saw Kaia and Steve approaching through the shadowed clutter of backstage. My smile got even bigger. With apologies to the tech nerds, I started to push my way toward them.

". . . and then he did that thing with his hips and . . . wow." Kaia excitedly waved her arms for emphasis. Overhearing her praise made my insides feel like a half-baked chocolate chip cookie. I had to stop and collect myself behind a plywood apple tree as she continued, "You have to admit it was incredible."

"So incredible. It was basically his coming out performance, right?" Steve snorted.

Kaia's arms dropped. "Wow. You really can't handle anything but twentieth-century gender norms, can you?"

"What? Come on, Kaia, it was a little gay."

Kaia stiffened. "I'm sorry. Are you using the word 'gay' like it's a bad thing?"

"Uh . . . no?" Steve floundered. I felt a stab of pity for him and stepped back into the shadows. But I was still a little excited to hear Kaia tear into him.

"Because I'm really not sure what you're trying to say here." Kaia crossed her arms, waiting.

"Oh, don't act like that was normal."

"*Excuse* me?"

"Not that being gay isn't normal . . . I mean . . . um. Come on, he was in a dress!" Steve said this last bit as if it was proof of something, though he was obviously no longer sure what. Kaia shook her head in disgust.

"You know what? Why don't you go home? You look really tired from being so threatened."

"Whatever. If that's what you want. God. You're being—"

"What?" Kaia stepped close, her eyes ice, her voice low. "What am I being, Steve? Does it start with a 'B'?"

The moment seemed to stretch.

"Fine." Steve shoved his hands into his pockets and slunk away. Something clattered as he kicked it on his way out.

I turned and bent down to fiddle with my shoelace. I needed a second to process what had just happened. Because it seemed like Kaia and Steve just had a fight . . . about me.

Through the cutout branches of the fake tree, I saw Kaia ask the stage manager if he'd seen me. Not wanting to be caught hiding, I stood up.

"Kaia?"

Kaia's eyes lit and she bounded toward me. "Cam!" I took a bracing step back as she threw herself against me, squeezing me tight. "Holy shit! I mean . . . holy shit, Cam! That was . . . sexy!"

All the feelings I'd had since I stepped offstage rushed back. I was flying again. I could do anything. And Kaia Gonzales was hugging me. I wrapped my arms around her and twirled us once before releasing her. I stepped back, breathless. "I was so unfair to Cardi. I get it now. I mean, as long as stripping is by choice and not as a last resort due to systemic financial inequality—never mind. Screw it. That was insane." Something occurred to me, and I grinned. "Wait. Did you just call me sexy?"

Kaia blushed and knocked me on the shoulder. "Shut up. You know that was hot." Waggling my eyebrows, I popped my shoulder and rolled my hip like I had in the dance. A few stagehands hooted, and Kaia pretended to fan herself and laughed.

"Well, it was all for Steve."

Kaia's face fell and I inwardly cursed. Way to ruin the moment. "Yeah. Um, he had to go. He wasn't feeling well."

Now it was awkward. Great. "Oh. That's okay." I searched for something else to say and then came up empty. She'd probably leave.

"Um, anyway, what are you doing now?"

Hold on. Was that . . . Did she want me to . . . "I was going to take the dancers to Denny's as a thank-you."

"Oh. That's nice of you." She looked down at her feet.

I was still flying. I could do anything.

"Do you want to come?"

Twenty minutes later, we were all crammed in a booth, piles of food spread on the table: chocolate chip pancakes, fries, mozzarella sticks, a huge banana split. Our spoons clashed as we fought for the best bits. Kaia was pressed up beside me. Everyone was talking over each other. Our shrieks of laughter filled the dining room. The other customers stared at our glitter-smudged faces. We didn't care.

"And then when you threw your arms out—" Mei shouted.

"And everyone got super quiet—" Tamara said.

"But then we pulled off the dress—" Alyssa continued.

"And the whole place just went—" Lainey mimicked the roar of the crowd. The girls burst into delighted laughter. Kaia's eyes caught mine and she smiled.

"So how long have you guys been friends with Cam?" she asked when the laughter subsided.

"Oh, um, we aren't friends. I mean, we all danced together, but we didn't hang out outside of class." I realized how bad that sounded as soon as I said it. It wasn't that I hadn't wanted to be friends. Or that I didn't like them.

"Cam was a mystery to all of us," Alyssa said, popping a mozzarella stick into her mouth.

"We called him Disappearing Webber because he was gone as soon as class was over," Mei added. It was true. I'd always see them walking off together after class to get ice cream and I'd wanted to go. But every time I tried to ask if I could tag along, my stomach clenched.

"Poof! Like a magician." Mei wiggled her fingers.

"I was intimidated!" I attempted to defend myself from their laughing eyes. "You were all super good and my voice was cracking."

The girls laughed. "Whatever," Lainey said. "Just 'cause we didn't do sleepovers didn't mean we weren't friends."

"Wait, we *were* friends?" I was confused.

The girls dissolved into giggles again. "Oh my lord, Cam." Tamara sputtered. "You are so hopeless."

Mei placed a hand on my shoulder and explained it to me like I was a child. "We spent hours together every week, Cam. Yes. We were your friends." I blinked a few times, taking this in.

"Yeah," Alyssa added, "did you think we'd spend a week in that studio for just anyone? Did you see my blisters?"

"Oh no, mine were way worse," Lainey said.

Beside me, Kaia's phone buzzed. She picked it up and rolled her eyes.

"Your mom?" I asked.

"No," she said with a sigh. "It's just Steve. He said something stupid earlier and has been apologizing all night."

Mei perked up. "Ooh. Mute that shit. Make him suffer."

"Nah. I already told him it was fine, but he still feels bad." Kaia glanced at me, then looked away.

Alyssa shrugged and dug into the banana split. "Well, he is hot."

Lainey shoved her, sending ice cream splattering onto the table. "Alyssa! He's sick."

"So? He can't be hot?"

Tamara leaned back in her seat. "I'm with Alyssa on this one. Eleven out of ten. Would ride."

"Guys, stop. We're making our new friend blush," Mei said with a laugh. Then she dropped her fry. "Ooh! Idea! Who wants to go to the beach?"

There was an answering squeal from the table and suddenly money was being grabbed from wallets and thrown on the table. I turned to Kaia.

"You coming?"

Kaia slumped a bit. "I've got some yearbook pages to work on—"

"It's okay. You're busy." I wasn't surprised. In fact, I was still kind of in shock that she'd had the time to go to Denny's.

Kaia threw a wad of money onto the table. "Fuck it. Let's go."

* * *

We sprawled on an unlit stretch of sand. Behind us, the highway provided the occasional flash of light as cars passed and the drone of traffic mixed with the crash of the waves. In front of us, the ocean was almost invisible in the darkness. Only the occasional froth of white foam as the waves broke hinted that we weren't staring into an endless sky.

The girls had run straight to the water when we'd arrived. Now they were dancing and shrieking, kicking sand and salt water at each other as they ran from the waves. Beside me, Kaia watched them, her shoes off, her feet dug into the cool sand. But then she reached into her bag, pulled out her phone, and started typing. "Sorry, I just got a great idea for the yearbook cover. Footsteps on the sand." She paused, her fingers hovering over the screen. "Is that too cliché? I feel like it's been done. Maybe just a beach theme?" She groaned. "What am I doing? This is a beautiful night. I should be enjoying it, but instead I'm thinking about yearbook. Which, if Kendra had turned in her cover on time, would not be my problem." She sighed and dropped her phone. "I'm sorry. I'm not fun."

"Don't worry," I assured her, "neither am I."

Kaia turned. "What are you even talking about? You just did an entire Cardi B routine and a few weeks ago you wore a freakin' beard of bees."

What was I supposed to say? That's all Steve? Your boyfriend. Because on my own I was much more of a sit in the sand type than a run through the waves one. "I promise you. I'm more not-fun than you are. I spend most of my time thinking about how the world will end."

Kaia arched an eyebrow. "Really? Because when I look out there, all I see is rising sea levels." She gestured to the ocean.

"I see toxic runoff," I countered without blinking an eye.

"I see sea turtles in plastic bags."

"Extinction from overfishing."

"Underwater noise pollution."

"Bioluminescent algae blooms!" I finished, triumphant.

Kaia chuckled, then held out her fist. "Bummer Twins activate." We sadly bumped, then turned back to the dancers. They were twirling and taking long, graceful leaps over the water.

"Stand up."

"What?" Kaia frowned, confused, as I got to my feet.

I brushed the sand off my sweats and held out my hand. Kaia took it, still unsure. "Let's try it. Being fun." I pulled her up.

"I'm not dancing, Cam. I'm not g—"

I tapped her on the shoulder. "You're it." She stared at me, still not comprehending as I danced back a few steps.

"Oh my god. Are you eight years old?"

I smirked. "No. I'm fun."

Kaia shook her head but then, without warning, she swiped at me. I barely jumped back in time. She tried again and I darted out of her reach. She huffed, frustrated, then leaped for me. I dodged, but almost lost my footing. This time she laughed a little. "See," I said. "I'm laughing. You're laughing."

"No," Kaia growled, "you're it!" And she launched herself at me. With a spin, I dug my heels into the sand and pushed off, feet pounding, flying down the beach. Kaia charged after me, a spray of sand in her wake. I stretched the distance between us, digging my toes into the damp grit with each step, feeling the cool night breeze wash over my face. "How do you run so fast?" Kaia called after me.

"I've been dancing three hours a day for a week! I can keep this up all night!" I laughed and kept going, loving how the beach stretched before me, seemingly infinite in the dark.

"Slow down!"

"And let you tag me?" I called. She wasn't far behind, though she was struggling to keep up.

"Look! Litter!"

"Where?" I whipped my head around to see where she was pointing. *Whumph!* Kaia grabbed me around my waist and tackled me to the ground. We crashed in the sand, both cackling helplessly. Finally, a little breathless, I sat up and shook my hair, sending bits of beach debris flying. "Oh, ow."

Kaia sat up, sand caked to her cheek. "Yeah. Sand. Despite appearances, not soft."

"Nope." I looked down the beach. I could barely see Alyssa and the other dancers now, though I could hear their shrieks occasionally breaking through the crash of the waves. I turned back to Kaia. She was staring at me. I wondered what she saw. Probably someone whose hair was a mess, with a scrape on their elbow, and sand mixed up in the glitter ringing their eyes. I knew what I saw when I looked at her: someone who knew me well enough that she could beat me at tag by pretending there was trash on the ground.

"See," I said, though it came out a little too soft, "that was fun." Neither of us moved. We just hung there, suspended.

"That's why, you know." She said it quietly.

"What?" I blinked a bit, like I was coming out of a dream.

"Why I'm with Steve."

Oh.

For just a second I'd forgotten about Steve. For just a second it had been only me and Kaia on an almost empty beach.

"Fun." There was a funny twist to her lips as she said it. "That's why I started dating him. Because he seemed like fun. There's no big story, no huge romance. We had a class project together. When I got paired with Steve, I was sure I'd get stuck doing everything. But he actually did the work. Except while I worried about everything, he just laughed. And then he asked me out. And I thought, *Maybe this is what I need.* He wasn't ever who I imagined dating . . . but maybe that was okay. And I didn't want to hurt his feelings, so I said yes."

It was so simple. After everything I'd planned and worried about, waiting for just the right time, Steve had just asked her out, like it was nothing, probably on the way to lunch while half thinking about the Tater Tots he was going to eat. Did he even care what her answer was? Was that why it was so easy? I realized Kaia was still talking.

". . . and we started dating. And I kept hoping maybe there'd be more to him. Because I liked him. I did. I do. But . . . he's not . . ." She looked down.

He's not what, Kaia? My heart was in my throat. *HE'S NOT WHAT??*

"And then I figured, well, it'll be short. He's broken up with how many girls?"

"Six last year." Not that I'd counted or anything.

"Right. But then he didn't. And I'm not much of a breaker-upper. I mean, I haven't even had a real boyfriend except him. And then he got cancer. What was I supposed to do? You can't break up with a guy with cancer."

All I could hear was *break up*. Over and over, like the crashing waves.

Kaia scrubbed her eyes. "Sorry, I—"

I wanted to put my arms around her, but instead I went with a joke. "Hold on. I'm still stuck on the part where you thought Steve Stevenson has feelings."

Kaia burst out with a laugh that turned into a sob. "Cam! This isn't funny!" She flopped back down and threw an arm across her eyes. "I'm dating a guy who calls his penis 'Stevie Wonder.'"

I choked. "I did not hear that."

Kaia pulled her arm halfway off her eye and peered at me. "Will people hate me if I break up with him?" There were those two words again. The two words I'd been desperate to hear. I'd worn a diaper and bees and danced and gotten tattooed just to get to this moment. Kaia continued, "It's not like he'd be alone for long. I mean, have you seen the comment section on the website?"

"Unfortunately." As the campaign had grown more popular, random girls had been leaving messages of "support" for Steve that implied they'd be willing to nurse him back to health in some very nontraditional ways.

"Is it horrible I imagined if we somehow got to twenty thousand and his family was taken care of, that breaking up with him would be okay? And we're pretty close to our goal, right? I mean, not twenty thousand . . . but would people still hate me?" She took her arm all the way off her eyes and stared at me, eyes shining and hopeful in the dark. I answered her the only way I could.

"I wouldn't hate you."

With a sigh, Kaia closed her eyes. There was a smile on her lips again. It was a little wobbly, but it was there. She opened her eyes and sat up. "Can I tell you a secret?"

"Of course."

"I got you named Best Person in the yearbook."

"Really?" I couldn't quite meet her gaze. It was everything I wanted. Well, not *everything*, everything, but it was how I wanted Kaia to see me. So why wasn't I leaping through the waves? Why did I feel guilty?

"Oh, don't give me that humble bullshit. You know you are."

"I'm not."

"Tell me one bad thing you've ever done. And forgetting to recycle something doesn't count."

I looked out at the ocean. "Okay, here's one thing: I pretended to want to help your boyfriend in order to impress you. And then even though he tortured me, my plan worked out perfectly and now we're sitting here on a beach while your hair floats around you in an ocean breeze and you're telling me you want to break up with him, and while I feel really, really happy about that, I also feel a little confused and guilty and I'm not sure why." I could have said that. But I settled on, "I've done some bad stuff."

"Really?" Kaia scooted closer. "Please tell me it was something really terrible because then . . ." She drifted off, her face inches from mine.

"What?" Suddenly whatever thoughts were in my head vanished. She was so close.

Kaia reached out and wiped some glitter and sand off my cheek with her finger, watching it sparkle in the dark. "You wouldn't be Best Person . . ." Wait, what did that mean? Did she not want me to be Best Person? Was it okay if I wasn't? And how did I not notice she had freckles? "And also . . ."

"What?" The word came out a bit strangled.

She dropped her hand gently to my shoulder and leaned forward to whisper in my ear. ". . . now you're *IT!*" With a cry she sprang up and darted away. I sat back with a thud. Kaia spun around to face me, her bare feet dancing in the sand. "Come on. Aren't you going to get me?"

14

As my mom made a massive stack of celebratory pancakes, I snuck a peek at the site. What was I going to have to do now? Skydive? Run with the bulls? Burn down a rain forest?

But when the site popped up, I was shocked to see it was still unchanged. I assumed Steve must have slept in. It was Saturday. I exhaled and tried to enjoy this rare moment of peace. Closing my eyes, I basked in the memory of the beach and Kaia and being the Best Person. Had that really happened? Had she really said she was going to break up with him?

The next day, the website was still the same. I wandered around my house in a daze while my mom blasted Cardi B and danced in celebration. I still couldn't completely relax. The longer he took to change the site, the worse I imagined it would be. He probably wanted to unveil it on a Monday when he could get the full impact of my humiliation. Or maybe he'd finally given up. Or maybe Kaia had broken up with him. That thought had caused me to drop my phone again, finally fracturing the screen so badly it was useless. But then I figured the lack of internet connection was probably good for me. Inspired by the peace it brought, I even let my laptop battery drain so that I couldn't check the site on it either. I was going off the grid, living in ignorance and bliss. Last night, I'd read the copy of *The Five Love Languages* that I had bought my mom for Christmas last year. I hoped Kaia's language was number two: Acts of Service.

This morning I still hadn't plugged in my laptop. I'd finally had a full night's sleep and just wanted to keep the good vibes going. But as I arrived at school, something seemed off. Usually when I walked toward my locker in the morning I was ignored. But today, people were smiling at me. Someone high-fived me. Then another. Two guys from the basketball team congratulated me. Then, so did Mark, the class president, and even my art history teacher, who I was sure hated me. I mean, I knew my dance was good, but I wasn't expecting this.

It must be a prank! Steve had gotten everyone at school to be nice to me and then . . . what? Were they slapping stupid notes on my back? I felt around but nothing was there. Maybe they were snipping my hair secretly. But my hair looked okay in the awards case reflection. Was there some other level of humiliation I couldn't conceive of? A lot of them *had* already seen me covered in vomit and with my diaper erection.

I pushed through the crowd, looking for air and someone I could trust. Finally, near the entrance to the multipurpose room, I saw Kaia selling prom tickets. I started toward her, but she caught sight of me first.

"Cam! Cam! Oh my god!" She stood up and rushed over to me.

"What's going on? Why are these people . . . ," I asked, and kept watch for the prank I thought was still coming.

"Didn't you see the site this morning?"

"What? No. My phone and laptop are dead."

"Dude, you did it!" She thrust her phone at me.

"Did what?" Confused, I took it. SaveSteve.org was displayed and it said something truly insane.

"The goal. We made it!" This couldn't be right. I was sure her screen was broken. But Kaia kept explaining, "The video of your 'Money' dance went viral over the weekend! It's got like sixty thousand views on YouTube and bits of it are blowing up on TikTok!"

I stared at the ticker on-screen. We hadn't just made our goal. We had blown right past it! It was now at $29,342.

"There's so much money," I said, gaping at the screen.

"I know. I can't believe it, Cam. You saved Steve!" I put down the phone and looked at Kaia. She had tears in her eyes and a smile so wide that I thought little flying hearts would appear. This was exactly how I'd first imagined Kaia would look if I could somehow pull this off. I had done it. And she was looking at me. Like this.

"And Cam . . . did you see?" Kaia took her phone back, excited. She flicked some windows and then handed it to me. "Look who retweeted your video."

"Furrydick15?" I read, confused.

"Below that." She pointed. "The one who watches over you at night!"

And sure enough, right below Furrydick15, was . . .

"Michelle . . . Oh . . . What the . . . Oh my god . . ." I started to hyperventilate. "Oh my god."

Kaia enjoyed watching my complete respiratory collapse and finished what I could not. "Michelle motherfuckin' Obama!" Then she hugged me so hard I thought I would pop.

Michelle Obama had retweeted me! Because of my dance! Because I'd raised thirty thousand dollars! Because I had saved Steve. Because I was amazing. And I was holding Kaia. My eyes welled. And this time, it was *my* tears that dropped on Kaia's shoulder. Tears of joy and amazement.

And victory.

Steve was history.

I ripped some tape from my roll and slapped the Save the Shark flyer to the lamppost. It was a good mindless task to do as I considered how to finally ask Kaia to prom. She might even be breaking up with Steve right now. I'd need to wait a little bit for the dust to settle, but not too long. Prom was just a few weeks away. And however I asked, it shouldn't be something public. I'd done enough stunts for Steve. I didn't want her to think I was just addicted to the spectacle. And she was in a tricky emotional space. I didn't want it to look like I was too celebratory. It would need to be perfect. Maybe the wetlands! I could make a picnic, pull out a copy of *The Uninhabitable Earth* as a joke, and then just ask, "So, Kaia, I was wondering if you'd go to prom with me?" No, I needed to sound more confident. "Would you like to go to prom with me . . . How about—"

"Hey there," I heard from behind me, and a Natty Ice chill ran down my back. "Kaia said you might be out here." Had he just heard what I was rehearsing? Had she just broken up with him? Was he here to kick my ass?

"Oh, hey, Steve . . ." I tried to sound like I had no idea what was going on. "It's been a while. I know because I haven't been stung or stabbed or rolled in bodily fluids."

"You did that to yourself," he said coolly.

"Because I was trying to help you!"

"Because you have a sequoia-sized boner for Kaia."

"I do not have—"

"God. Just admit it, okay? You won. Congrats," he said, a little defeated. Oh my god, she'd broken up with him. I was beginning to feel a little sequoia-sized. "I underestimated you and your little nice guy act. Kaia is barely speaking to me. Happy?" Hold on, that didn't sound like a breakup. That sounded more like a fight.

"Look. That's not why I'm here." Now I was totally confused. Why else would he be here? He seemed calm and a little tired. "I'm trying to be different. I'm trying . . . Well, I came

159

here because . . . I just wanted to say . . . thanks, okay?"

"What?" I said, and worried it sounded rude. But seriously, what the hell was going on?

"The money. It really helped. My parents . . . Let's just say it was nice to see my mom cry from happiness for a change."

No. No. I was not falling for this nice guy routine. I'd seen too many dicks scrawled on too many lockers to forget that quickly. I had a tattoo in Comic Sans on my ass. I was just going to play along and keep an eye open. "Oh. You're welcome."

"And I have a favor to ask." He quickly saw the massive amount of skepticism on my face. "Don't be like that. It's nothing bad."

"Sorry. For some reason I don't trust you."

"Just . . . can you be at school a little early tomorrow?" I tilted my head sideways to clearly indicate, "Really?" He laughed. "It's nothing bad. I promise." The way he said it, with a hint of vulnerability and a tinge of apology, I couldn't help but wonder if he actually meant it.

Steve started to walk away but stopped, remembering something. "Oh, by the way," he said, and pulled a piece of paper from his pocket and held it out to me. "Here." I stared at it for a moment, confused.

"A free pass to the aqua park?"

"They donated it to me. But I don't want to support the shark."

"Then just throw it out."

"I wrote the password for the website on the back." He pushed the ticket closer. "I'm done torturing you." And then he walked away.

I stared at the ticket for too long, trying to figure out what had just happened.

Finally, I turned it over, revealing the words: CamIsAnA$$hole!!

The password had actually worked. So why was I here? At the aqua park? I should have just thrown away the ticket. But for some reason, I wanted to see the shark. I needed to see him. For all the time I'd spent trying to save him, I'd never actually visited him in the flesh. Probably because I was actually terrified of sharks. While some kids had gone through a shark stage when they were little, I thought even toy sharks were scary. And it was shark specific. I loved monsters and aliens. I wasn't scared of a T. rex or the snow creature in *Frozen*. It was just sharks. One of the few memories I had of my dad was watching *Jaws* with him. When I was four. He said it was an old cheesy movie. He was a fucking idiot.

It was late afternoon on a Tuesday and the place was pretty empty. I hid my face in my hoodie, just in case they recognized me from the protest. Slinking past the gift store and the IMAX theater, I made my way through the aqua park, looking for the shark exhibit. I passed huge tanks filled with turquoise-colored water where schools of fish commuted in circles. An instrumental version of that Disney song, "Under the Sea," murmured through hidden speakers. A trio of human-sized animatronic fish with smiling faces and top hats sang along to the song. I hated how these places always anthropomorphized the sea life. They couldn't just be the magical and mysterious creatures that they were. They seemed to think they had to present them as human so we could relate to them. Couldn't a fish just be a fish?

I followed signs of a bloody-toothed shark pointing the way, finally coming to the exhibit. The area was crammed with families, shrieking and shouting as they strained to see the great white. On the surface of the massive pool, a few surfboards drifted aimlessly, cheekily implying their riders had already been eaten. To one side there was an amphitheater-like viewing deck from where you could presumably see the iconic fin skulking, or if you were lucky, where the shark would burst out of the water for the terrified entertainment of children. Fear sold tickets. But I knew he was really just a rare, beautiful creature who needed to be free.

To one side a cave advertised the entrance to an underwater viewing area. It was decorated with more smiling fish. I entered a very dark hallway and the piped-in music became more ominous. Of course they had to make the shark a monster. That made keeping him in a cage easier. Oversized warning signs were plastered everywhere to underscore the danger. Finally, I emerged from the hallway into the Shark Zone. It was a massive glass wall that allowed a view into the special tank that connected to the open ocean. This was how they fooled everyone into thinking it was humane. The shark could look at the ocean that he would never be able to swim in.

I gawked into the dusky green tank to find him. Smaller fish, doomed to be his lunch, swam about anxiously. One school passed close by the glass and then darted away. Beyond them, floating bored in the middle of the tank, was the shark. He was even larger than I'd imagined, like a zeppelin in a bird cage. His two-toned gray skin looked weathered. There were small gashes on his fins. And he had that great white smile. The one that revealed a row of jagged teeth. The one that said he would enjoy eating you at any moment. The one that reminded me of Steve.

Steve.

Why had he given me the password? Why was he being so nice? What was this "favor"? What was I missing? Was he going to eat me?

I shook it off. He wasn't a shark. He was just Steve. We'd hit the fundraising goal. There was nothing else he could do.

I refocused on the great white and how depressed he seemed to be as he lazily coasted toward the side of the aquarium.

"Hey, poor fella," I said calmly, as if he could hear. "We're gonna get you out of here." I took a tentative step to the tank. "There's nothing to be afraid of, is there?" I took another step. The way he moved was so effortless and confident. He knew his strength and how to use it. Kaia would probably like him. Especially if he had cancer.

Stop!

"You're just a fish," I reminded myself. "You're not going to suddenly come around the corner and eat me, right?" I took a deep breath and absorbed the calm of nature. The way the water undulated. The dance of seagrass as it swayed in the tide. The white noise of distant crashing waves. The way the shark suddenly jerked toward me. His eyes wide! His power surging! His jaws agape! Grinning! Laughing! Plotting!

I stumbled away.

And fell ass backward over a toddler. The little boy screamed. The dad barked, "What the hell are you doing?" I scrambled to my feet and apologized.

"Shark!" the kid announced with delight as he pointed at the tank. Excited, he held up his own toy shark that he was definitely not afraid of.

A van that exclaimed "KYET—Ventura's #1 Local News Team" was parked in front of our school. My mind raced as I tried to imagine how this was part of Steve's "favor." But it must be. The only other time we'd had a news van here was when Mr. Jenkins locked himself in the women's locker room.

Walking into the quad, I came upon a crowd of students milling around a stage where a podium was set up. On the stage with his parents was Steve. In a suit. My prank radar was peaking.

"Oh great, you're here," said a heavily made up woman in a blazer, holding a KYET microphone. She grabbed my arm and led me forward. Steve waved to me and smiled.

"What is this?" I asked, but she was all business as she led me onto the stage. "You're gonna stand on that X next to Steve." We approached him. His face was inscrutable. I stood on the X and turned to Steve. "What are you doing?"

"Be chill. It's a surprise." He flashed that grin and a familiar vomit-like taste appeared in my mouth.

"Steve? Cam?" It was Kaia at the foot of the stage. "What's going on?"

I shrugged. Steve smiled. "Get a spot in front." She furrowed her brow. She seemed tired of Steve's antics, too. But she went to the foot of the stage and waited.

Steve approached the podium and grabbed the microphone. "Hey, everyone. Thanks for being here today. Not that you have a choice. School and all." The crowd laughed and a guy called out, "We love you, Steve." Steve gave the kid a thumbs-up. With his bald head, Steve had an air of class to him that his swooping mop usually hid. "I have a little announcement to make."

There was a gasp and a girl cried out, "Don't die, Steve!" Kaia looked a little stunned.

Steve held up a hand to quiet her and continued, "I'm not dying." There was an audible exhale of relief from the students. "Most of you already know that my cancer is highly curable and I'm down to my last round of chemo. And thanks to all you generous people"—he motioned to the crowd—"my girl-friend, Kaia"—he nodded to her—"and especially my good friend Cam"—he held his arm out in my direction—"my family has all the money they need to pay my medical bills and then some." There was a burst of applause and some whoops. Kaia smiled at me and I tried to return it, still unsure where this was going. Steve's voice then dropped lower and, with uncharacteristic sincerity, he explained, "But there are a lot of kids out there with cancer who aren't as fortunate as me. I've sat in waiting rooms with them. Had chemo with them. I've learned a lot about how our medical system works. And how even if you have insurance, there are still tons of costs that don't get covered." The crowd had become silent. Kaia was looking up at Steve in a way I hadn't seen before. Like she was seeing someone new. With a bright inflection, Steve then announced, "So with the extra money from Save Steve, I've started a new foundation: the Cam Webber Hero Fund." I had heard my name but didn't register it until I saw Kaia mouthing, "Oh my god." The crowd burst into a cheer. "Cam Webber has been by my side. He has been steady. He has been brave. He has done things no person should ever have to do!" With each word of praise he gave me, I saw Kaia's face soften. Steve turned back to me and flashed a toothy grin. "You deserve all of this and more." He picked up a plaque that was on the podium and walked it over to me.

"Thanks. I . . . Uh . . . ." I took the plaque, stunned. I could feel the news camera zoom in. He motioned for his parents to come over. They both hugged me, his dad a little too hard. I caught Kaia wiping away a tear.

"You're welcome!" Steve said, and grabbed my shoulder the way a politician running for office would. He then turned back to the crowd. "Oh yeah, and before we get off this stage, one more thing." He bounced up to the podium like Ellen DeGeneres and screamed, "CARDI B CALLED AND SAID SHE WANTS TO PLAY PROM!!!!!!!"

Pandemonium. Steve triumphantly raised his hands in the air. I saw Kaia say, "Holy shit!" And I felt the floor slipping out from underneath me. The crowd chanted, "Steve! Steve! Steve!" Steve surfed on their tsunami of excitement.

Then, just when things couldn't get any more surreal, Steve jumped off the stage, right in front of Kaia. From absolutely nowhere, he produced a long-stemmed red rose. "Hey there, Kaia . . . ," he said in his smokiest voice.

She blushed.

Uh-oh.

"I think you know what's coming next." On a little Bluetooth speaker, Jay-Z's apology song to Beyoncé came on. Steve got down on one knee. Whoops and cheers came from the crowd. Kaia looked away, shy but smiling. "I know I messed up. And I know you got a little mad. But I'm sorry." Kaia looked back at him, right into his super apologetic eyes. The entire student body melted. "I was kind of hoping, if you don't mind going with a bald, disease-riddled cancer boy—"

"Steve . . . ," she whispered.

"Who also happens to be a terrible dancer . . ."

"Stop . . . ," she playfully objected.

". . . you might go to prom with me?" He held out the rose. She mooned over him and then nodded, too moved for words.

Steve teased, "I think the TV cameras need to hear you say it." The crowd cheered in agreement. He held the mic up.

"Oh my god, yes. Yes!" The crowd had a collective fucking orgasm as Steve pulled Kaia close and kissed her.

I stood, holding my plaque. Helpless. Disintegrating. And then Steve pulled out the final dagger. He looked into Kaia's eyes and, even though it was off mic and only for Kaia, I could clearly see he said, "I love you." Kaia's mouth slacked open. I could feel the emotion in her welling up. And I could see she was just about to say something.

But then Steve's body became stiff. And Kaia's swooning turned to concern. "Steve?" His eyes rolled back. "Steve?" The crowd gasped. And then Kaia couldn't hold him, and he slid to the ground. "Steve!"

Steve's dad jumped into action. "Someone call 911!" His mom followed and soon there was a crowd around him. I rushed to the end of the stage but couldn't make out anything. "Get back, everyone. Get back!" Steve's dad demanded.

I took a step back. Then another. Until I was invisible.

Moments later I was in the parking lot by the ambulance, waiting for Steve. I needed to see if he was okay. I hadn't organized the event, but I felt somehow responsible. And so confused. Had he really made a fund in my name? Had he really been that thankful? Had he really changed?

There was a surge of activity and then I saw the medics rolling Steve on a gurney toward the ambulance. Kaia and Steve's parents were close behind. I rushed over to him.

"Steve? Steve?" I pleaded, praying he'd respond, but he didn't move. My heart slammed against my chest. Was he dead? "Steve . . ." Panic spread through me. Darkness. Void.

Just then, Steve turned his head to the side and opened his eyes.

"Thank god!" I exclaimed.

And then he . . . was that . . . did he just . . . wink?

I stumbled over a crack in the concrete. Hold the fuck on. "Are you faking it?" I said, still not really believing it.

Steve beckoned me to get closer and then he whispered, "You can't beat the dying guy." And then he winked again. My organs iced over.

The gurney stopped. And before I could form any words in response, Steve was shoved into the ambulance. He weakly raised his head and cried out, "Kaia!"

She scrambled into the back. "Steve. Oh my god. Steve. Shhhhh. I love—"

SLAM! The van doors closed.

Steve's parents ran to their car and before I knew it, the ambulance was rushing away.

A few minutes later I hadn't moved. Instead, I just stood there holding my plaque. And thinking about how right Patrice had been all along.

15

Shailene Woodley sat in her car and read the letter Ansel wrote before he died. Lying on the grass, her oxygen tube in her nose, she looked up at the stars and said, "Okay."

Click.

Tears slid down Keanu Reeves's cheeks as he stood alone in a park. Charlize was gone. She couldn't bear to let Keanu see her die.

Click.

"I told you not to fall in love with me," Mandy Moore whispered in the night. Then she got married and died.

Click.

I shoved my laptop off my lap and grabbed for another tissue. Dammit, Patrice was right. She was so, so, right. (I blew my nose.) A cancer love story was an unstoppable force. No one could resist the combination of true love and untimely death.

And you know who else knew that? Steve. Steve the faking fucking faker. He was like an evil version of that kid from my mom's favorite movie—*Ferris Bueller's Day Off*. But instead of faking a head cold to get out of school, Steve was faking complications with cancer to manipulate Kaia.

Then it hit me. Ferris Bueller had only taken one day off. Was Steve going to fake these extra symptoms forever? How could he be Steve if he was always fainting and drooling and droopy eyed? How could he always be awesome? His plan was unsustainable.

I took a deep breath, blew my nose one last time, and told myself to stop worrying. Kaia was almost ready to break up with him that night on the beach. This was just the act of a desperate man.

The next day, I walked through the halls to my locker, head down, hoodie up. I wished I had some earbuds on me because the whole day, no matter where I went, there was only one topic of conversation.

"Dude, Steve looked like shit, man."

"Did you hear? Steve's on a feeding tube."

"Kaia had to hold his hand all night."

"He can't even speak anymore. He just blinks in Morse code. And he only says one thing: 'I love you, Kaia.'"

A guy from econ watched as I took a drink from the water fountain. When I finished, he came closer, put both hands on my shoulders, looked me in the eye, and said, "I'm so sorry for your loss," then walked away.

"He's not dead!" I called after him. "He's fine. He was in the hospital for an hour and then went home! He's playing video games right now!" But the guy had already disappeared down the hall. "Ugh." I kicked the wall.

"Let me guess, everyone thinks Steve is dead."

I turned. Kaia was holding a piece of poster board, her backpack slung over one shoulder. "You too?"

"I had three girls cry on my shoulder this morning because I'll never love again."

"Wow. It must be hard to realize that at only sixteen you're basically a husk of a human being, facing an endless desert of sadness."

"I bought a bunch of black lace veils on Amazon." Kaia's eyes danced with laughter and I relaxed, sensing that she hadn't been taken in by Steve. She saw how ridiculous this all was. Her "I love you" had just been a heat of the moment thing. "Anyway," Kaia continued, "I'm glad I ran into you. There's something I want to ask."

"Go for it." She looked nervous. Was nervous good or bad? Good, right?

"I know it's weird. We had that whole talk on the beach, but I was wondering if maybe . . . ?"

She mentioned the beach! This was definitely good. I tried my best to sound casual. "Yeah?"

"Kaia! There you are." A skinny guy from student council

came barreling toward us. I watched helplessly as Kaia turned.

"Hey, Cole! I got the poster board."

No! No! The poster board can wait!

Cole's face fell. "That's not poster board."

"Yes, it is."

Enough with the poster board! Let's get back to the beach.

"No, it's too thin. It needs to be thicker. It's, like, you know, made out of . . . foam."

I cleared my throat. "What were you wondering, Kaia? About the beach?"

Kaia tilted her head at Cole. "You mean, foam core?"

"Oh, is that what it's called? Sorry, I told you the wrong thing. Can you get foam core?"

"Sure." Kaia's smile seemed a little strained.

"We need it by tonight. Thanks!" Cole bounced away. Kaia crumpled the poster board and threw it in the trash but then instantly regretted it. Pulling it back out, she mumbled to herself, "I'll just glue some cardboard to the back after prom committee."

"Just for the record," I said, "I know the difference between foam core and poster board."

Kaia laughed. "See, that's why I like you."

Oh my god, she said she liked me. I needed to get this back on track. "So . . . there was something you wanted to ask me?"

Kaia shook her head, remembering. "Oh, that's right. I was just wondering, if it was okay with you . . ."

Anything she said would be okay with me.

". . . and you could totally say no."

Like I would ever say no to her.

"Maybe you could share Best Person with Steve?"

I'd never been punched, but I knew what it felt like now. Suddenly there was no air in my lungs. "Oh . . ." My voice came from somewhere far away. "The yearbook thing."

"I feel terrible. I don't want to hurt your feelings or anything. You're still really great. It's just . . ."

"Steve."

"Yeah. It's just, the last twenty-four hours really changed things. I think I saw for the first time who Steve really is, and I'm pretty sure I've never met anyone more thoughtful or selfless."

Not only had I been punched, now someone was taking a blowtorch to my face. At close range.

"Steve is selfless." I thought if I said it out loud it would make sense. It did not. Somehow, in one pratfall, he had stolen my entire identity.

"Right? Of course, you'd have seen it. You spend all that time with him. Please, please, forget all those things I said on the beach. I'm so embarrassed. I can't believe I was thinking of breaking up with him. If I had . . . God, I never would have known. He explained everything to me at the hospital. He's really hurting, you know? It took so much courage for him to come out and do that."

"Collapse?" I couldn't help myself. This was ridiculous. How could Kaia have fallen for a rose and a stumble?

"What? No. To be so vulnerable in front of everyone. In front of me. But god, seeing him crumple like that . . . it made me realize how fragile life is."

Fucking. Cancer. Love story.

"Have you ever seen *Ferris Bueller's Day Off*?"

"What? No. What's that have to do with this?"

"Nothing. I just . . . I mean, Steve got better kind of quickly, though."

"I know. The doctors were surprised. But he's so strong." She got a little misty on the last word. Like she was lost in a memory of Steve's weirdly undiminished biceps being wrapped around her.

"But, like, don't you think it might have been a little, I don't know, too fast?"

"What? No. What are you saying?"

"I'm not—"

"You don't think he passed out?"

I should lie. I should bail on this whole conversation. "Not really."

"YOU THINK HE'S FAKING CANCER?"

I retreated from Kaia's death glare. "What? No! Of course not!" Heads were turning our way. "Of course Steve has cancer!" How could I take it back?

"So what? You think he faked losing his hair?"

"No!" I took another step back and held up my hands.

She crowded close to me. "You think he's been faking throwing up from chemotherapy?"

"No! Of course not!" I took another step, and banged against the lockers.

"Then what?" She crossed her arms and waited. She was at a rage level she usually reserved for oil companies.

I wanted to crawl inside the locker behind me. I whimpered, "Nothing."

But I couldn't erase what I'd said.

"What possible reason would someone have to fake passing out?"

"Toimpressyou?"

She stared at me with disbelief.

"I think maybe you shouldn't share Best Person after all."

I didn't see Kaia the next day or the day after. I'd checked my newly repaired phone a hundred times to see if I'd gotten a text from her. The only message I'd missed was from my mom asking me to pick up bok choy. I couldn't text Kaia, because the idea of texting her and not getting a response was somehow worse.

At least now it was the night of the city council meeting, where I would definitely see her. They were voting on our ordinance banning large marine animals, and Todd had asked me to speak for the group, for reasons of "youth culture," "Gen Z," and something about "being in the zeitgeist." I could apologize to her right before I gave my speech. And maybe if I crushed the aqua park tonight, Kaia would start to forget our last encounter.

That small sliver of hope propelled me to Main Street. Unfortunately, I was running a little late. Checking the Save Steve site, which had now been renamed the Cam Webber Hero Fund, had been a mistake. I had become distracted scrolling through the comments. There were hundreds of them, all praising Steve and his generosity. If the random girls had been bad before, it had been kicked up to a whole new level now. There had been poetry. Dirty poetry. And despite the fact that the fund had my name on it, not one single person had bothered to comment on me.

A horn blared. I swerved my Prius out of the way as a pickup truck ran a red light. I skidded to a stop, breathing hard.

"Asshole!" the driver yelled.

My head snapped up. "Are you kidding me?" I shouted through my window. I'd been the one with the right of way.

The driver gave me the finger.

I rolled down my window. "No! You're the asshole! Not me! You're the asshole." But the driver sped away and left me yelling at an empty street.

"The aquarium has already poured hundreds of thousands of dollars into a state-of-the-art tank providing ocean access for the shark and putting our own economic interest at risk . . ." The lobbyist for Channel Islands Aqua Park stood in front of the city council and presented his case. On the projection screen behind him, numbers and data flashed.

I sat in one of the old scratchy chairs that must have been in the city council chambers since the 90s and tried to pay attention. My backpack was on the seat next to me to save a spot for Kaia. She wasn't here yet. I hadn't worried at first. She was always running a little late. But when, an hour and a half in, the council called the representative from the aqua park to the front, it had finally occurred to me: Kaia might not be coming at all. For the hundredth time, I tried to subtly turn my head toward the back entrance to see if she had slipped in.

"Still no Kaia?" Todd asked. I turned back and shook my head. "What's up? She's usually glued to your side."

"Oh, um, we had a fight."

Patrice leaned over from the row behind us. "Told you," she singsonged. *"Here on Earth."*

"It's not the same!" I hissed. I'd watched the movie now, so I knew. It was so not the same. For one thing, Steve would never wear a shirt as baggy as Chris Klein's. I couldn't take it. I had to finally text her. I couldn't go up there with this hanging between us.

Me: Hey, I'm sorry for what I said.

Send.

I waited, only half listening to the lobbyist spew his lies. My phone buzzed.

Mom: Best son ever! I'm watching on the livestream!

I thumbed a thanks to my mom, my heart sinking. Still nothing from Kaia. The lobbyist was wrapping up. Maybe she was on her way. If she was driving, she wouldn't be checking her phone. I was sure Kaia wasn't a text and drive type.

Me: I'm up soon.

That wasn't too pushy. Even if she was mad at me, she wouldn't miss this, right? We'd been working on it for months. One little fight couldn't ruin it. True, she seemed to be more into Steve now than ever before, but that didn't mean she was suddenly going to give up everything she cared about. She wouldn't just forget about the shark.

"Cam, brah, you're up." Todd nudged me.

I stepped to the front of the room, feeling a hush fall over the crowd. The seats were about a third full. There was no sign of Kaia.

Someone cleared their throat. I realized I'd just been standing there. I picked up my notes.

"Members of the city council, this aqua park lobbyist tells you that the special habitat with ocean access has been a successful means of keeping sharks in captivity. But he didn't tell you the context of the statistics he pulled. He said captive sharks were now living triple the length of time in captivity. But triple from what? From a wild shark? No, of course not! He means triple from the absurdly short lifespan that sharks survived in theme parks in the 90s. Those sharks often died within months. So best-case scenario, they live a few years? But a white shark in the wild can have a lifespan of seventy years!"

My phone buzzed. I'd laid it on the podium. I could see it glowing, the little bubble of text on my lock screen. I angled it toward me so I could see the words.

Kaia: It's fine. This whole thing's been crazy. Steve wasn't feeling great so I'm over at his place. We're watching on the livestream. Good luck!

She was never coming.

Because she was with Steve.

Lying liar falling down faker who for sure felt just fine Steve. They were curled up on the couch watching me. I could practically see the smirk on his face through the public access camera.

"Is that all?" one of the city council members asked.

Hell no, that wasn't all. I stared back at the camera. At Kaia. "Don't you see? He's trying to trick you to gain your support. How can you even trust someone like that? This isn't just about the shark. This is about what's wrong and what's right!" I slammed my fist down on the podium and shifted my eyes to in-camera Steve. "Aren't we all tired of the bad guys winning?"

There was a cheer from our section, and even a few of the other people sitting in the audience nodded and clapped.

Feeling the energy in the room, I turned to the seated crowd. "Aren't you?"

This time the cheer was bigger. "Yes!" An old man in a Hawaiian shirt stood up.

"Then we can't let the bad guys win again! We're sick of it!" I pounded the podium harder. This time everyone stood and cheered. I stepped off the stage and strode through the crowd, accepting back slaps and congratulations.

"Thank you, young man, for your passionate remarks," the

city council member said as she shuffled the papers before her. "If there are no more public comments, we can commence the vote."

I took my seat, a little out of breath. My phone buzzed.

Kaia: Great speech. 🎉 Gonna win for sure!

Take that, faker Steve.

"No!" Next to me, Todd half started from his seat and sat down. I looked up.

"What?"

I turned around, taking in everyone's reactions. They were muttering and frowning. Patrice sat in her seat, her expression closed off. "We lost."

"What? How?" Around me, the other protesters got to their feet and started to boo. The city council members called for quiet, but instead they just got louder.

"The system's rigged, Cam!" Todd shouted over the howls. "That's what we get for playing by the rules!"

"If you disrupt the meeting any further, we will be forced to bring in the police." Near the emergency exit, a uniformed police officer stepped forward. The protesters didn't quiet, but they began to disperse and move toward the exits. Todd shouted out a Nelson Mandela quote and something about this not being over.

I bumped along with everyone else, but couldn't find the energy to add my voice to the throng. I didn't understand what had just happened. We were in the right. How could the city council not see that? Around me people began to chant, "This isn't over." In my pocket, my phone buzzed. I took it out.

Steve: So sorry, good guy. 😊 Guess it's time to let the shark go.

And just like that, I found myself shouting along as we marched through the halls, down the front steps, and out onto the streets. "This isn't over. This isn't over."

Among his Instagram dumpster of Shaggy memes, Deadpool GIFs, and reposted videos mocking Marie Kondo was the real Steve. Steve in a car with his bros, giving the peace sign with their tongues out. Steve stealing liquor. Steve doing a keg stand with a Viking hat taped on his ass. Steve igniting his farts. Steve lighting fireworks on a wall that formed the word *FART*. Steve obscenely straddling the kiddie rocket ride at the mall. Steve writing "Jiz" over the "Sha" on a *Shazam* movie poster. "Best person, my ass," I said out loud.

Every few months he was seen taking a goofy-grinned selfie with another girl. Madeline Fields. Angelie Shishbangar. Nancy-Lee Nguyen. Brianna Stonebrook. Emma Napolitano. Emma Montoyez. Emma Chan. Emma Bumgartener. Emma-Grace Hurwitz III.

Kaia was just another in the string. Or worse, she was only a pawn in his game. He just wanted to beat me. To prove he could get whatever he wanted. I bet he already had another girlfriend on the side. Oh man, I'd pay to see whatever Kaia would do to him if she found him with some random. Then she'd see who he really was. The real Steve Stevenson. Then she would drop him like an old gym sock.

But I couldn't just tell her to look through his Instagram. She'd say that was before and that he was different now. She'd say cancer had changed him. I needed to show her that he was still the same. Cancer Steve was still Asshole Steve. The thought of them going to prom together made me nauseated.

Then an idea sparked.

I opened a new browser, popped up the Save Steve site, and whizzed down to the comment section. Scanning feverishly, I searched for what I needed. This would work if I found just the right post. Not too crazy. No poems rhyming the word *chemotherapy* with *come and sleep with me*. Boom! *StevesGirls.* That was their login name. A photo of three very cute college girls underscored it. Their post read: Can we buy you a beer, Steve? 🖤🖤👯🍺

"You can't always play by the rules," I said like an evil villain. But I wasn't the villain. I was the Best Person. And I was going to show Kaia who was the Worst.

16

The sun went down behind Steve's house as I sat in my car rehearsing. I had one shot at this. And I knew it was gonna be weird just showing up out of nowhere to see if he'd hang out with me.

"Hey, Steve, I just wanted to thank you for naming the fund in my . . . uh . . . name. It was really touching . . ." No. He'd never buy that. Not after that wink. It needed to seem realistic. Maybe work related? KYET wanted to do a follow-up interview with Steve, Kaia, and me on the Cardi B thing. "I thought we could go over what we wanted to say in the interview?" I tried. Eh. We could do that standing awkwardly in the doorway. Why would he go out to do that? What possible reason would we go out at all?

It was getting dark. I was going to have to wing it. Shit.

Winging it was not my strong suit. But the trap had already been set. I needed to act now.

A few uncertain knocks on his door later and it opened. For the first time, his dad answered. His chest strained his CrossFit shirt. But he seemed really happy to see me. "Oh, hey, Cam, buddy! Just the guy I wanted to see!"

Caught even more off guard than usual, I stammered, "Really?"

He grabbed my arm, just like Steve would, and led me into the house. "Come on, you got to see this. You're gonna love it."

Four eighty-inch LED TVs mounted like a command center. A Sub-Zero mini fridge. A pulsing *Pulp Fiction*–themed jukebox. A row of neon gaming chairs. An electric Ping-Pong table.

"Look what you got Steve!" his dad said as he ushered me into the newly upgraded man cave. Steve sat in the center of it all. Seeing me, he raised a confused eyebrow. His dad trotted over to him and shook him playfully by the shoulders. "We couldn't waste all that money on bills. Look at how happy it makes my boy!"

So instead of paying off their bills, they had just given their man cave a large dose of Viagra. This was what all my pain and suffering paid for? More than ever, I wanted to take Steve down.

"Come on in, have a seat and kill something," Steve's dad urged.

"Oh no. I just . . ." How was I going to get him out of this man-topia? "I, uh . . . I actually wanted to take Steve out," I offered weakly. "To . . . uh . . . celebrate."

"Well, celebrate here," his dad countered. "What could be better than this?" He fired up the electric Ping-Pong table, a Tetris-like light display cascading across the surface.

"Cam's a pacifist, socialist vegan. This isn't his particular scene," Steve explained.

"I'm a pescatarian." I felt the need to clarify even though we weren't ordering food.

Steve frowned at me. "We don't need Cam judging our slaughter-fest, do we, Dad?" He was doing a good job trying to get rid of me. And I was at a loss for what could get him out of here.

"No one ever had fun without someone else getting killed, Cam," his dad joked, and slammed a Ping-Pong on the table, which caused a digital explosion.

"I'm not sure that's true," I said.

Steve bounced up from his chair. I was sure he was going to just take me out by force. But instead, he dropped his controller and smiled, "All right, Cambo. Let's get out of here and get this celebration started."

A few minutes later we were in my car. I couldn't believe how easy it had been. Too easy, really. But Steve hadn't even known I was coming. How could he have plotted anything? Steve slammed his door closed and I strapped myself in.

"So, what'd you have in mind?" he asked.

"I . . . well . . . I thought we could play mini golf." I'd needed to find a fun place we could accidentally run into someone.

"Mini golf? Isn't Astroturf full of toxic chemicals? Are you sure windmills aren't racist?"

I resisted the urge to fire back. I needed to keep this thing friendly. "Come on, Steve. We don't need to keep repeating the same dynamic over and over, do we? Isn't it time for a fresh start?"

Steve stared at me for a long, probing moment and then fell back in his seat. "Sure. Why not? Let's fresh it up." He clicked his seat belt in and turned up the radio that had been playing Daft Punk's "Get Lucky."

The Golf N Stuff parking lot had a smattering of SUVs and family vans. Steve and I walked toward the entrance. A single go-kart whizzed by on the track that was adjacent to the parking lot. An eight-year-old literally screamed, "Wheeeee!"

"All right. Let's get turnt," Steve mocked.

We approached the entrance and a harried mom carrying a cake and balloons hurried past us. "Do you think Tyler will notice if we crash his seventh birthday party?" Steve asked.

"Look, you're not going to have fun with that attitude."

"Okay, Mom."

"You never know, something . . . exciting might happen."

"Doubt it."

Anonymous pop music thumped inside the dark, mildew-scented arcade. What was probably Tyler's birthday party raged in one corner. To our right, some junior high kids banged on the token machine, hoping to score more tickets. A six-year-old murdered digital zombies by the ball pit. I scanned the room for the girls. I'd told them to meet us by the golf course, but maybe they were early.

"You got any quarters for the claw game? I really need a new fidget spinner," Steve deadpanned.

"We need to get our clubs."

"You're the boss, party man."

I found the cashier and saw that a group of girls was already in line. I stiffened, anxious about my plan. We got in line behind them and I tried to get a good look. The picture from the comment section only gave me a vague idea what they looked like. One blonde. Two brunettes. One had glasses. One had freckles. I leaned in toward them, but their faces were buried in their phones. I slid a little out of line but one of them stepped forward, blocking my view further, her tiny Totoro backpack almost hitting my face.

I checked Steve to see if he noticed my interest. But he was laughing at a kid who had crawled up the Skee-Ball ramp and was trying to throw his fries in the holes.

I cleared my throat, but the girls didn't notice.

I leaned in a little closer, almost able to catch a glimpse of one of them. She did have freckles and brown hair. But I still couldn't tell. I was bending a little closer when a kid walking absently with his iPad ran into me. I stumbled into the freckled girl.

"Hey! What's your problem?" Finally, getting a good look at them, I knew they weren't the girls from the site. Instead, they were about thirteen and very creeped out by me.

"Sorry, I, uh, tripped."

"You tripped standing?" one of them asked, her hands propped on her hips.

"Damn, Cam. If this is your move, we need to talk," Steve giggled. "Haven't you heard of Me Too? You can't just rub up on random chicks."

I blushed and backpedaled. "I was not— I would never— I've read Simone de Beauvoir."

That didn't help. They clearly had no idea who the twentieth-century French intellectual was and how she related to them. Instead, the girls all stared at me like I had just exposed myself. "Gross." The muttonchopped employee behind the counter handed them their clubs and they flounced away.

We stepped up to the hairy cashier who had just overheard the whole thing. Certain he also thought I was some creepy girl-rubber, I explained, "That was not a move."

He rolled his eyes and said, "No shit."

Steve watched me fumble, exasperated. "We know, Cam. Everyone knows. Your reputation is intact." He patted me on the back. "Anyway, your move is more like an elaborate long-running scheme that allows you to hang out with other people's girlfriends, right?" He then addressed Mr. Mutton-chop. "Two thrilling games of mini golf, please."

Blue and green dome lights made a path to the first hole. I

scoped out the course for the girls. It was more sprawling than I'd remembered from when I was eight. There was a family putting at the Old West hole, a gaggle of girls whacking balls at the princess castle, and a teenage couple making out by the crocodile pond. But *StevesGirls* were nowhere in sight.

"That's a lot of walking," Steve said, and stopped. As we took in the course, I realized that there were a lot of stairs and ramps. Steve seemed to wilt a bit at the thought. Somehow, I kept forgetting he had cancer. "Sorry, I didn't even think about the chemo. You always seemed so indestructible, you know."

"And you always seemed so destructible." He smirked.

For a moment we stared at each other. Part of me was waiting to see if he wanted to go home. I might have been a little relieved. Standing here together at the mini golf course, my rage toward him had diminished a little.

"Is it too much?" I offered him a way out.

Considering it, he looked back at the arcade where we had come from. Then he exhaled. "Cam, eighty-year-old dudes with heart failure play real golf. I think I can manage." He then headed down a series of steps to the first hole.

"Think I can beat cancer?" Steve asked.

"I . . . uh . . ." Did I miss something? I thought it was highly curable. . . .

"I mean the hole," he clarified. And I realized he was talking about the smiling animatronic crab whose orange claws were swiping slowly back and forth, blocking the path to the hole.

"Oh, right," I said, and laughed, relieved.

190

"So serious," he said, and tapped his ball toward the crab. It scooted between the pendulating claws, under its belly, and right into the hole. "Eagle!" he cheered.

Of course he'd get a hole in one.

I put my ball down; it dribbled out of the tiny groove in the Astroturf and I had to replace it. Then I tapped it but not hard enough, and it rolled back to me.

"One," Steve counted.

I stopped the ball's return and put it back on the groove. I tapped it again. It rolled back.

"Two."

With increasing annoyance, I put it back on the groove. Tapped it harder. The crab smacked it back.

"Three."

"I know!"

Groove. Tap. Roll back.

"Four."

"I can count."

Grove. Tap. Roll back.

"Does your ball need training wheels?"

"Shut up."

Groove. Tap. Smack. Roll back.

"Should I get a chair?"

Groove. Hard tap. Bounce. Onto the concrete. Hit a post. Tapped a ceramic bird. Banked off the corner of a bench. Was guided by a discarded Slurpee cup. And wobbled onto the green.

"Of course," Steve said. "You had to find the most convoluted way."

"Ha. Ha," I said as we followed the path to the hole. We came around the other side of the crab and I saw three girls heading down the main stairs. They were wearing tight black dresses and seemed ready for a more exciting night than eighteen holes of mini golf. They were checking out the crowd, looking for someone. This had to be them. They had texted me their names—Nika, Haedyn, and Sophie—but I didn't know which was which. Then they stopped and saw me. I think it was Nika who gave me a look that said, "Is that you?" I nodded and motioned for them to follow us. I had told them to pretend not to know me. Steve would be too embarrassed if he thought I was setting him up, I'd explained.

"Finish your awesome shot off, Tiger Woods," Steve said.

I turned back to him and tried to pretend nothing was up. My ball plopped into the hole just as the girls appeared behind the crab claw. "Steve Stevenson?" Maybe-Nika asked.

Steve glanced up, surprised. He took them in for a moment, clearly confused. "Yes?"

I plucked my ball out of the hole as the girls made their way toward him. "Oh my god, how are you?" asked Maybe-Haedyn.

Steve watched them approach cautiously. "I'm good . . . and . . . do I know you?"

As they reached our green, the heavily made up girls whispered to each other, seeming to confer on who was going to speak first.

Steve looked at me and joked beneath his breath, "Do we need security?"

Finally, Maybe-Sophie stepped forward. "You don't know us, but we've been following your brave journey online and . . . we're, like, your biggest fans."

Hearing the word *fans*, Steve lit up, accepting the role of celebrity with ease.

"You're cuter in person," Maybe-Haedyn added.

"I think so, too," he flirted. The girls laughed way too loud. This was working exactly as I'd imagined.

Maybe-Sophie approached Steve. "You look amazing without hair."

"Like a bald Ansel Elgort." Maybe-Nika swooned.

"Can I touch it?" giggled Maybe-Haedyn.

"Why not?" Steve said, and tilted his head a little to make it easier for them. Maybe-Haedyn rubbed her hands gently all over it, being sure to keep her bright red nails safe from scratching him.

"Are you smooth all over?" she asked suggestively.

Maybe-Nika leaned in and raised her hands. "Let me feel." Now they were both running their hands over his head and Steve was purring. The girls tittered and "awwwed."

"I should have shaved my head a long time ago," Steve said. He was totally eating it up. If he'd had a wedding ring on, he would have pocketed it.

"Well, time for the next hole," Steve said. "You guys wanna join?"

"Yes!" they all agreed at once. Operation The Real Steve was a go.

I pulled out my phone, ready to snap the picture that would take him down. Over the next few holes, there was no shortage of flirty shots. Steve bought them all sodas. The girls couldn't stop touching his arm. They laughed at his dumb jokes about balls and putters. But none of my pictures would be proof enough to get Kaia to dump his ass. He could easily explain them away. I needed the money shot.

At the circus-themed hole, I saw Maybe-Haedyn standing by herself, sipping her Coke. Maybe-Nika and Maybe-Sophie were taking a selfie with Steve and the giant clown. I felt the need to push things forward.

"Isn't Steve amazing?" I asked Maybe-Haedyn.

"He really is. It must be so hard," she said as she watched Steve with a dreamy glaze in her eye. "His girlfriend must feel so lucky to have this time with him." I was surprised that she was even considering Kaia, since the girls had clearly come out to paw all over Steve.

"Oh . . . yeah . . . ," I agreed softly. Then added (somewhat truthfully), "But I heard they were having problems."

Maybe-Haedyn's eyes lit up and she looked over to me with a sly smile. "Really? That's terrible." But she clearly didn't think it was.

At the pirate ship hole, the girls huddled together in a cluster, whispering. Maybe-Haedyn was filling them in. They eyed Steve speculatively as he lined up his next shot. "You're awfully quiet, Cambo." He swung, but his ball rolled right past the hole.

"I'm focused on my game." I held up my scorecard. "And now I'm only one shot behind."

"I've been a little distracted," he said with a goofy smile, and nodded in the girls' direction.

"Well, you're going down," I said in my best playful jock tone. I had never really done the whole competitive dude joking thing. But I figured it was the best way to keep him from suspecting anything.

"Getting a little cocky. That's how you make a mistake."

"Just sink your ball," I teased. It was weird to banter like this. I kind of liked it, even though I was in the middle of a sting.

At the Dutch windmill, Maybe-Haedyn swung and missed three times. "I suck at this," she said helplessly, and looked to Steve. "Can you help me?" My talk had worked. She was now untethered by the guilt of a sad girlfriend at home.

Steve willingly took up the offer and sidled up behind her. He brought his arms around her and adjusted the way she held the club. "It must be so hard being sick," she said.

"It's really just a wee bit of cancer. It's not so bad." His casual words only made her more moony. She leaned back into him and then they hit the ball together. It rolled up the bridge and onto the main green. "There you go!" Steve cheered.

But she did not celebrate. Instead, she turned to look at Steve with longing, thoughtful eyes and said, "Life is so short, isn't it?"

"It really is," Steve agreed. She placed her hand on his arm and he looked over at me. "You're up, buddy."

He then stepped off the course and took Maybe-Haedyn's hand. "Come here." He led her into a corner and brought her close. In love with Kaia, my ass! What a phony.

This was the shot I needed. But the other girls were blocking my view and it would be too obvious to get in a better position, especially since I was up next. "Hey . . . you guys want a picture?" I asked Maybe-Nika and Maybe-Sophie. They jumped at the opportunity and leaned in close together, held up their drinks, and made the usual selfie faces. "The light's better to your left." They shuffled to the edge of my frame. Now, clearly in the background, were Steve and Maybe-Haedyn, backlit by the red lava of the volcano. He leaned into her and whispered something. *Snap!* Maybe-Haedyn giggled. *Snap!* She whispered something to him, her hand on his neck. *Snap!* Then Steve led her behind the volcano and out of my sight line.

I took one more photo of the girls. "Awesome." Then I put the phone down and they instantly resumed their normal expressions. I needed to get to the other side of that volcano. Quickly I putted, knocking the ball off the course and into a pond, where I might be able to spy better. The other photos would probably do the trick, but if I could get one that was fully incriminating, my plan would be bulletproof. I climbed over the railing but still couldn't see them. Shuffling toward the edge of the shallow pond, I held my phone out, hoping to catch a glimpse of Steve and Maybe-Haedyn in full make-out mode. There was an elbow . . . and maybe a bit of knee . . . I inched a bit closer. My foot wobbled on the mossy edge. Was that a hand? My foot slipped and slid into the water. "Shoot." I pulled my shoe out of the swampy muck and shook it off. Just then, Steve and Maybe-Haedyn emerged from their dark corner. Dammit.

I kneeled down, plucked my ball from the stupid pond, and then returned to the group. The girls were again clustered together and Maybe-Haedyn was whispering something to them. "Two-shot water penalty," Steve said, and motioned to my scorecard. "Mark it down." I pulled it out and penciled in the score. But when I was finished, I found Maybe-Haedyn right up in my face.

"You're so fucking brave."

"I am?" I asked.

"You've done so much for Steve," Maybe-Sophie added. She was also right in front of me. Their proximity, their perfume, and their cleavage overwhelmed me.

"It's the least I—"

"And you're the one who's really dying!" Maybe-Nika said. *What the what?*

"I'm sorry. I'm not—"

Maybe-Haedyn put her hand on my arm. "Stop. He said you'd deny it." I looked over at Steve and he nodded with a little smile. "He said you wouldn't want a pity party."

"No, I don't—" I tried to squeeze my words through theirs.

"Only three months to live!" Maybe-Sophie said, and touched her hand to her chest.

"And you're still trying to cheer up your best friend," said Maybe-Nika.

"Steve . . ." I tried to get his attention, to clear things up. But he stood over his ball, looked at me with a big grin, and tapped his shot in without looking.

"You know what? You two deserve a toast!" exclaimed Maybe-Haedyn, and held up her soda.

"Ah ah ah. Hold on. We need a top-off." Maybe-Sophie dug into her purse and pulled out a small bottle of vodka.

I felt things spinning out of control. I didn't even consider that they'd be drinking. That was not part of the plan. But it also explained so much. The glaze in their eyes. The wobble in their steps. What I now recognized was the liquor smell on their breath.

Maybe-Sophie tried to spike my cup, but I pulled it away. She immediately realized her error. "Oh, shit. I'm sorry. You can't drink on chemo."

My head swam, trying to figure out a way to explain that I wasn't on chemo and I wasn't dying and, even more importantly, drunk girls weren't part of my plan to get Steve to cheat on Kaia.

"Oh well, more for me." Maybe-Sophie splashed another shot into her cup.

"Wait," I objected, trying to get this under control. "You can't be drinking."

"Really? What else do you do at mini golf?" Maybe-Nika chugged what was left in her cup.

"Exactly!" Steve encouraged. "Now let's do the volcano!"

For the next three holes I couldn't shake the girls. My "terminal cancer" was apparently way more romantic than Steve's real cancer. As a light fog rolled in, the girls doted on me, put their hands on my arm thoughtfully, and laughed at what they thought were my jokes. They were a drunken whirlwind of attention that made me sweat and stumble and babble incoherently. All the while, Steve basked in my discomfort.

Maybe-Nika pulled at my hair for the third time. "Seriously, it's not a wig," I explained again.

"But it'll probably start falling out soon, you poor thing."

"It won't. I'm not on chemo. I'm fine."

"I totally believe in positive thinking, too," Maybe-Haedyn said. "I've been telling myself that I could be a server at Olive Garden for six months and yesterday I got an interview!"

"Hey, girls, can I borrow Mr. Camtastic for a bit?" It was Steve, and for some reason he had decided to save me.

"No. He's ours now," slurred Maybe-Haedyn. She leaned forward and whispered, "I really like bread sticks . . ." A gust of vodka breath almost knocked me out.

"Oh, okay. Which one of you ladies wants to help apply the steroid cream on his rash? It's time for an application. He'll flare up otherwise."

"Rash?" Maybe-Haedyn said. The word seemed to instantly puncture her fantasy.

Steve pulled out a tube and held it up. "Yeah. Chemo side effect. Kind of an unusual one. The doctors said they'd never seen one this bad, right, Cam?"

"Um, yeah," I sputtered, going along with the plan.

"Though it is around the groin," he offered. "So maybe that's of some interest. But be warned, it does get a little crusty and you'll have to make sure you get the cream in all the crevices. Otherwise, the sores will burst. Right, buddy?"

The drunken girls made squishy faces. Apparently, their cancer fantasy only involved looking longingly into my dying eyes.

"Uh, that seems private."

"We don't want to intrude."

"Of course not," Steve said with a smile, and pulled me away.

Once we were safely inside the bathroom, Steve dropped my arm, sauntered over to the urinal, and unzipped.

"Cancer groupies? Really, Cam?"

I looked away. "I don't know what you're—"

"Kinda a dick move for such a nice guy. Again."

"No, no. They just—"

He shook off and zipped up. "Cut the shit, Cam. You're a terrible liar. Sincere people always are." He turned to face me. There was a coldness in his expression I hadn't seen before. He flushed the urinal with more force than necessary.

"I—"

He stepped toward me. "Did you really think I was going to cheat on Kaia with some randoms at mini golf?" I'd never realized before just how big Steve was. But in the tiny bathroom with its dirty fluorescent light buzzing, he was suddenly huge.

I wanted to say something, but my mouth just kind of flopped open and hung there. Something flickered across Steve's face as he studied my expression. "Wow. You really do have a low opinion of me."

I knew he could see the truth in my eyes. "I—"

But Steve just shrugged and turned on the faucet to wash his hands. "So what was the plan? Let me guess. You were going to livestream the whole thing, so Kaia would break up with me and fall into your spaghetti-strand arms. I mean, I gotta give you credit. You come up with the most convoluted Rube Goldberg type schemes to get a girl to go out with you." He shook off his hands and punched on the hand dryer. "And yes, Cam. I know who Rube Goldberg is. Let's not underestimate me again."

"I'm not trying to get Kaia to go out with me!" I shouted over the sound of the blower.

Steve whirled around. "Then why else would you honeypot me!"

"I'm not—"

He stepped toward me. The dryer continued to scream. "Come on. It's over. Give up."

I stepped back and bumped up against the sink. "I don't know what you're talking about."

"You're going to deny it? Seriously?"

"You're just confu—"

He leaned forward, inches from me, and curled his fingers around the scuffed white porcelain. "JUST FUCKING ADMIT IT!"

"WELL, WHAT WAS I SUPPOSED TO DO?" The dryer suddenly cut off and my words bounced off the tiled walls. I cringed as Steve hovered over me, both of us breathing hard. For a moment, neither of us seemed to know what to do. Then Steve released his grip on the sink and stepped back.

With space between us again, I blinked away humiliated tears. Steve turned his back to me. "Do not. Fucking. Cry."

"You tricked her."

Steve spun, surprise and fury warring on his face. "*I* tricked her?"

"The Cam Webber Hero Fund! Pretending to care about people! To be a good person!" I spread my arms trying to express the enormity, the everythingness, of what he'd done.

Steve's expression was strangely blank. "Maybe I am a good person. Ever consider that? Maybe hanging out with you and Kaia all the time made me think about things. The foundation's real, Cam. Maybe setting it up made me feel all warm and gooey inside."

"What about collapsing in front of everyone? What about 'You can't beat a dying guy'?" I moved forward, closing the space between us.

Steve's mouth twisted. "Oh yeah. I faked that part. Totally wrenched my shoulder, if it makes you feel better."

There wasn't even a trace of shame. God, I hated him. Even with cancer, it was like he'd never felt pain. I really wanted to make him feel pain. "She was just staying with you because she felt bad you had cancer! She was going to break up with you!"

Steve stared at me for a long moment. He cocked his head. "Yeah. I know. She told me all about that."

I stumbled back. "What?" I'd heard exactly what he said, but my world was kind of crumbling.

"She told me. Because we talk about stuff. Because she's my girlfriend." He said it slowly, like a teacher helping a particularly confused student with a remedial concept. And he was looking at me with a feeling I didn't know he was capable of: pity. Steve Stevenson pitied me. It was the most horrible feeling in the world.

I wanted to say something devastating. But what was there to say? I had nothing left. I was standing in a mini golf bathroom and everything I thought was true, wasn't. They were in a real relationship. They talked about things. Kaia might actually really love him. "God. You aren't even angry with me, are you?" The words were bitter in my mouth.

"It's hard to get angry with someone who is so ineffective." It was true. Anger was a feeling you reserved for someone who could hurt you. And I wasn't that to Steve. Because I wasn't anything to Kaia. Steve patted me on the shoulder as he opened the bathroom door. "Anyway, you torture yourself enough for both of us."

A blast of alcohol-scented air wafted in. The girls were clustered right outside the door. "We were so worried!" Maybe-Nika shout-slurred. Steve and I both flinched.

Maybe-Sophie caught sight of my red eyes. "Oh no! Were you crying?"

Maybe-Haedyn held out her arms and stumbled forward. "Do you need a hug?" At this, the other two girls raised their arms in offer, wobbling toward us. Maybe-Nika burped, long and juicy. Steve jerked back, bumping into me.

"Nope! We're good!"

"No hugs needed," I added as Steve slammed the door in their faces. We both turned and leaned against it, holding it shut, as the girls pushed the door and we dug in our feet. Through the heavy metal of the door, we could hear muffled shouts of "Hey" and "We just want to hug."

"Just to be clear," I huffed, "I didn't think they'd be drinking."

Steve rolled his eyes as a particularly forceful push jerked us forward. "Cam, they're college girls. It's Friday."

"Do you think they'll break in? Should we try to jam the door somehow and go through the window?" I jerked my chin toward the small opening near the top of the tiled wall. "We're near the edge of the course. We can hop the fence into the industrial park next door."

"Jesus, Cam. They're drunk, not zombies. Give them a minute and they'll get bored."

He was right. The pounding got more and more half-hearted, tapering off into a final shove that barely bounced us forward. Some muttering filtered through for a moment longer and then the only thing we could hear was the distant sound of the go-karts through the open window. We slid to the ground.

I studied the pattern in the tile on the floor. It repeated over and over. "Why do you like her?" I wasn't sure I'd even meant to ask the question out loud.

Steve sighed, as if he'd expected this. "Same reasons you do."

I shook my head. "Nope. Not possible."

Steve tilted his head back against the door and stared at the ceiling. "She's smart. She's hot. She goes with the flow." He counted them off on his fingers one by one.

"Those are some pretty generic reasons."

"They're the reasons most people go out, Cam," Steve sighed.

"But"—I tucked my knees up and half turned to Steve— "Kaia's not a generic person, Steve. She's amazing."

Steve rolled his eyes. "Like that's super specific."

"Fine. You want specific?" I turned all the way to face him now. "Kaia is honest. She thinks the best of people. She's kind but she's never fake nice. She is passionate but not righteous. You can tell she wakes up in the morning and thinks about how she can make the world a better place."

"And she's hot." Steve turned to face me all the way, too, a hint of challenge in his eyes.

"Yes, Steve, she's hot." I threw my arms up. "But even if she was burned horribly in an explosion at a fracking mine she had barricaded herself to in protest, I wouldn't care."

Steve slowly shook his head from side to side. "God, do you lube yourself up with superiority when you masturbate?" Before I could answer, Steve rolled away and pulled the door open a crack. He peered out. "All clear." He hopped to his feet, yanked open the door, and left without bothering to see if I would follow.

I caught up to him near the windmill. He waited for me, twirling his golf club under the lazily rotating vanes outlined with cheery yellow lightbulbs.

"Sure you don't want to finish our round?" Steve asked.

"Positive."

Steve swung his club over his shoulder. "Too bad. I really enjoy beating you." With a little skip in his step, he walked toward the exit.

We crossed the parking lot in silence. A few rows in, under the glare of a streetlamp, I could see my Prius. We'd get in, and I'd take Steve home. It was over. My stupid, half-baked plan had failed. Honestly, I was probably lucky that the night hadn't ended with me getting a black eye.

I still couldn't wrap my head around it—Steve and Kaia talked. They shared things. They were a couple. I might be able to handle it, this new reality where Steve and Kaia were together for real, if I just knew one thing.

"At least admit I'm better for her."

Ahead of me, Steve paused. For a moment I didn't think he would answer. Then he turned and arched an eyebrow. "It doesn't matter if you're better for her, Cam. I'm the one who asked her out."

I wish he had kicked me in the nuts. It would have hurt less.

"Let's go, bitches!"

We both turned to see a rust-orange El Camino lurch to

life and rumble forward. At the wheel was Maybe-Sophie. She stuck out her arm and chucked something out the window. It gleamed and flashed as it spun through the air under the streetlight before hitting the pavement and exploding into a thousand pieces. The fifth of vodka.

I was already running by the time my brain caught up to what was happening. My Nikes skidded as I squeezed through some parked cars, then dashed across the lane, veering to intercept the car. I slammed my hands down on the hood. There was an answering *thunk* next to me. Steve was beside me, hands on the car, breathing heavily.

"What?" he asked, looking slightly annoyed at my obvious surprise.

"Move, cancer assholes!" A horn blared. We both peered through the windshield. The three girls were squished in the front seat.

"We hate you," Maybe-Haedyn wailed. "You ditched us!"

"Get an Uber!" Steve shouted over the rumble of the engine.

"My roommate needs her car back for work in the morning!" Maybe-Sophie yelled.

"Not if it's destroyed." Steve was patient but immovable.

"I promised her! She's gonna hate me." Tears spilled down Maybe-Sophie's cheeks. She dropped her head on the steering wheel. "She already hates me."

Maybe-Nika shoved her from the middle seat. "Let's go! I'm STARVING. Need food."

But Maybe-Sophie just cried harder. Maybe-Haedyn

stretched her arms out and yawned. "Can we go home? Need bed. Me ty-ty."

I dropped my head. "Oh boy." I looked up at Steve. "Divide them up?"

He nodded. "Yep. I'll take Weepy. You take Sleepy and Hungry."

I followed the taillights of the El Camino down Victoria Avenue. Maybe-Nika was slumped in the passenger seat, clutching her stomach and grumbling intermittently about food. Maybe-Haedyn was sprawled in the seat behind me, moaning.

"I need my blankey."

Holding my phone, I spoke into the receiver. "We got an address yet?"

Steve's voice answered, "Not exactly. Somewhere off Telegraph. But Weepy put on Kelly Clarkson and now I can't get anything more out of her."

Through the speaker I heard, tinny and thin, Maybe-Sophie sing-wailing, *"I watched you die/I heard you cry/Every night in your sleep."*

"Okay, well, that's a mile or so up. After the song ends, ask her left or right." Maybe-Sophie continued her serenade through the speakers, occasionally just dissolving into sobs.

"Why didn't you just ask Kaia out?" Steve's voice was quiet, but it cut through the wailing. I couldn't tell if Steve was playing me, but his tone lacked any of its usual mockery.

"Um . . . she was dating you?"

Steve huffed, rueful. "Nuh-uh. You know what I mean. Before that. Sounds like you've had a boner for her since sophomore year."

"I have not had—"

"Don't worry. I'm sure it's a very respectful boner."

Maybe-Nika perked up. "Wienerschnitzel sounds good."

I sighed, my shoulders drooping. "Look, I tried to ask her out a thousand times." All the almost perfect moments flashed in my mind.

"But you shit the bed."

"Beeeeedddddd," groaned Maybe-Haedyn.

"I didn't— It was never the right time." It hadn't been. There was no way Kaia would have said yes. Right?

In front of us, the light turned red and we stopped. I watched as cars slid through the intersection.

But then Steve had asked her, apparently without any special moment at all, and she'd said yes. If I had tried that, if I had taken a chance on one of those messed-up perfect moments, would it have worked? I closed my eyes for a second, gathering my thoughts. "I just—"

"DEL TACCOOOOOOOOOOOOOOOOOOOOO!"

"Whaaa?" I whipped my head around to see Maybe-Nika flinging the passenger door open and tumbling into the street. She scrambled up to standing and then weaved her way across the road toward the red, white, and green glowing sign of Del Taco. "Steve! We've got a problem!" I turned the wheel, angling my Prius toward the fast-food restaurant.

"Already on it!" The El Camino lurched forward.

Seconds later we pulled into the parking lot. I punched off the Prius and turned to look behind me. Maybe-Haedyn was asleep, drooling in the back seat. "Okay. Cool. Stay there." I climbed out of the car. Maybe-Nika was easy to find. I just had to follow the sound of a fist pounding on glass.

"Give me a burrito with red sauce now!" Maybe-Nika was half hanging off the ledge of the service window in the drive-through as she repeatedly banged on the window. The glare of lights reflecting on the glass made it impossible to see inside, but I thought I saw the silhouette of the cashier shaking with laughter.

Arms out in front of me, I slowly approached Maybe-Nika like she was a deer who might bolt at any second. "Hey . . . there . . ." I didn't dare say her name in case I was wrong and it might set her off. "Why don't you get back in the car and I'll drive you through."

Maybe-Nika whipped around, snarling. "No! I am not leaving until I get a fucking burrito!" Then without warning she slumped, laying her cheek on the cold metal of the ledge, arms dangling. "I'm so hungry." Her voice was barely a whisper.

Footsteps pounded on the asphalt. Steve had gotten out of the El Camino and was jogging to the drive-through. He stopped a little ways away, taking in the scene. "You take six o'clock. I take twelve. We herd her toward the Prius. Copy?"

I nodded once. "Yeah. Got it."

The speaker by the menu board crackled to life. "Ma'am.

This is a drive-through." The worker managed to choke out their words through breathless giggles. "You need a car . . ."

Like she'd been jolted with electricity, Maybe-Nika came alive and flung herself on the window. "YOU WILL GIVE ME A BURRITO!" Through the raspy speaker there was a short shriek of terror.

Steve and I inched closer, eyes locked on each other. I held up my hand. "On the count of three. One . . . Two . . ."

The service window slid open with a screech. "Screw it. Here." And then a burrito was sailing out, flipping end over end. Maybe-Nika's eyes widened as they traced its perfect arc.

"BURRRRITTOOOOOOOOO!"

She bounded after it.

"Shit!" Steve yelled. "Hungry's on the move!" As one, we dashed after her.

Reaching the grass partition, Maybe-Nika scooped up the burrito from the damp ground and thrust it into the air, triumphant. "I'm gonna run for the border!" she exclaimed.

"That's Taco Bell," Steve said, lunging for her.

Maybe-Nika leaped to the sidewalk and took off down the street, holding the burrito high overhead. I tore after her, jumping a bush to land a few yards behind her. Steve followed a few seconds later. We pounded down the sidewalk, back toward the parked Prius and the El Camino.

As we got closer, we could see Maybe-Sophie hanging halfway out the window of the front seat of the El Camino. "I'm alone. I'll always be alone," she wailed.

We kept running a few more feet, then stopped. There was no sign of Maybe-Nika. "Where'd she go?" I panted. The streets were empty and quiet, not even an echo of a Mexican fast-food slogan.

Beside me, Steve scanned the darkness. "No idea." He sighed. "Back to the car?"

"Yeah. Maybe if we drive slow we'll spot her." We trudged back toward the waiting vehicles.

"So, what does the Cam Webber 'perfect moment' look like?" Steve mused, his hand stroking his chin. It took me a minute to remember what he meant. That we'd been talking about my inability to ask Kaia out. I'd hoped we'd been done with the conversation, but judging by the glint in Steve's eye, I feared it was just beginning.

"So, is it swimming with dolphins after spending a day building homes for Habitat for Humanity?" Steve chirped through my phone's speaker. He was on his one thousandth guess as we slowly drove down the street, hoping to spot a drunk burrito-munching fiend. Behind me, Maybe-Haedyn snored softly.

"First, humans should never swim with dolphins for entertainment—"

"What? But they're so magical!"

"Second. Do you see Hungry anywhere?

"That's a negative." There was a beat of silence. "Oh. Got it. Candlelight dinner on a compost heap. Yes, it's a little stinky, but you'll be stuffed full of self-satisfaction."

"Steve?"

"Yes?"

"Fuck off."

I heard Steve stifle a snort of laughter when, through the phone, came a heartbreaking sob. "Oh my god! What if she's deeeeeeeeaaaaaaad? It's all my fauuuuuult." Maybe-Sophie howled. Through the rearview mirror of the Prius, I saw Steve pull Maybe-Sophie back up to a seated position.

"Shhhhh," Steve said. "It's okay, Weepy. She's fine. You're a good friend."

"I am?" She sniffed.

"Of course."

I smiled, then gripped the wheel. "Wait! Steve! Is that . . . ? Up there . . ." A little ways ahead in front of a bus bench was a huddled figure. I thought I could see the bright white corner of a Del Taco wrapper fluttering in the gutter nearby.

"Yep. That's her," Steve confirmed.

"Okay. I'm pulling over." I put on my emergencies as I angled the car toward the side of the road. Just as I reached the right lane, arms wrapped around my neck, crushing my windpipe.

"What the—" I wheezed, and the car swerved.

"I had a nightmare!" A now awake Maybe-Haedyn squeezed me tighter.

"Let go!" I scrabbled at the arms around my neck. With no hands on the wheel, the car bounced onto the curb. Maybe-Haedyn let out a surprised shriek. The seat belt bit into my shoulder. I slammed on the brakes, throwing us both forward.

We skidded toward the bus stop.

I pressed down as hard as I could and yanked the wheel. We jerked to a stop. In front of the car, illuminated in a pool of yellow from the headlights, was Maybe-Nika, snoring, red sauce smeared on her face.

I picked up my phone. "Got her."

Twenty minutes later, I pushed a passed-out Maybe-Haedyn into the girls' apartment on a wobbly, rolling desk chair. Steve shoved a glittery pile of clothing onto the floor, then gestured to the now clear space. I tipped Maybe-Haedyn onto the cushions. "Wow. This place is Forever 21 after the apocalypse."

There were empty pizza boxes, beer cans, and piles of clothes flung on every available surface. "Right?" Steve said. "Guys get so much shit for being slobs, but this is some *Mad Max*–like destruction here."

"Is there a bed anywhere?" I asked.

"I think I saw a mattress on the floor in the bedroom, but it might just have been a pile of laundry. I made Weepy a nest."

I nodded. "Well, I guess that's—"

"Ooooooh!" Steve interrupted. "I got it! Your perfect moment is watching the last iceberg melt in Alaska and the impending planetary doom gets you so horny you fall into each other's arms and start humping!"

I groaned. "I don't know, okay?" Steve was just being Steve, but every time he made a guess, I relived every moment with Kaia where I had messed up. "That's the problem. I thought

214

I had the right moment. A few times. But then something would happen. And I'd have to wait for another chance. For a moment where I could . . ." What was I hoping would happen? "I could . . ."

"Guarantee success?" Steve was watching me carefully, his arm resting on a bookcase. I looked away.

"Go home, Uber drivers," Maybe-Haedyn mumbled from the couch, then rolled over. "Haedyn sleep sleep now."

"I knew she looked like a Haedyn!" I grinned at Steve, who returned my look with mild confusion. "Anyway . . ."

I started to walk to the door. Steve grabbed my arm as I passed. "So what if Kaia said no? Would it kill you?" The look on my face must have said enough. Steve ran his hand over his bald head. "Well, I'll give you one thing, Cam. You really do care about shit."

We stared at each other for a moment.

There was a clatter in the kitchen. We turned. Maybe-Nika stumbled into the living room, an empty family-sized bag of potato chips clutched in her fist, burrito sauce still on her face.

"I need some fucking bacon cheese fries!"

Steve squealed, "Run, Cam! Ruuuuuuuuun!"

17

We took the stairs two at a time, checking behind us to see if we were being chased. And we were laughing. Both of us. Which was really weird, because it felt natural in a way I'd never imagined it could.

We reached the central courtyard of the apartment complex and caught our breath. The windows of most of the other apartments were dark, though a few glowed yellow through their drawn curtains. "I feel terrible for whoever's on call for Postmates tonight," I said.

"Wow, that was like half a joke, Cam. You deserve a prize." He reached into his pants and pulled out a sparkly headband with kitty ears and placed it gently on my head.

"Did you steal that?"

"I wanted a memento to commemorate the night. I got one

for me, too." He pulled a second one out and placed it on his head. "Despite the fact that you are a complete asshole, that was fucking fun." Still breathing heavy, he put his hands on his knees. "God, I used to be able to wrangle three crazy girls no problem. This cancer is no joke. I gotta sit down." He wandered over to the community pool, pulled off his shoes and socks, and stuck his feet in.

I inspected the stairwell back up toward the girls' apartment, still afraid they might make an appearance. Meanwhile, Steve pulled out some weed, took a long drag, and exhaled. A plume of smoke drifted into invisibility. Concern jumped in my stomach. "Are you feeling nauseous?"

"No. I'm fine. Relax. This is the only cancer perk I have," he said, and brought it to his lips again.

I was relieved and let myself relax. It had been a crazy night. And I had been such an idiot. But with the rest of the apartment complex asleep, the quiet of the night and the damp air were inviting. I looked down at Steve and his kitty ears illuminated by the pool light and thought maybe I'd join him. I slid off my shoes.

Steve took another puff. "Well, this definitely beats a night at home."

"Really?" I said as I dipped my bare feet into the warm pool. "I'm surprised you'd want to leave your fancy new man cave."

"Dude, that's all my dad." The way he said it echoed his anger from the bee café. I thought I'd better not push it.

"It's cool. You don't have to explain."

We had already been through enough tonight. We didn't need another fight. Instead we sat in a long silence. Steve let out a tired exhale.

"I mean, you've heard them fighting. My mom's pissed he spent all that money on the room, but Dad tells her that I shouldn't be worried about bills and stuff because staying positive is more important. After I set up the foundation, he wanted to make sure I got something fun for myself. I need to keep"—and he switched into his "dad voice"—"killing it. He's not some cancer kid, Cheryl."

"Your dad seems like he doesn't worry about much."

Steve laughed. "He's worried to death. If it doesn't look like I'm living it up, he thinks I'm dying, and when he thinks I'm dying . . . Jesus . . ." He put his head down. The weight of all the effort he was putting in living up to his dad's expectations bore down on him. "I'm just glad my cancer's one of the good ones. I don't know what I'd do if I was actually terminal or whatever."

"I'd think you'd be kind of worried about yourself then."

"You'd think that, right? But I actually think I'd be more worried about them. I mean, I'd be dead so who cares, but they'd have to live the rest of their lives with a dead son. Fuck, that's the worst."

"I guess I never thought of that." I also never thought Steve would sound so selfless. I stared at him for a moment to see if he really was the same Steve.

Then he looked up at me. "What would your parents do if you died?"

"It's just me and my mom. My dad left when I was seven."

"Left? Like you don't see him anymore?" Steve took a long inhale.

"Yep. I think he moved to Georgia or something. I don't care. It's not like he's in contact. It's better this way."

"Really?" Steve exhaled, sending a cloud of smoke over the surface of the pool.

"I mean, yeah, there was, like, this black hole for a while after he left. Like a space where he used to be. But it went away. And he was an asshole. Even a black hole in my life is better than an asshole." Steve looked at me like he didn't quite believe me and for a moment, I wasn't quite sure I believed myself. I shook off the thought. "But my mom? If I died? I can't even imagine." The thought of my mom without me seemed impossible. It actually hurt too much to consider. "I can't die."

"I don't think that's your choice."

"No, seriously, I mean, she's, like . . . she takes so much pride in what I do. I'm like a vindication that she didn't need my dad." I tried to think of a situation where my death wouldn't completely destroy her. "Okay, maybe if I went out for some noble cause, like jumping in front of a school shooter or saving a village from Ebola."

"Both likely."

"But if it was something like alcohol poisoning at a frat party, she might move away and pretend she never had a kid."

"She sounds intense," he said with a hint of sympathy.

"You should talk," I said. It was weird to have something

in common with Steve. I wondered if he felt the same. For a moment we both watched the water lap against the chipped tile of the pool.

Steve offered his weed to me.

"What? I don't. I mean, I'm totally for legalization and think it's ridiculous that people believe alcohol is safer. Not to mention the medicinal benefits of CBD . . ."

"Man, you're exhausting," he said, taking a hit to counteract my babbling.

I laughed at myself. "Sorry."

"Are all your friends this fun?"

The question caught me off guard. "Yes. No . . . I mean . . ." My stomach clenched. "They're fun . . . Not like yours . . ." My breathing got shorter. "I'm so busy and . . . there's not a lot of time . . . We mainly hang out at protests . . . City council meetings . . ."

"You don't have any friends, do you?"

"Of course I do. I just told you."

"Friends don't just sign petitions together."

"Whatever," I said, desperate to change the subject. "I don't see a ton of people hanging out with you anymore." I winced as soon as I said it, but Steve didn't seem to care.

"So? I don't want anyone to see me lying around puking into a bucket. I mean, at least not from chemo. They've seen me do it plenty of times from tequila." He laughed, but it was half-hearted. He kicked at the water and watched the ripples float away.

"Did any of them even ask to come by?" I said as sensitively as I could.

"At the beginning some of them did. But most of them didn't. And it's been a while since anyone asked." I didn't know what to say. How could they abandon him like that? As if he heard my thoughts, he answered, "I think they were happy you were doing all the work for them." He said it casually, but the pain in his voice was unavoidable. "Fuck . . . Cam, does that mean you're my only friend?" I tried to find the sarcasm or mockery in his voice, but it wasn't there.

"I don't think we're friends," I joked, but wished I hadn't.

"You're probably right. You did just try to steal my girlfriend. And you're trying to save that shark."

"What's the shark got to do with anything?"

"I need your shark to stay in that tank. That big fish is my whole cancer backup plan. I always figured if shit went sideways, I'd just take a nice dive into old sharky's lair and call it a day."

"You're going to kill yourself by shark?" I asked, only half joking, because he seemed half serious.

"Awesome, right? I wouldn't have to watch my parents fall apart as I waste away. I'd go fast and furious. And I mean, I kind of think my dad would even be proud of that. His boy didn't die of cancer, but of a glorious shark attack!" He laughed, but his shoulders dropped and he looked down. It seemed like he wished he could take the whole thing back. Like he had said too much. Been too honest. The way I always was.

I thought about putting my arm around him, but then worried it would be weird. Or worse, that he'd shrug it off. Instead we stared at the sparkling pool and let its reflection dance on our faces.

"You sure we're not f-friends?" he stuttered. Maybe we were after all? Was that possible? Why did the thought of it not repel me? Why did it actually feel kind of nice?

As I considered this, he slumped onto my arm as if he'd passed out.

"Oh. Ha ha. I'm the one who should be passing out. Being friends with you . . ." I nudged him, but he refused to let up on his joke. His kitten ears tickled my face. "You're really committing to this, huh?" I shoved him harder, but he just fell back on my arm and the kitten ears fell off. I resisted my urge to panic. That's what he wanted. I checked his face but didn't see even a hint of a smile. "Seriously, this is not funny." I added some intensity to my voice, but didn't want him to think I'd actually fallen for it.

No response.

"Steve? Really?"

He moaned.

"I'm not falling for that again."

But his face looked ashen and there was no way he could fake that, could he? Were things going "sideways" right now? I listened for his breathing and was relieved to hear it. Then his eyes fluttered open. "Cam? I don't . . ." The sound of his voice was the clincher. It sounded so weak and thin. Maybe he was that amazing an actor. Maybe he was going to pop up in a second and laugh his ass off at my overreaction. But, screw it, my gut told me I had to do something. And if it turned out he was faking it, then we were definitely not friends.

I pulled out my phone. "I'm going to call an ambulance."

"No . . ." My suggestion stirred him, but he still seemed unsteady.

"Fuck yes."

He found just enough strength to sit up and took a deep breath. "Don't bother. S'happened before. Fine. Just a side effect. Get dizzy sometimes. Sexy, right?"

"Nothing about this is fine!"

"Just take me home. Please." My finger hovered over the call button, but now that he was conscious, maybe it was better to get him in the car. It would take forever for an ambulance. And I could always take him to the emergency room if it got worse.

I helped him up and he took my arm to help stabilize himself. "Your elbows are really soft," he observed.

"My mom moisturizes them while I sleep."

"Fucking . . . intense . . . ," he said weakly, and we made our way to my car.

I raced down Victoria Avenue, relieved that the streets were empty and not caring about the cops. Getting pulled over actually sounded like a decent idea at this point. They'd see how Steve was and make him go to the hospital. But, slumped against the car door, he kept insisting I take him home.

223

"I'm gonna be fine."

"Is it hard to breathe?" I asked, splitting my attention between him and the road.

"Just tired."

"Okay. We'll get you home. Just don't . . . No going sideways, got it?"

He didn't respond, just looked away. Little blooms of mist came and went on the window with his nose pressed against it.

This was exactly what would happen, wouldn't it? I'd make a friend and then he'd die. And I'd have killed him by taking him out and trying to frame him. By being an asshole. "Just don't die, okay? Please. I'm sorry I tried to steal Kaia from you. You were right. You've been right the whole time. I only did the fundraiser to impress her. But shit, Steve, I'd do it just for you now. If you needed it. Which you don't. Because you have a really good prognosis. Right? But if you did. Or if I could start over again, which I really wish I could, so much . . . But I can't . . . But if I could. I would. Just for you. Because . . . Just don't die?"

To my relief, he shook his head a little. "Told you. Not dying. Side effect. I'm fine."

I needed to do something to show that I cared. That things were different between us. That there was an "us." "Look, I promise, I'll let go of the whole Kaia thing."

That perked him up a little bit and he turned to me, surprised. "Really?"

"Yes," I said, and still felt like maybe it wasn't enough. "I'm sorry . . ." I added, and the "for everything" was obvious, even if I didn't speak it.

"You are a nice guy, Cam."

I opened my door even before I fully stopped in Steve's driveway. Rushing around the car, I got to his side. I knocked on his window to make sure he was alert before I opened it. He sat up, bleary eyed, and I pulled the door handle. To my surprise, he began getting himself out of the car without my help.

"I'm good."

"Dude . . ."

"I got it." He hit my hand away.

"Let me walk you to the door," I insisted as I helped him to his feet.

"I told you, I'm good," he said, and took a deep, steadying breath.

"You are not good."

"Fine. I'm not good. Just . . . let me do this, okay?" He held my gaze for a moment to be sure I understood he was serious.

"Okay, but if I see you stumble, I'm walking you all the way to your bed."

"Sure thing, Florence Nightingale." He smiled, a little of his usual glint back in his eye, and then walked slowly but surely toward his door. "Thanks for everything tonight, Cam. What you said. You have no idea."

I watched as he made his way up the long, lit path to his front door. He didn't look great, but he didn't falter. As he opened the door, I breathed a sigh of relief. He'd made it home. His parents could help him now. At least his mom could.

I sat in his driveway for ten minutes just in case.

Still raw, I drove home at a snail's pace, listening to Rex Orange County. I would show up tomorrow morning and check on Steve for sure. And maybe bring him some of that honey he liked. Maybe I'd even play *Grand Theft Auto* with him. I could protect the sex workers. Ha.

I felt a little selfish having these thoughts. They were as much about me worrying about Steve as they were about me not wanting the night to end. How had that happened? How had my stupid plan turned around so completely that I now wanted to hang out with Steve instead of kill him?

It didn't matter. It had happened. I just basked in the warm surprise and turned up Rex.

Buzz.

There was a text on my phone. I pulled over to the side of the road and checked. It was from Steve. I was immediately prepared to turn around and get him to the hospital, but it wasn't an emergency.

Steve: I made it in alive. Thanks for a night I'll never forget, friend.

I reread the word *friend* and smiled. I needed to respond in a fun way. My heartbeat began to accelerate as I struggled to find the right thing. It should be funny. But I didn't want to just ignore that he'd said *friend*. He was taking the first step. I needed to have the courage to meet him there. So, a

226

"thumbs-up" or a "crying laughing" emoji seemed too slight. Like I was trying to be cool. But he would be totally freaked out if I wrote something too sincere. My fingers hovered over the screen with nervous excitement. But then, out of the corner of my eye, I noticed something.

On the car seat beside me, next to my discarded kitty ears, was Steve's jacket.

Once again, I pulled up to Steve's house and turned off the car. It was so late that I figured I would just leave the jacket on the doorstep. The forgotten coat had given me an idea of how to respond. I'd send a picture of it with: Friends don't let friends get cold.

But through the front bay window, I saw that the lights were still on. And then I saw Steve. He was up and looked a little better. I could knock and bring it to him. We could relive the night one more time.

But then he grabbed a Nerf gun and did a barrel roll over the coach, disappearing for a moment before jumping back up victoriously. In his underwear, he hopped onto the couch and bounced and bounced with the gun raised in the air. He looked more than better.

He looked . . . fine.

My stomach clenched.

Then I heard something through the window. Music. Steve seemed to be singing along to it. *"Nooo time for looosers/'Cause weeeee are the champions, of the wooooorld!"*

227

My legs braced.

I squeezed the steering wheel tight as pressure began to build in my head. Like the house lights coming on after a movie, the whole artifice of the night disappeared. Reality blinded me. And a new movie began to replay itself in my mind. One that a not-sick-at-all Steve had directed.

Steve asking, "Does this mean we're f . . . f . . . friends . . . ?"

Me saying to him, "I'll let go of the whole Kaia thing."

Steve saying, "Thanks for everything tonight, Cam. What you said. You have no idea."

He had been manipulating me. Pretending to be my friend, opening up, sharing stuff about his family, so I would start to like him. So I would feel guilty. So that I would give up Kaia.

My chest seized.

Watching Steve do a victory dance through his window, I burned with embarrassment. My vision went bright white with rage and I felt the terrifying void open up below me, threatening to swallow me whole. He knew my weakness and he had exploited it. So easily. Because I was desperate. Because I'd really wanted it.

"You idiot! You're such an idiot!" I screamed at myself as I drove home. I held back tears because Steve didn't deserve my tears. He didn't deserve anything I had done for him. "Fuck!" I wailed again. "Soooo stupid!" And tried to rip the steering wheel off the car. "How come you're so stupid?"

As I let an old lady in a Nissan Maxima pass me, the answer

became clear. "Because I'm a good person. I'm compassionate. And he took advantage of that. He's literally the worst person I've ever met!" I grabbed the kitty ears and hurled them out the window. In my rearview mirror, I saw them bounce a few times before coming to rest in the gutter. Goddammit. Steve had even made me litter.

Once home, I crept upstairs into my bedroom, not wanting my mom to see the pain that I was certain was still on my face. Luckily, it was my mom's romance novel book club night and the delighted cackling of middle-aged ladies echoed through the house, masking my entrance. Safely inside, the wall of Save Steve mocked me. His stupid face glowered as if to tease, "Can't we be friends? Hahahahah . . ." I thought about tearing it down, but instead I took a Sharpie and drew devil horns on it. I needed to leave it up to remind me that he could never, ever be trusted again.

I then fell face-first onto my bed and screamed into my pillow. "FUUUUUUUUUUCK!"

Knock, knock.

I sat up and tried to look semi-normal before my mom barged in. "Were we being too loud?" she asked, her face flushed, a glass of rosé in her hand.

"No, I just stubbed my toe."

"Oh. You okay?"

"I'm fine."

She took a sip of wine. "We're loving this month's book. You should read it; it's a fabulous example of how consent can be sexy. When Prince Thabiso checks in and asks Naledi, 'Do you like that?' . . ." My mom swooned, overwhelmed, then caught herself. "Ignore me. Sorry to scar you." And closed the door behind her. I could hear her giggling as she went downstairs.

I fell back on my bed and the whole Steve nightmare came rushing back. I couldn't believe I'd admitted that I liked Kaia. That I'd done the whole Save Steve thing just for her. He'd manipulated me into admitting everything. I needed to get back at him.

The pictures.

I flicked on my phone and opened my photos. The very last shot I took was of Steve nuzzling up to Maybe-Haedyn. I zoomed in to crop out the other girls and make it look more like a selfie. A suggestive caption would help. I could make it work. But I had to do it now. "I can't let the bad guy win." I refused to think about how I had set up the whole honeypotting thing. He'd basically forced me to do that because he'd tricked Kaia into falling in love with him. I was the good guy here. I was.

I vaulted from my bed to my desk, tapped my laptop on, and brought up the Save Steve site. I scrolled to the comment section. I knew Kaia had been looking at them. She would find this. Hopefully soon.

I felt something next to me. Someone.

"Don't look at me like that, Michelle," I said without looking at her. I took her photo and placed it facedown. I just needed to beat Steve. For once. For good. "Even if she's not with me, she shouldn't be with him."

Click.

I uploaded the photo.

Click.

In the message window below, I typed: Had so much fun last night. Hee hee. Xoxo.

I stared at the post button and laughed. *It should say* toast, I thought to myself. Because that's what Steve was gonna be when Kaia saw this.

Toast.

Click.

I half-heartedly spread almond butter onto a slice of bread. A Steve-induced hangover had slowed my school-lunch-making to a crawl. I didn't want to think about last night, but flashes of it kept interrupting me. The drunk girls. Del Taco. The pool. The kitty ears. Steve. *No time for losers.* Laughing. Mocking. The comment section. The photo. I folded the bread in half and shoved it into a reusable container. Then I slammed a whole bag of sriracha chickpeas into a brown paper sack.

"You okay, honey?" my mom asked as she pulled on her Realtor's jacket.

"I'm fine," I said.

"You sure?"

"Just still mad about the shark situation."

"I know it was disappointing. Did I tell you I got one hundred likes on my Facebook post about it?" Her pride in even my defeat rankled me for some reason. "Hey, just remember what your other mother says. You got to go high, right?"

I looked away and mumbled, "I know." She would definitely think I was an asshole after what I did last night. The drunk girls. The photo. The comment section. The revenge. Especially the anger that was boiling up inside me. But she definitely didn't need to know about any of it.

As I walked into school, I tried to deep breathe out of my anxiety, but my emotions were like a Whac-A-Mole of sadness, righteousness, and the tantalizing hope that Steve would soon be taken down. That hope tasted so good. Better than any stupid honey. On my way to my locker, I passed under a million banners with brightly colored mermaids extolling us to go to the Junior/Senior Under the Sea Prom. "Now with Cardi B!" someone had added after Steve's big announcement. And there were cartoon drawings of Steve and Kaia, too. People had been swept up in his dramatic fucking promposal. It might as well be called "Under the Steve!" I quickly wiped that image out of my mind.

I hadn't bought a ticket to prom. I wasn't going to pay money to spend a night getting humiliated. And buying a single ticket would mean it was over. But maybe I wouldn't have to now. Maybe I *would* be buying two tickets.

Because Kaia was gonna dump Steve right before prom. And he would be the one with the single ticket. And Steve would finally see the power of my spaghetti-strand arms.

I spent much of the day looking for Kaia. I thought about

texting her a "how r things?" but stopped myself. The last time we'd talked face-to-face, we'd fought, and even if she said she was over it, the fact that she hadn't bothered to text me since the shark night said otherwise. But I needed to know if she'd seen the photo.

At the end of the day, I ran into her. Not literally this time. We were both at the Wall of Service again. We said "hey" but she had to rush off, as she always did. In that "hey" I tried to decipher everything. Had she seen the post? Had she confronted Steve? Ripped him a new asshole the way only she could? I replayed the moment in my mind for the next day, trying to see if there was any hint that she'd seen the photo.

Almost a whole week passed and nothing happened. Kaia seemed busy, but not angry or sad. And now it was the day before prom and my post was buried deep in the comment section. Once again, Steve had won.

"Cam!" It was Kaia's voice. She was calling to me even though I was halfway down the hall. It sounded urgent. Had she finally seen it? Was it starting? The Steve undoing?

She was sitting behind the prom ticket booth, waving at me. I headed toward her, all the while flipping through scenarios. Breakup. Nothing. Breakup. Nothing.

"Hey," I said, sounding as uncertain as I was.

"How are you?" She looked exhausted. Weary. Heartbroken?

"Oh, I'm . . . the usual."

"Cool. Cool." She fiddled with some papers. This small talk

couldn't be why she had called me over.

"Is everything okay?" I ventured.

"Oh yeah. I . . . uh . . . just noticed you haven't bought your ticket yet." My pulse quickened. She wanted to know if I was going to prom?

"Oh, uh . . ." I stammered. "I haven't?"

"Not according to our records."

"Oh, shoot—"

Just then, a guy in a student council T-shirt pushed past me. "Kaia, sorry, can you check over this flyer for Senior Spirit Week?"

Kaia snatched the neon flyer from his hand. She looked pissed. Had she seen the photo? It was Kaia—she wouldn't just be weeping at the prom ticket table. She was too proud. She wouldn't want everyone to know. But there was definitely an agitation to her. Something was up.

Kaia handed the guy back his flyer. "Looks fine." He mumbled thanks and dashed away. Kaia smiled up at me. "Sorry. So look, I wanted to talk to you about something?" The photo, please be the photo. "This whole Cardi thing wouldn't have happened without you." Okay, not the photo.

"We all kind of owe you. So, I talked to the prom committee, and they want to give you a free ticket. If you want to go."

"Wow, that's . . ." Was she making sure I went to prom because she'd broken up with Steve and didn't want to be alone? No, she was too nonchalant. But she had to be the one who had asked the committee. She wanted me to be at prom.

She was thinking of me. "That's so nice. Sure."

"Oh, thank god. I was worried you didn't want to go," she said, and held out an envelope with my ticket. I took it in my hand and a small amount of confidence came back to me.

"No, no. I just hope it's cheesy enough," I joked. She laughed. And it was a sweet, knowing laugh. Like she'd had on the beach. She brushed hair out of her face, and even from here I could smell the coconut.

"I'll just be happy when it's over," she said.

Had she seen the photo?

"Did they get the right balloons?" I asked.

"Who knows? I'll probably have to blow them up myself anyway."

A girl squeezed by me to reach Kaia. "Disaster, Kai! Academic Decathlon booked the study room the same time we did."

"Are you kidding me? Whatever. I'll text Khaled. He owes me."

"Thanks!" she said, and hurried off.

With a growl, Kaia tapped away on her phone. "Sorry, Cam. As usual, no one knows what the hell they're doing."

"No worries."

She sighed. "I miss working with you."

She did? I had to ask. "So . . . how's Steve?"

"Good." And the way she said it, I could tell she hadn't recently dismembered Steve and hidden his body parts in black garbage bags. "He had a bunch of doctor's appointments this week to wrap up treatment, so I haven't seen him much. But he's doing good, I think."

"Good. That's good." I was sure my disappointment was melting down my face.

"He's excited about doing the TV interview tomorrow." Crap. The interview. I'd forgotten. We were all supposed to be there—Steve, his girlfriend, and his best friend talking about their favorite artist, Cardi B. Double crap. "And did you see that they want us there in full prom attire?"

"Oh, uh . . . no . . ."

"Ugh. I'm going to have to get up so early to be ready. Though I'll probably be up all night decorating the ballroom by myself anyway," she said, exasperated.

"Hey, Kaia. Just need a second . . ." Another girl pushed her way to the table with another urgent thing for Kaia to do.

This time I was grateful. I mumbled, "Well, see you in the morning," and shoved my single ticket into my pocket for a prom I was going to go to all by myself because my plan had failed.

18

I crossed the parking lot to the squat gray building of the local ABC affiliate, already a bit sweaty in my rented tux. It was way too early to be in formal wear. I was late because there were more parts to putting on a suit than I had anticipated. Cuff links should not be a thing.

I opened the door to the lobby and was met with a blast of cold air and a very perky woman with a headset.

"Cam Webber?"

"Yeah."

She broke into a huge grin. "Everyone is so impressed with what you did! And Cardi B! Oh my gosh! The others are in the greenroom! Follow me!" She was like a human exclamation point. I hurried along after her as she rattled off the schedule, occasionally pausing to answer a question on her headset. We turned down corridor after corridor, my eyes swinging wildly as I got glimpses of coiled cables, oversized props, tables of food being fussed over to look perfect on camera, and racks of clothes.

We squeezed by an arch of brightly colored flowers. "For our summer wedding segment!" Exclamation Lady explained, and she led me down a hallway until she was suddenly stopped by someone in her headset. "Shoot. Be right there." Flustered, she gestured to an open door a few feet down the hall. "Greenroom's over there! There's water and snacks inside! Should be about fifteen minutes!" And she was gone.

I took a few steps toward the room when a loud clatter startled me.

"Why did you lie to me? You told me you stayed home Saturday!"

I knew that voice: Kaia. Or more specifically—Angry Kaia. Furious Kaia. Apoplectic Kaia.

She had seen the photo. She'd actually seen it. This was it. The Steve evisceration! It was happening!

I edged closer to the door and saw a toppled-over folding chair. Another few steps revealed Kaia in a sparkly yellow dress and Steve in his tux and Air Jordans facing off in the tiny greenroom. The rhinestones on Kaia's dress shimmered, because she was literally shaking with anger. Steve stood with his arms crossed, looking mulish.

"Aren't you going to say something?" she growled. But Steve just shrugged. "Say something, Steve!" She grabbed her phone out of a tiny beaded purse resting on the bagel table. "What's up with this girl? What were you doing with her? Did you . . . Did something happen that night?" Kaia's shoulders were hunched inward, the phone clutched in her hand.

Kaia's fury always melted him. I waited for the stammered, cotton-mouthed jumble of denial. Something like, "It's not what it looks like. . . . It was Cam . . . and cancer groupies . . . and mini golf . . ." Steve Stevenson was finished.

But instead Steve gave another little shrug. "I was hoping you wouldn't find out until after prom, but fuck it. Yeah. We hooked up."

"WHAT?" Kaia yelled.

WHAT??? Where was the stammering and the cotton-mouthing and the denials?

Steve uncrossed his arms and stuck his hands into his pockets like he didn't have a care in the world. "But come on, we've been going out awhile." He grabbed a bagel off the platter and munched on it like he wasn't lying. I was reeling. And confused. And panicked. However, Kaia's feelings on the situation were much clearer. She plucked the bagel out of Steve's hand and tossed it aside.

"And what? You got bored?"

Steve swallowed his bite, not seeming to mind that he'd lost his breakfast or that he was about to be murdered. "I mean, a little. You're busy all the time. And, you know, she was a little more adventurous than you." Kaia bristled. Steve added, "Which isn't saying much."

"ARE YOU SERIOUS RIGHT NOW?"

Steve's smile was unrepentant. "I'm saying she rubbed my bald head. Both of them."

Kaia grabbed a fresh bagel and threw it at him as hard as she could. "You fucking asshole!" she yelled. Those were the words I had always dreamed she'd say. And just like that. With fire in her eyes. And rage in her heart. But instead of elated, I felt confused. Because Steve was going along with it. He wasn't fighting back. Why?

"You said you loved me!" I couldn't see Kaia's face, but I saw her shoulders trembling. She was crying. And I was responsible. Why hadn't I realized until this moment that she'd be hurt, too?

Steve merely looked down at her with an expression of utter boredom. "Did I?"

Kaia made a sound halfway between a scream and a sob. "I can't believe I fell for your bullshit! I don't know why I let myself believe— Why I thought—" She ripped the corsage from her wrist and threw it in the trash. It bounced off the rim and onto the floor. "Cancer hasn't changed you a fucking bit."

I stumbled a few steps back, not sure where to go. Before I could formulate a plan of escape, Kaia burst from the green-room, clutching her beaded purse. And then she saw me.

"Cam . . ."

I couldn't look away.

"Kaia . . ."

She paused for half a second and then rushed toward me,

grabbed me on the shoulders, and pushed me back. I trip-walked a step back until I was up against the arch of wedding flowers. My vision suddenly narrowed to a blur of color, except for Kaia's shining brown eyes right in front of me. I inhaled a sharp, surprised breath, tasting flowers on my tongue. Her eyes darted down to my lips for a second, then back up to mine, and I saw the moment she decided.

Her warm lips pressed to mine, softer than the petals surrounding us. A river of coconut swirled in my head.

My mind whited.

When I came back, we were kissing. Actually kissing. And I tried not to think about why. Just that it was happening. Really happening. And that our kiss was like our conversations: easy, familiar, and yet each moment a surprise.

When she finally pulled back, Steve was standing in the doorway behind her. A flick of my eyes must have tipped Kaia off, because she turned.

"See, Steve," she said, her voice ringing with triumph. "*This* is a good guy." And she took my cheeks in her hands. And pulled me closer. She was going to kiss me again. In front of Steve. That was a thing that was going to happen. Right now. Her lips touched mine. And she kissed me harder. Deeper. Angrier.

Then she pulled apart and looked up at me. And burst into tears.

I just stared, slack jawed and goofy faced until, miraculously, my last functioning brain cell was able to suggest that I console her. I gathered her in my arms and she sobbed into the shiny satin on my tux lapel. Through her curls, I could see Steve standing at the end of the hall watching us, an inscrutable expression on his face. He gave me a thumbs-up. It sent a shiver through me.

Kaia gave a sniff and mumbled into my shoulder, "You must have heard us fighting, right?" I nodded, still trying to process the thumbs-up. "How could he do this? And on fucking prom?"

"Uh . . ." I looked back to where Steve had stood, but he was gone.

"Cam?" Kaia had stopped crying. She looked like she was waiting for me to say something, but my eyes kept darting back to the empty space where Steve had been. Kaia's expression clouded. "I'm such an idiot."

"What? No, you aren't."

"You tried to tell me about Steve. I mean, you said he was faking, which was crazy, but you must have sensed something. And you tried to be a good friend and warn me. And I was so mean to you. I yelled. And I didn't go to the shark thing. And I didn't text you. And . . . I'm sorry." Kaia wiped her eyes, smearing mascara everywhere.

"Oh." I tried to think of something else to say, but before I could, she heaved a huge sigh.

"Crap. I still have to go to prom. I'm on the freaking committee. I have to check everyone in. And I have this stupid dress." She smiled at me, a little uncertain. "I know this is lame and you totally don't have to, but . . . would you maybe want to be no fun with me at prom?"

I couldn't get Steve's thumbs-up out of my mind.

"Cam?"

I realized I was leaving her hanging. And while everything seemed twisted in a Gordian knot, I couldn't hurt her more. "Of course I'll take you to prom."

Kaia smiled and sniffed. "Well, taking isn't necessary. I'm on decorating duty, too. Just . . . meet me there? And dance with me?"

"Yeah. Yeah, I'd . . . I'd love that."

Kaia stepped back, releasing me. "I need to go and fix myself up. And punch something Steve-shaped. But see you later?"

"Yeah."

She reached up and pulled a crushed flower from my hair, then kissed me softly on the cheek. "You're the best." Her words pierced me as she walked away. I stood under the wedding arc, realizing I was going to prom with Kaia. Just like I'd dreamed. And I had no idea why.

Wobbly and confused, I walked to the greenroom. Steve was sitting on the fake leather couch, his head in his hands. He looked up as I entered.

"Did you know cancer was supposed to change me? That I was supposed to grow and blossom as a person? I thought it was just my body making mutant cells that would slowly shut down my organs and kill me, but apparently, I was supposed to learn shit, too. Oh well, missed that memo."

"Why did you do that?"

Steve's smile was bleak. "It's exactly what you wanted, right? Happy?"

It was. And I wasn't. "But . . . why?"

Steve stood and started to pace. "Oh, no big reason. Just . . . got some test results back. Shit was supposed to be all gone, but I guess there's some left. Apparently, my cancer might be 'resistant to chemo.' Kinda surprised everyone, even my doc. Cool, huh?" He grabbed another bagel off the plate and took a bite.

"But . . . it has a ninety-four percent cure rate." I'd read the statistics over and over. It was the good cancer. It was the good—

"Looks like I might be the other six percent!" Crumbs fell from his lips and he pumped his fist and made his voice sound like his dad's. "Killin' it. Or it's killing me." He swallowed. "Did I tell you, you and Kaia look super cute together? You make such an adorable uptight couple." He tossed the mostly uneaten bagel in the trash with such force the basket almost tipped over.

I grabbed Steve's arm, stopping him. "But . . . no. This doesn't make any sense. Why did you fake being sick the other night?" None of this was right. This was another of Steve's games. There must be something I wasn't seeing. Some advantage he was working.

Steve blinked. "Fake?"

"At the pool. After I dropped you off, I came back to give you your jacket and saw you. You were dancing. You made me admit all that stuff, pretended to be my friend, just so I would give up on Kaia. You were jumping around singing 'We Are the Champions.' You were laughing at me!" My voice cracked on the last sentence.

Steve studied me for a long moment. "Wow. That's a lot to unpack, Cam."

"Why did you do it?!"

Steve flinched. The room seemed suddenly, eerily quiet after my outburst. "I wasn't faking being sick with you, Cam," Steve finally said, his voice low. "I was faking being well with my dad."

I stepped back. "No . . . that's not . . ."

Steve shook his head. "I guess you'd have a hard time believing me after what I did to you. But, honestly, would you have ever believed anything good about me?" Steve paused, waiting for an answer that wasn't going to come. "Anyway, it actually works out. Once I got those results, I knew how sad Kaia would be and I . . . I didn't want that. I was going to break up with her. Make her really hate me. Hating me is so much better than being sad, right?" He flashed the bitterest smile I'd ever seen. When I didn't react, he started to pace again. "I was kinda stumped on how to do that, being all pukey and shaky and shit. Makes it hard to truly misbehave. But then you gave me such a perfect opportunity. Nice job. Anyway, when she confronted me, I was thinking, *Thank you, Cam, for being such a fucking dick! You're saving me so much work!*" He spread his arms wide in a grand gesture.

I stared. This wasn't possible. This wasn't what was supposed to happened. It was some sort of terrible joke. Because if it wasn't, it meant that night was real. It meant Steve had been—

"Guys, we're ready for you!" Exclamation Lady was back. "Where's"—she checked her notebook—"Kaia?"

"She had to go. Emergency." Steve's tone was wooden.

"Oh well!" she said brightly. "It's you two people we want to see anyway! Cam, are you going to dance for us?"

I didn't respond.

Exclamation Lady clapped her hands together, taking my catatonic state for consent. "Okay! Let's do this!"

She herded us into the hall. We weaved through various set pieces, past more props and some guy in a hot dog suit, all the while getting closer to the bright white lights of the stage. I could feel a blast of heat coming off them, warming my face. It was the only thing I could feel. Just as we were about to cross the boundary from the dark shadows of backstage to the blinding glow of the set, Steve leaned in close and whispered in my ear.

"Congratulations, Cam. You win."

Something happened after that. I couldn't remember what. A lady with really thick fake eyelashes asked questions. A man who was a lot older than her and slightly orange laughed too loud when I stood up and danced a little. Steve smiled at me. He called me "buddy" and "Cam my man" and "bro." He never called me friend.

Then it was over.

"You are such an amazing guy, Cam!" Exclamation Lady was making me sign some paperwork. My tux felt too tight. "Steve is lucky to have someone like you!" My head jerked up at the sound of his name. Where was Steve? We'd walked off the set side by side. I looked around, searching, but I already knew he was gone.

Outside, the marine layer had cleared and the sun flashed off the rows of parked cars. But other than a few seagulls, the parking lot was empty.

I drove home.

Down Main Street.

Past the posters Kaia and I had hung.

Steve's face repeated in the windows of every shop.

Somehow, I got back to my room. As I stood in the center of it, still wearing my prom tux, the full weight of what had happened this morning became crystal clear—I had ruined everything.

The photo of Steve caught my eye. Sick Steve. Selfless Steve. Good Steve. I had tried to take advantage of a kid with cancer. I had tried to steal his girlfriend. I was the one who should be wearing the devil horns.

"Local Hero!" proclaimed an article about me that I had proudly tacked next to his picture. Bullshit. BULL. SHIT. I stomped over, ripped it from the wall, crushed it into a wad, and chucked it into the trash. The trash. Where my good deeds belonged.

The Save Steve wall loomed over me. There was the poster again. The T-shirts I'd designed. Letters from people telling me how great I was. How thoughtful. Articles. Praise. It wasn't a wall for Steve. It was a wall of my own self-importance. A wall of my lies.

With sudden fury, I tore at the wall. "The Fundraising Genius." Rip! "You're an inspiration!" Rip! "SuperCam!" Rip! All of it, down . . . down . . . down. Into the fucking trash. Until all that was left were bits of paper under a constellation of thumbtacks.

My breathing was heavy and my blood rushing. It felt good. But it didn't feel like enough. I spun to the other walls. Save the shark. The wetlands. The straws. The sand dunes. It was all bullshit. Because I was bullshit. I couldn't look at that bullshit anymore.

It had to go. My arms whirled like propellers, ridding the walls of my arrogance. Citizenship awards torn into pieces. A letter from the Sierra Club, dismembered. My Amnesty International merit badge, discarded. All the conceited do-goodery, eradicated. But there were still shelves of pseudo-accomplishments that needed to be destroyed. I whizzed around my room. The trophy from Junior United Nations, shattered. A plaque from the Lions Club, smashed. A commemorative tree from the Arbor Day Foundation, snapped in two. The trash overflowed. I stomped on it. Hard. I needed to obliterate any remnant of my smugness.

The top of my dresser was cleared. The walls bare. The shelves empty. All of it gone. Except one thing.

With shaking hands, I gripped the framed photo of Michelle Obama. I held it for a brief moment and then discarded it, facedown into the trash. I heard the glass crack and, for a moment, thought that was it. I was done.

But I needed full erasure.

Clutching my pile of hypocrisy and our fire extinguisher, I walked out of our town house and into the backyard. I looked for a place to set the garbage pile down, but the area was too exposed. The fence behind us was too low for privacy and I could hear the neighbors' kids splashing and shrieking in their pool. It wasn't the right place for my final act.

I headed down the side yard until I reached the door to the garage.

Inside, I flipped on the light and closed the door behind me. Quiet. My mom wasn't home so there was plenty of space. I placed the pile in the center, sat down in front of it with the extinguisher next to me, and pulled a lighter out of my tux jacket. I stared at the pile. In transporting it, Michelle's photo had shifted, and her face was now visible in the clutter.

"I went low." I snapped the lighter to life. Tipping the flame to the corner of the "Local Hero" article, I watched as it took the fire and quickly spread to my other unworthy achievements. Sierra Club. Surfrider Foundation. Pride parade. Gun control. All catching the flame.

"I went fucking low."

The heat grew and I slid back. This was what my efforts were worth. Destruction. Immolation. Eradication. I hugged my knees, hoping it would make the pain in my chest hurt a little less.

Ash floated out of the pile and danced in the air. The clear plastic covers on the Save Steve buttons turned a burnt caramel and curled inward. The raised hands on plastic trophies singed and melted. The heat and smoke caused my eyes to water. I wiped the wet away and then I saw it—the flickering red flame licking the edge of Michelle Obama's photo. She was still staring at me and I forced myself to look at her. To watch. The paper curled as it accepted the fire's full rage. The words *Go high* burned to a crisp. My name, in smooth black Sharpie, eaten away. Unable to watch as the flames spread to her proud smile, I closed my eyes.

The darkness felt right. I coughed. That was where I belonged. A perfect void for the worst person. I coughed, again.

After a moment, the air started to feel thicker and I opened my eyes. The flames had grown even higher and, above me, a dense cloud of smoke threatened. I felt the particles in my lungs and coughed deeper. A sharp jab of panic gripped me. I reached for the fire extinguisher. But I moved too fast and knocked it over. Its metal cylinder clanged across the floor. Shit.

The smoke descended and the toxic plume was beginning to make me light-headed. Vinyl acetate. Polyacrylonitriles. Polyethylene. I was unleashing them into the world. Fuck. I couldn't even get this right.

I let out another thunderous cough and pawed around for the extinguisher, but I couldn't see it. Or the door. Or the ceiling. I could only make out the glow of the flames as I gasped for air. In the miasma, I saw what looked like a monstrous hurricane swirling toward me. A hurricane? Yes. And its wind pushed me down to the ground. From the oily cement, I felt debris crash over me. When I looked up, I witnessed glaciers collapsing. Forests engulfed in flames. The environment in full apocalyptic disintegration. And I was the cause. I had brought about climate change. It was me. All of it was me. Me.

"Are you fucking kidding?"

I sat up and peered through the vapor. There, drifting into view, I saw her. Michelle Obama. And she looked pissed.

"I'm so sorry, Michelle. I failed you." I prostrated myself at her feet. "I went low."

Her thick waves of black hair blew in the breeze and she looked down at me, full of disappointment, the fire reflected in her eyes. "This is what you brought me here for?"

I averted my gaze, ashamed, and mumbled something meek. But she wasn't satisfied and continued, pausing dramatically after each word.

"I.

"Don't.

"Have.

"Time.

"For.

"Your.

"Privileged.

"Little.

"Butt."

I coughed and tried to catch my breath. There was nothing I could say. I deserved it. All of it.

"Oh damn." Another voice with a New York accent floated through the smoke. Lying on my side and clutching my chest, I slowly made out a curvy silhouette and I knew who it had to be.

Cardi B. Wearing a very classy pantsuit and looking pissed as hell, she sauntered to Michelle's side. "He's got us trapped here in some sort of weird toxic-chemical-induced shaming ritual."

"That's right," Michelle agreed. "Because apparently, he can't figure out shit on his own." I coughed.

Cardi crouched over me to examine my patheticness at close range. "Damn, you seriously hallucinated two women of color to do your emotional labor? That is next level."

"Oh god. I'm so, so sorry," I moaned. "I can't believe I did that. Um, please, go . . . back . . . to whatever you were doing. I'll just . . . lie here . . ." I flapped my hand weakly and hoped they would just evaporate back to their more important lives. "I'm the worst."

"Oh my fucking god!" Michelle exclaimed, and threw her hands in the air. "Just stop! Can you get more arrogant? You really think you, Cam Webber, are the absolute worst human on the planet? Do you have any idea the number of assholes I've met?"

"Um . . ."

Cardi B sighed, a tad bit sympathetic. "Kid, listen. I used to drug motherfuckers and rob them. Does that make me the worst? No. Sometimes you do shit you're not proud of. But that's not all of you. Understand? You're not the worst."

"But you're not the best either. Not even close," Michelle made sure to clarify.

"That's me." Cardi reached up and Michelle gave her a fist bump.

"But then . . . what am I?" I asked, squinting a bit. It was getting difficult to see through the oily smoke.

"You're just afraid," Michelle said. I thought I heard a little of her usual compassion slip through.

"I know. I'm so afraid . . ," I agreed. "But of what?" I tried to wave the smoke away to see better, but it was hard to lift my hand.

"I think you know," Cardi said.

"I do?"

And just then, a bright light bloomed and I had to shut my eyes to block it out.

"Oh my god. Cam? Cam!" a familiar voice screamed. And I knew this one was real—my mom. Panicked, I sprang to my feet, hacking violently.

"No! Mom!" I needed to cover this up. She couldn't know. As the smoke began to clear and oxygen once again entered my lungs, I searched for the words that would make it all disappear. But I was too dizzy. All I could come up with was, "I'm fine."

Through the haze, I made out the form of my mom rushing in. "What are you doing?" The fire extinguisher was in her hand, terror in her eyes.

"It's fine," I repeated, but was unable to move. She couldn't see this. The embarrassment. The failure. The shame. She couldn't see any of this. I needed to explain it away, but how? It was all there at my feet. Floating in the rafters. Swirling around us. Undeniable. "I'm fine."

With a whoosh, she smothered the fire. Immobile, I stood like a statue of humiliation with a white mist settling around me.

"Are you okay?" she asked, still distraught.

"I'm fine." I needed her to go away. To forget she'd seen this. "I'm fine." Because how could she ever forget seeing this?

"What's going on?" She dropped the extinguisher.

I would have flinched if I could. But all I could manage was to turn my eyes away from her, to the smoldering pile of stupidity that I thought made me okay. "I'm fine," I repeated. I needed her to believe it was true. "I'm fine."

"It's okay, Cam. It's okay." But it wasn't okay. I had failed her. And now she had failed. And now we were two failures in a town house garage, trying to bury the lie that we weren't. I could hear her moving very slowly toward me. My insides clenched tighter, wanting to hide what she could never see. She reached out and said, "And it's okay if it's not okay, honey," and put her hand on my shoulder.

It was hardly there, but even its delicate touch sent fissures through my stone facade, shattering it. My stomach uncoiled. The brace on my legs snapped. My chest swelled. Tears streamed from my eyes. I was unable to hold it back any longer.

The truth.

"I'm not fine."

* * *

It took a few minutes, a box of tissues, and a round of warm hugs for me to finally breath normally again. As I curled on the couch, a weird buzz tingled through my muscles. With a crusty nose and blotted eyes, I finished telling my mom the whole damn story. ". . . I sat through the entire interview like an asshole. And now Kaia thinks I'm the good guy and she doesn't even know Steve's cancer isn't getting better. It's all my fault. God, you must hate me."

"Hate you? Why do you think I would hate you? Nothing you could ever do would make me hate you."

"Are you serious?" I wiped my nose again and looked at her. "There's a million things I could do to make you hate me. I hear it every time I walk past you when the news is on."

"Oh, come on." She grimaced in disbelief. "You know I'm kidding about that."

"Are you?" I felt a wave of anger rear up. "Because you don't sound like you're joking. And don't get me started about Dad."

She recoiled, confused. "What's that asshole got to do with this?"

"That's it. That's exactly the problem! You're always calling him an asshole. Telling me how terrible he is."

"I'm doing that to make you feel better. I didn't want you to be sad he wasn't around."

"Yeah, well. It worked. I don't care that he's not around. But I'm also terrified I'll end up like him."

"Oh, come on." She laughed the idea off. "You could never end up like him."

"And what if I did? Would you disown me?" I watched as

the thought of it played out in her eyes—her son, the deadbeat asshole.

And she hesitated.

I sat up and pointed at her, at the truth she had let slip. "See! See!" I felt tears returning and I needed to get the words out fast. "You have to think about it?! How do you think that makes me feel? Like at any minute you would . . ." and then the tears caught up and I couldn't finish.

She sat forward as if to catch me. "No. No. No. No . . . Never, Cam. Sweetheart." Regret rattled her voice. "Shit. Shit. What did I do . . . I'm sorry . . ." And now her eyes began to well up. "I'm just trying so hard to do this right and . . ."

"I know you are . . ." I didn't want her to cry, too. I didn't want either of us to cry. Still, I had to get it out now. "But all that pressure to be the best, all the time, to never mess up—"

"God, I pushed you too hard." She sounded so angry at herself.

"And I know you wouldn't disown me, but I'm so tired of being scared all the time. I'm so scared . . ." I looked away and felt the emptiness rearing up to swallow me.

"Oh, Cam. No . . ." She grabbed my hand and sat close, so close, like when I was little. When I had let her get that close and comfort me. "Are you scared that I don't love you?"

I didn't say anything. Because I didn't know how to say the whole of it.

"Cam . . . ," she pleaded.

"Not just you," I said, my voice fragile.

"Who? Kaia? Steve?"

I held it in for one last moment and then, finally, let it go. "Anyone."

I could swear I heard my mom's heart break.

"Oh, Cam . . . ," she said, and hugged me tight. "Everyone's not your father."

"I know. I know. And it doesn't make it any better." In fact, it made it worse. Because it reduced me to something so small. A person who couldn't get over his father. A person who was nothing, just a little kid who believed he wasn't worth hanging around for. And now, thanks to Dad, that void roared to life with every possible rejection, with every opportunity to change the story. Now that was all I was. A stupid, broken victim. A walking void. As I started to fall back into it myself, another wave of despair crashed down.

"I'm the wors—" I started to say through the tears.

But something stopped me. A voice (or two) in my head. I couldn't keep doing this. It took some effort, but I finally found the words to accurately describe how I felt. "I think I'm a little fucked up." It came out sounding like a joke, and my mom laughed. I wiped away tears and laughed as well.

"Oh, Cam. Even if you're 'a little fucked up' right now, you're still the best kid anyone could ever want." I normally cringed at those words, but today they weren't so bad.

"And you're still the best mom, even though you are a little fucked up, too."

She smiled and shook her head. "You have no idea." She gave me a noogie and I squirmed away.

Then I sighed once more, letting as much go as I could in one breath. Fuck, that was a lot. Just because I couldn't ask a girl out.

"God, I should never have done any of this."

But my mom took my hand. "Hey, listen . . . ," she started, but then dropped her voice to make something very clear. "And don't mistake this for me approving or condoning anything, but . . ." She squeezed my hand. "You weren't happy. You were busy, but I never saw you with friends your age. You know? And you need people. More than just your annoying mother." I nodded and she continued, "It may have been the wrong solution to the problem, but . . . at least you know what the problem is now."

"Yeah. I think so," I said. At least, I hoped I did.

"And if some dumb girl or guy doesn't like you? Fuck them. They are not your father, right?"

"Right," I said. "But I still need to fix this, if I can. Steve and Kaia should be together. The only reason they aren't is because of me. He broke up with her to protect her from having to see him in pain. If that isn't an act of love, I don't know what is."

"That does sound stupidly romantic. Totally misguided, and he should respect Kaia enough to let her judge for herself, but, yeah, sounds like they deserve a chance."

I stood up, a new urgency pumping through me.

"And if it doesn't work out and everything is messed up and you can't fix it . . ." My mom paused and waited, until I turned to listen. "I'll still love you."

258

"Thanks." We exchanged a moment of understanding. I headed for the door but then stopped, wanting to get one last thing off my chest. "Mom . . ." She leaned in, ready to say yes to anything. "You've got to stop moisturizing my elbows at night."

She put up her hands, offended. "I don't—"

"Mom."

"I don't—"

"They're unnaturally soft!"

"They're perfect!" I raised my eyebrows at her. "Fine." I waited. "I'll stop." I crossed my arms. She rolled her eyes. "I'll stop! Okay?"

"Good." I turned and opened the door.

As I left, she called out, "But seriously, Cam . . . lotion! Every night. I put a lot of work into those things and I'm not seeing my masterpiece destroyed."

19

I was already texting Kaia as I hurried to my car.

Me: You around? Need to talk.

There wasn't an answer by the time I'd buckled up and turned on the car. Not wanting to wait, I called her number. The phone rang a few times and then went to voicemail.

"Kaia? It's Cam. Um, can you give me a call? It's important." I hung up. I couldn't exactly say "I'm responsible for your boyfriend breaking up with you. Also, you should talk to Steve because he might be dying" in a voicemail. Maybe I could go find her? But it was the middle of the day. She could be anywhere. Her house, setting up for prom at the Radisson, getting her hair done, squeezing in some extra time at the food bank—it was Kaia; with her schedule, there was no way to know. And I couldn't just drive over to her house and ask her parents, because, I realized, I didn't know her address. We'd always been at Steve's.

Steve. At least I knew where he lived. And as far as I could tell, he pretty much never left. I thumbed out a text to Steve and threw the car into reverse. It might actually be better this way. I could apologize to him and then we could explain things to Kaia, together.

There was no response from Steve by the time I pulled up to his house. I leaped up the stairs to his front door and hit the doorbell. It was only after I heard the ring echo through the foyer that it occurred to me: Steve might not want to hear my apology. There might be a reason he hadn't answered my text. There was a very good chance Steve hated me and never wanted to see me again. But then the door swung open. I squeezed my eyes shut in reflex, bracing for Steve to yell. I wouldn't even blame him for a punch. I kind of deserved it.

But there was no fist to my face. There was a hug. A really manly hug.

"Cam! My boy!" My eyes flew open as Steve's dad crushed me in his arms. I could smell beer.

"Mr. Stevenson," I choked out. "Hi." He released me and I stumbled back a step. "Um, it's nice to see you. Is Steve around?"

"He's not here, bud. Left to get Kaia a while back. You're lookin' sharp in your tux, though." He made guns with his fingers and shot me. Now that I wasn't being anaconda'd, I could see that his eyes were a little bleary.

"To get Kaia?" I repeated, not sure I'd heard right.

"She's something else, right? My boy landed the hottest chick in class." I nodded uncomfortably, meanwhile thinking there was no way Steve had left to get Kaia. Not with the way they'd left things. But if he wasn't home, where was he? "And you!" he continued. "Steve told me about the other night. Three college girls! That's my man." He held out a fist and waited. I realized he wasn't putting it down until I tapped it. I rapped my knuckles weakly against his. He grinned. "Steve said you've been a really great friend through all of this."

"He did?" That hurt a lot. It was too easy to picture Steve sitting at the dinner table, his bald head shining under those giant chandeliers, telling his family over forkfuls of lasagna that I was his friend. Oh god, I had screwed things up so bad.

Steve's dad must have read something in my expression, because his eyes got watery. "Yeah. Glad you're around." He tried to hide a sniff. "I'm sure he told you, but shit went a little sideways this week."

Sideways.

Oh no.

Steve's dad kept talking for a moment. I must have responded, because he nodded. Then with a final fist bump, he shut the door.

Sideways.

It was just a turn of phrase. It didn't mean . . . Steve wouldn't . . .

I started driving. My phone rang. It was Kaia. She was

262

probably calling to say she and Steve had made up. That's why she hadn't answered before. They'd been too busy making out and talking about what a jerk I was, and I didn't care because Steve was fine.

"Hello?"

"Cam? Just got your message. I'm in the middle of setting up. Purple balloons showed up instead of aqua. People are freaking out."

"Is Steve with you?" He was. Right? Putting up balloons. That seemed like a totally Steve thing to do.

"What?"

"Is Steve with you?"

"Sorry! Can't hear you! Reception is terrible! Text me."

One hand on the steering wheel, I tapped out:

Me: Steve with u?

I'd barely pressed send when Kaia's response buzzed back. And then kept buzzing.

Kaia: Fuck no! That cheating ballsack!

Kaia: He on his way here?

Kaia: Assbooger is not trying to apologize is he?

Kaia: Do I need a restraining order?

Kaia: Maybe just a bat?

Me: Np

Me: *No!

I pulled over to the side of the road.

Kaia: He should have got cancer in his junk. Anyway, if it's not about my loser ex, why'd you call?

I stared at my phone. Should I do this over text? Where did I start? Before I could decide which disastrous piece of news to lead with, my phone buzzed again.

Kaia: Sorry. Can this wait till tonight? It's crazy here. Gotta go. Aqua balloons arrived. 🖤

"Oh god!" I slammed my head against the headrest. Steve wasn't with Kaia. That meant . . . that meant he might . . . he could have . . . Picking up my phone, I typed:

Me: Steve. Call me. I will do anything to make this right.

Please let him respond.

Please let me be wrong.

Please don't let it be too late.

My text sat at the bottom of the screen. I waited. I closed my eyes and counted to ten, then looked again. Nothing. I closed them again. He was going to respond. He was. I opened my eyes.

There was a little bubble and three dots at the bottom of the screen. My heart started to beat again. I'd been panicking over nothing.

Steve: You can't always save the shark.

And then a photo of the aquarium.

No.

No no no no no no no no no no no no no no.

I was still miles away from the aquarium.

But I could get there.

I had to.

The engine of the Prius whined in protest as I weaved in and out of traffic, my phone propped against the steering wheel.

Me: Steve. Do not do this.

Me: Steve. Listen to me.

Me: Steve!

Three dots popped up on the screen, and I breathed easier for a moment knowing he was still on the other side, but then they eventually disappeared.

Shit. I called his number. It went straight to voicemail.

"Steve! You stay away from that shark! You stay away." I clicked off and punched on the gas just in time to sail through a yellow light. I was almost there.

I needed to call Steve's parents. Scrolling through my phone, I searched for any sort of contact info. Finally, I found his dad's email and typed out a quick message telling them to come to the aquarium and that Steve needed help.

I could see the entrance to the parking lot of the aqua park up ahead, blue and yellow flags fluttering in the breeze. A cheerful cartoon dolphin helpfully pointed the way with his fin. Yanking on the wheel, I made a hard left and turned in, ignoring the angry blast of a horn as another driver had to swerve out of my way.

It was late enough in the day that the parking lot was clearing out. Parents dragged sticky, sugared-up children back to their cars, defeated and exhausted by a day of fun. I took the first open spot I could find and jumped out of the car, pounding across the vast expanse of asphalt toward the entrance. The archway, made to look like a giant wave with happy sea creatures cavorting in it, seemed impossibly far away. My stupid shiny patent leather shoes that came with my tux skidded every time I tried to pick up speed, their slick soles providing no traction.

Finally, I made it to the wide paved entrance with its trio of ticket booths and giant clamshell fountain squirting water into the air. There was only one worker slumped by the turnstiles, her aqua park baseball cap pulled low over her eyes.

"Cam?"

I whipped my head around but didn't stop running. Todd, Patrice, and a handful of protesters were camped near the edge of the entrance where the aqua park property ended and became public beach access again, battered signs at their feet. They'd been out here nearly every day since the city council meeting, though recently fewer and fewer people were showing up. Todd waved, eyes hopeful. "Cam! You joining us?"

"No," I panted. "Got to save him."

I turned my attention to the turnstile and picked up speed, even as I heard Todd's confused shouts. The park worker snoozed on, her chin tucked on her chest. I judged the height of the metal bars. Yeah. I could do it. With one final burst of speed I ran forward, slamming my hand onto the silver metal column for leverage and twisting my body to the side, flying up and over the turnstile. I landed with a thud, nearly losing my balance as my shoes slipped on the pavement.

"Hey!" The aqua park worker startled awake, but I was already running. Behind me I could hear Todd's and Patrice's surprised cheers.

The light was fading as I ran deeper into the park, the shadows slicing across the wide manicured paths. I passed signs for sea lion tanks and jellyfish exhibits, gift shops with stuffed dolphins in the window, and snack stands promising penguin pops and fish-shaped fries. A few janitorial workers looked up in surprise as I thundered past.

I followed the signs to the shark exhibit, a cartoon shark with bloody teeth pointing the way, still burning with rage each time I passed one. Finally, I reached the tank. It looked even bigger than I remembered, a wide glassy pool that seamlessly blended into the ocean beyond, the only obvious thing separating the two a discreet row of buoys far in the distance. I could hear the quiet hum of the generator that filtered impurities out of the ocean water but kept the pen at the correct salination point. I scanned the amphitheater. With the sun inching toward the horizon and reflecting off the gently rippling water, it was hard to see through the glare, but even so, there was no sign of Steve.

I stood for a moment, too scared to move. I'd thought for sure once I'd rounded the corner, I'd find him standing by the pool—and in my most panicked moments, about to jump in. But there was nothing. Just the lapping water. I edged closer to the tank and looked over the ledge. There was murky green ocean, some algae, and not much else.

"Steve?" I called. There was no answer. Was I too late? I couldn't be. There'd be some sign, some evidence, something to show what had happened. Not just this shining, placid nothingness.

Numb, I walked to the underwater viewing area. The adorable fiberglass fish smiled, cruel and oblivious, as I passed under them. Inside, I could see a faint greenish glow. I hurried down, my shoes slipping on the slick ground. The deeper I went, the colder it became, smelling faintly of dead fish and mildew. My footsteps echoed as I stepped into the main viewing area. When I'd been here before, the space had been filled with families, but now it was empty except for me. No sign of Steve. My stomach sank, even though I hadn't really been expecting him to be there. The glass separating the viewing area from the tank was smudged with a day's worth of handprints. I stepped forward and peered into the murk.

At first all I could see was greenish-brown water and the couple of rays of late afternoon sun that penetrated the surface. Then, as my eyes adjusted, I could make out shapes. Rocks, small silver fish darting through the water . . . and a shoe.

It was one of Steve's Air Jordans, tipped to one side, its laces gently waving in the current.

"STEVE!" I pounded on the glass. "STEVE!" I called out his name again. But then, as if in answer, a shape appeared in the gloom.

The shark.

Its body undulating silently, it slid through the water, too far away to be anything more than a shadow. But it was there. And so was Steve's shoe. Which meant, somewhere in that tank, Steve was, too.

I pounded back up the ramp leading out of the cave to the surface.

"Is anybody here?" I shouted as I ran. "I think my friend is in the shark tank!" I cursed the understaffed theme park when there was no answer.

The setting sun blinded me after being in the cave, but I didn't stop. I ran to the side of the tank closest to where I'd seen the shoe. The wall was about four feet high on my side, with the water about six feet below on the other, a half-"eaten" surfboard drifting by. I ripped off my tux jacket, tossing it to the ground, and kicked off my shoes and socks. Then, gripping the rough concrete of the wall, I pulled myself up, throwing one leg over first and then the other. Perched on the ledge, I squinted, trying to see through the reflections on the surface to the depths beneath me. If I angled my head right, I could just make out the bright white of the shoe. Behind it, around an outcropping of decorative sea rock, only a few feet under the surface, was another shape, one I hadn't been able to see from the angle I'd been at below. It was too small to be the shark and too big to be a fish. And it was moving.

"STEVE!"

I scanned the water one more time, looking for the shark, but there was nothing else moving below the surface.

Okay. I was going to do this. I carefully turned so my belly was pressed against the ledge and my feet were dangling over the surface of the water. After I jumped in, a few quick strokes would get me over to where I thought Steve was. The rock outcropping was only a few feet under the surface. No more than the deep end of a swimming pool. I could do this. And I definitely wasn't going to think about how territorial white sharks were. Or how they had three hundred teeth. I was going to think about orange blossom honey, and Del Taco, and sparkly kitty ears.

I slid down, holding on only by my hands now, and felt the first bite of cold ocean water on my toes.

"What the fuck are you doing?"

Steve? Why wasn't Steve in the tank? His shoe was in the tank.

My hands slipped on the concrete ledge and then my legs swung wildly, my toes kicking at the water.

"Steve?" My arms were pressed up against my ears as I struggled to hold on, but from the corner of my eye I saw Steve, whole, uneaten, and wearing only one shoe, running toward me from the amphitheater side of the exhibit.

"Cam?"

I tried to yank myself back up by the fingertips, but only managed to slide farther down. "Steve, can you . . . ?" I asked. "I'm slipping." My ankles were in the water now, which was soaking the cuffs of my tux. Its fabric clung to my skin as I continued to flail. Steve rounded the corner and raced up to me, his own tux askew. Leaning over, he gripped my forearms and tugged.

"What the hell are you doing?" he grunted as he tried to pull me up.

"Trying to save you!" I flopped uselessly against the side of the tank. Above me, Steve's eyes widened, seeing something. "What?" I tried to turn my head to where he was looking.

"Shit. Shit shit shit shit shit. Come on, Cam." He pulled harder, but instead of inching upward, his hand slipped on the fabric of my dress shirt and I slid back down. My shins dipped into the water. "Oh god."

"What? What is it?" But I knew exactly what it was. There was only one thing it could be. I finally managed to turn my head enough to see over my shoulder. A long shadow glided under the surface of the water, right toward my very edible toes.

"Pullmeuppullmeup!"

"I'm trying!"

An alarm screeched and then repeated on loudspeakers all over the park. All around us, I saw red lights flash on. "Oh my god, I'm going to get eaten, then arrested!" I dug my toes into the wall and tried to scrabble up the side of the tank. But it was slick with algae and I kept slipping down. All I was doing was undoubtedly interesting the shark.

Steve gripped his hands into my forearms and tugged. "Shut"—I slid upward—"the fuck"—my feet cleared the water—"up." With one final massive tug, Steve pulled me over the side of the railing. I toppled onto him and we landed with a thump on the ground.

"Oh my god." I rolled off him and faced the sky. "Oh my god."

Steve sat up, panting. "You are insane!" He yelled it so loud I could hear it over the blare of the still-sounding alarm.

"Me?" I sat up as well. "Why was your shoe in the water?"

"I wanted to see what the shark would do before I—"

Footsteps sounded on the pavement. I scrambled to my feet, grabbing my discarded jacket and shoes. "Go!"

"Where?" Steve stood, looking for a place to hide.

I took his arm and pointed over toward the cave that led to the underwater viewing area. There was a small indentation in the rock with a bush in front of it. "Over there."

The leaves scratched our faces as we pushed behind the bush just in time to see Todd, Patrice, and the other protesters round the corner. Todd held heavy-duty bolt cutters in his hand and the others had various intimidating power tools.

"Save the shark! Save the shark!" they chanted. Arriving at the pool, Todd thrust his bolt cutters into the sky. "I know this is a little earlier than we planned, but you've studied the schematics. You know what to do. Commence Operation Open Ocean!" The protesters split apart, running for various parts of the exhibit just as a handful of security officers dashed onto the scene, mouths to walkie-talkies.

"Send backup! Repeat, send backup!"

As soon as the guards passed us, Steve tugged my arm and pointed through the bushes. Just across from us, near the amphitheater, was a door labeled "Emergency Exit." I nodded. As one, we dashed across the open space, running for the door. Reaching it, Steve stopped suddenly.

"Wait. It says emergency use only. Are you cool with breaking a rule?" He managed to keep his expression serious, but I could see the laughter in his eyes again.

"Shut up." I was pretty sure Steve could see my smile as I

slammed through the door.

We hurried down a set of rusty metal stairs, slippery with salt spray from the ocean crashing just a few yards away. The exit was near the part of the park that backed onto the beach, though there wasn't much sand here, just rough black sea rock. As we stepped onto a narrow walkway that ran parallel to the beach, there was an enormous *ka-chunk*, followed by the sound of metal cables snapping, and then a loud cheer.

Abruptly, the alarms stopped and the only sound became the whoosh of the ocean as it met the rocks. In the last few minutes of our escape, the sun had dipped below the horizon, leaving the sky a mix of orange, pink, and blue. Between the waves, the rocks, and the cotton candy clouds, it was stupidly beautiful. I rested my hands on my knees and breathed. A few feet away, Steve did the same.

Then Steve started to laugh. He doubled over, wheezing. "I'm going to get eaten, then arrested," he said in his usual high-pitched "Cam voice," then laughed harder. "Your face— The shark—" His laughter turned into a cough and he sat down on the bottom step.

I stood over him. "It's not funny, Steve. You were trying to kill yourself."

Steve's coughs subsided and he stared at his feet, one bare, one still wearing an Air Jordan. "I wasn't going to kill myself."

"Yes. You were."

"No. I wasn't." The next words were so quiet they were almost lost to the waves. "Not here, anyway." Before I could respond, he jumped up, stretched his arms overhead, then shook them out. "Man, that shark was terrifying, right?" He flashed me a bright, false grin and began to walk along the beach path.

Jamming my shoes back on my feet, I hopped along after him. "Steve . . ."

"You shouldn't be saving it. You should fucking murder it."

"Steve!"

"Die, shark! Die!" He made finger guns and pretended to shoot, making *pew pew* sounds. The path became rougher, more a rocky track in the sand than an actual walkway. I could see sharp stones cutting into Steve's bare foot. In front of us, the path split, one part going straight along the coastline, the other veering off to a long jetty that thrust into the bay. Steve paused. "Did you hear those people cheering a minute ago? I wonder what happened." He bounded off toward the jetty. "I think if I walk to the end, I'll be able to see the shark enclosure!"

"STEVE!" I called after him.

Already partway on the jetty, he spun around and threw his arms wide. "What, Cam? What?" I nearly twisted my ankle as I followed him, trying to navigate the rough black stones. But a few feet in, I stopped, realizing I had no idea what I was going to say beyond just repeating his name. Steve gave a quick, tight nod, like this was exactly what he'd expected. "Let me guess. You're gonna tell me it's all going to be okay? That the odds are in my favor?" I opened my mouth and then closed it, because yeah, that was pretty much where I was going to start. "Then what?" Steve challenged. "You'll be by my side while I turn into a withering raisin boy? Well, fuck you. I don't want to do that lame-ass show. I don't want months of my mom in tears or my dad's disappointment now that I'm no longer me. I can't do it. I'm not strong like you, okay?"

I looked up from the piece of rock I'd been staring at. "Like . . . me?"

Steve groaned and grabbed the back of his neck. "Yes, Cam, you! Look, I admit when all this started, I could not imagine a more pathetic person."

"Hey!"

Steve shrugged, unapologetic. "That's why I liked being around you. Because why should I feel bad about being some broken-ass cancer boy when someone like you exists in the world? But then, no matter how I humiliated or embarrassed you, you just kept coming. Despite what anyone thought. Who does that?"

Steve kicked at the rocks with his sneakered foot. How could he have gotten it so wrong? So utterly, stupidly, completely wrong. I stumbled a few steps forward, my arms out for balance. "Dude, it's not a positive. Trust me. It's not bravery or anything like that. It's what I thought I had to do to earn someone. I had to practically save the world because I was too terrified to find out if anyone would care about me if I didn't. If just being me was worthy of love."

Steve snorted. "Wow. Did you just actually say 'worthy of love'?"

I scowled. "Shut up."

"Sorry, did we wander into a period piece? Should I be wearing a corset?"

"Steve—"

"Are smelling salts a real thing because—"

"Oh my god, Steve! Just . . . would you . . ." I was glad there were still a few boulders separating us because otherwise I would strangle him and that was kinda the opposite of the point right now. "What I'm saying is, I'm not brave. I'm basically nothing but fear. All the time. But . . . I think that's okay."

Steve looked at me for a moment, his expression unreadable. Then he turned and stared out at the ocean. "Maybe for you."

I crossed the last several rocks separating us. "For me. For you. For anyone. Pretending you're not afraid isn't being strong. Fuck fearless."

Steve laughed, short and sharp. "Sure. Fuck it. Like it's just that simple."

"Maybe it is."

Steve whirled, getting right in my face. "It's not okay! Not for me. I don't want to be you, Cam. I'm fucking Steve Stevenson!" He punctuated this with a thump on his chest.

"So what?" I shouted, refusing to back down. "You'd rather die than let people see that you're scared?"

"Yes!" Steve waved his hands. "Yes, okay? Yes." Then his shoulders sank, crumpling forward in the tux jacket as he curled in on himself. "I'd rather be dead," he mumbled. "Not by shark. I realize that may have been a mistake. But by . . .

276

something. And if I go now, at least I go out as me."

Below us the waves crashed against the rocks, the water swirling in the pockets and crannies before being pulled out to sea again. The cycle repeated, over and over. I reached out to Steve, then dropped my arm. "Getting sick doesn't change who you are."

Steve's eyes hardened and I knew I'd said the wrong thing. "That's such bullshit," he spat.

"Come on, Steve, you——"

He stepped back. "Cancer totally changes you. I am changed forever because of this. I know what T cells are now. I know chemo makes my mouth taste like pennies. I know the sound of my mom praying outside my door at night. And I don't want to change anymore, okay?" His voice broke on the last word, but he kept going. "Because who will I be then? Huh? Tell me!" Steve stood on the black rock, the ocean spray misting his face, and waited for an answer. I knew everything I could say would be wrong. I was going to screw this up. I might hurt him more. But I couldn't leave him standing on a rock all alone. Carefully, I picked my way toward him.

"Steve, I get it. You're scared." I reached for Steve's shoulder, but my fingers barely ghosted the damp fabric when he jerked away.

"Don't." He stumbled forward over the last few rocks to the end of the jetty, putting as much space between us as possible. "You have no idea. It's easy to say 'fuck fearless' when all you have to be afraid of is asking some girl out. Your problems are so small. I'm looking at needles and CAT scans, vomit and shit and . . ." He made a choking sound. "I don't . . ." He squeezed his eyes shut and tilted his head up. "I don't . . ." But despite all his efforts, tears still leaked out, tracking down his cheeks. "I don't want to fucking die, okay?" Bending over, he yanked his remaining shoe off his foot and hurled it into the ocean. "Fuuuuuuuuck!" It landed with an insignificant plop, floated for a moment, and disappeared.

Steve crumpled, burying his head in his knees. "I don't want to die."

I crossed the last few boulders to where Steve sat. This far away from shore, everything seemed small. The distant beach, the palm trees; even the aqua park looked toy-sized. In front of us, the ocean expanded endlessly in all directions. The light had faded to a soft purple, the sun now well below the horizon, and the only sound was the constant white noise of the waves. We were suspended, alone, two fucked-up people in a twilight world. I sat down next to Steve, letting my legs dangle off the rocks.

"I can't keep doing this." Steve's voice was muffled by his knees. Then he uncurled a little and looked up, not at me, but at the ocean. "I can't go back into that house and pretend it's all okay. That I'm a fighter. That I'm going to kick cancer's ass." His fingers dug into the folds of his pants. "What if I'm not strong enough? What if that's not me anymore? What if I can't do it?"

"Steve, it's okay if you can't." I could see the moment the words registered. Anger, pain, embarrassment, but then . . .

something else. Something like peace. Finally. I'd found the right words. "It's okay if you can't," I repeated.

Steve broke down. His whole body was shaking. He wasn't even trying to hold anything back now. It was just endless racking sobs. And they were loud. Really loud. And there was snot. Everywhere. I should do something. My hand hovered uselessly over his shoulder. Did I? Should I? Okay, yeah. I was going to. I laid it down and patted gently. But it didn't seem to have any effect. Steve just cried harder.

"Um, Steve? Can I hug you?"

Steve choked on a laugh and sniffed. "Are you asking for consent?"

I huffed and smiled. "Yeah. I'm asking for hug consent."

Steve shrugged a bit, his face still buried in his hands. "I don't care."

So, I scooted closer, the side of my body pressing up along his. When he didn't flinch away, I carefully extended my arms, wrapping them around him. Then I pulled him toward me and . . . squeezed. At first it was weird; his tux jacket crunched up and the lapels kind of poked me. And Steve's bald head ended up smooshed against my nose. But then he sort of relaxed. And I sort of relaxed. And Steve moved his head down to my shoulder and we just stayed there. For a long time.

And it was just the ocean and us.

Eventually, Steve let out a sigh. "You know, you're stupid."

I pulled back, dropping my arms. "Wow. And I thought we just had a pretty touching moment."

Steve sat up, put his hands behind him, and leaned back a little, a faint grin on his face. "You said you were afraid no one would care about you if you weren't Save-the-World Cam all the time. But I knew you were an asshole from the moment I saw you and I still like you. So your big fear is pretty fucking stupid."

"Oh." That was the only word I could get out. I hadn't . . . That wasn't . . . How had I not . . .

Steve watched, enjoying my flailing. "Yeah." Then he stood up with a hop and sauntered back down the jetty. "Let's go, asshole."

"Whatever, coward," I muttered as I scrambled to catch up. From in front of me, Steve gave me the finger and kept walking.

When we reached the parking lot, both of us stopped.

"Whoa."

"Holy shit," Steve added.

The entrance to the aqua park was awash in flashing red and blue lights. Half a dozen cop cars were parked haphazardly, some halfway on the sidewalk. News vans with antennas raised formed a second ring. Police bustled under the welcome archway with its smiling sea creatures, walkie-talkies in hand. Beside the giant clam fountain, reporters clustered, microphones to their mouths as their nearby camerapeople crouched with their heavy black cameras, thick cables snaking on the ground.

". . . and we are hearing that a mass of protesters . . ."

"Channel Islands Aqua Park is refusing to comment. A number of arrests . . ."

". . . free. I repeat. The shark is free."

Careful to stay in the shadows, Steve and I skirted the chaos, dodging behind a group of onlookers who were jostling to get a better view of the action.

"Has anyone see my son, Steve?"

Across the lot, Steve's parents pushed their way through the crowd, looking concerned and confused. Beside me, Steve stiffened.

"Uh, I may have emailed your parents on the way here," I muttered.

"Oh god." Steve paled.

"I, uh, didn't tell them anything specific, if that helps. But, um, sorry." I cringed, but Steve just sighed.

"No. You did the right thing. I need to talk to them."

I watched the red and blue lights dance across his face as he stood, staring at his parents but not moving forward. "You want me to come with you?"

Steve snapped out of wherever he'd been and smiled at me, though it was a bit shaky. "Yeah. But I should do this on my own. Could you wait?" He looked at the ground, embarrassed.

"Of course. Sure. I'll be under that palm tree." I pointed to a palm a bit farther into the parking lot, away from the police's notice.

"Cool." He nodded, suddenly determined, and walked toward his parents, hands in his pockets, feet bare.

"Oh, um, maybe don't mention the shark part? Specifically? Because I think they're arresting people. But the feelings stuff. Share that," I called after him.

Steve gave me a thumbs-up.

I couldn't hear what Steve told them, but I saw his mom give a great heaving sob and pull him tight. He and his dad thumped each other on the arms and looked awkward, but they were talking. They talked for a long while. I crouched on the ground under the palm tree and waited. Eventually, Steve's dad hugged him and stepped back. Steve walked over to me.

"My dad admitted he was scared." He said it like the words were another language.

I nodded. "Yeah."

"It's . . . really weird. I never thought . . ." He trailed off.

"They okay?" I asked.

Steve shrugged. "Who the fuck knows? It's a total shit show. But I think it's going to be better now. Not good. But better."

"That's good. I'm glad."

"Thanks."

The moment stretched and became super awkward. I stood up, brushing off my pants. "So, um, I guess . . . good night? Are your parents going to drive you home?"

"What the hell are you talking about? It's prom."

"Yeah. I know." I gestured to our rumpled tuxes. "I just thought—"

"You thought I would miss this? It's Cardi fucking B, Cam. At our prom. You can tell how messed up I was earlier because there's no way I would have killed myself before seeing my girl Cardi if I was in my right mind."

"Are you sure?"

"Look. I asked my parents to get me a therapist or whatever. I'll deal with it. By the way, you should consider a therapist, too. Maybe we can get a Groupon?" I laughed but nodded; it was probably a good idea. Steve continued, "But right now, I'm feeling kind of okay. And there's no chance I'm sitting this out. Anyway, I should probably apologize to Kaia."

"Oh shit. Kaia." It was dark outside, which meant prom had started at least an hour ago. I pulled out my phone. There were a thousand text messages. And a lot of them were in caps lock. Steve looked at the screen and then back up at me.

"Uh-oh."

"Yeah."

Visions of Kaia ripping me limb from limb were interrupted when someone shouted, "Cam?" I turned. Nearby, an officer had thrown open the back doors of a paddy wagon and ushered a string of people in zip-tied handcuffs inside. One of the arrested shouted, "Cam! We did it!" It was Todd, a little scuffed up, but smiling.

I waved back. "Congrats."

"Oh my god. That must be Steve!" Behind Todd, Patrice bounced up and down in excitement, ignoring the frustrated admonishments of the police officer.

"Patrice!" I called. "You were right! It is *Fault in Our Stars*. Actually, it's a little more like *Here on Earth*. With a touch of *A*

Walk to Remember! And some *Sweet November!* Whatever. You get it. It's totally a cancer love story!"

Patrice punched her fists in the air. "Yes! Knew it!" She was grinning like a maniac as she climbed into the van.

Steve cocked his head. "Do I really want to know what you're talking about with those criminals?"

I grabbed his arm and tugged him toward my car. "Nope. Not important. What is important is that we are going to get you and Kaia back together."

20

Kaia was missing. Steve and I pushed our way through the crowd in the Radisson ballroom. We couldn't see her sparkly yellow dress anywhere. She hadn't answered any of our texts.

"Kaia?" I called.

"Anyone seen Kaia?" Steve added. Almost the entire junior and senior class milled under crepe paper kelp, and from the looks some people were giving Steve, Kaia hadn't exactly kept things a secret. A video projected fish on the dance floor, where clusters of kids showed off to some old funk, but she wasn't among them. I checked the tables scattered around the edges, but the aqua and indigo balloons that gave the impression of bubbles obstructed my view. So did the plastic crabs and octopuses that dangled from mobiles. The decorating committee had gone all out, but it wasn't making it easy to find one tiny and probably very pissed off girl.

A couple of guys from the baseball team pushed past Steve, knocking him into a life-sized papier-mâché mermaid, and I wasn't entirely sure it was an accident. I jerked my chin toward the stage and shouted over the 90s hip-hop. "Let's try up there."

We got past Cardi's security with Steve's easy grin and, "Recognize me? I'm the sad cancer boy." Once backstage, it was a swarm of very serious, very intimidating people in black shirts and zero sign of Kaia. Cardi's roadies were putting the final touches on her elaborate stage show and Steve was immediately distracted.

"Holy crap, is that a swing?" Steve asked a burly dude who was testing the wires attached to a glittery swing thing. The guy nodded. "What's Cardi do? Sit on it?" A grunt was the only response, but it was enough. Steve bounced. "Yes! That's my girl! Flying in like a superhero. Can I see?"

"Steve! Focus!" From behind the curtain, I scanned the crowd. Still no Kaia. "I'm going to go out onstage and see if I can spot her."

Steve didn't even bother looking at me as he examined an intimidating-looking harness with an excess of straps. "Cool. Sounds good." He held up the tangle of black fabric. "So this goes under her costume?"

I sighed, leaving him to his Cardi fanning, and stepped onto the stage. Squinting in the bright lights, I edged my way to the DJ and shouted a question in his ear. He handed me a mic and cut the music.

The crowd murmured and rustled uneasily. A few people began to chant, "Cardi! Cardi! Cardi!" but it petered out when they saw me.

"Hi, everyone. Sorry to interrupt your evening."

"We want Cardi!" yelled one of Steve's bro friends.

"Cardi will be on soon. I just need your attention for a second. Has anyone seen Kaia Gonzales?"

"Why are you always looking for Kaia?" It was the Cardi lover from Steve's party. And she had a point.

"I promise, this is probably the last time I'll be looking for her." After Kaia heard what I had to say, she'd never speak to me again. "But, um, has anyone seen her? Student council? Yearbook? Anyone?" Various clusters of people on the dance floor shook their heads. "Okay, well, um, if anyone finds her—"

"Cardi, Cardi, Cardi." The chant started again.

"If anyone finds her, can you tell her that Cam Webber has something to—"

"Sorry!" From the back of the ballroom I saw Kaia push her way through the double doors. She hurried forward, a few strands of hair from her tight bun slipping from their place. "I was just helping some people find the Lopez quinceañera. Someone said I was needed back—" She stopped when she saw me standing onstage. "Cam. Where have you been?"

Now that I was actually looking at her, I didn't know what to say. People had cleared out of Kaia's way, making a rough semicircle on the dance floor. Her dress shimmered softly under the wavy blue lights that were supposed to simulate the ocean. She looked up at me with annoyance and confusion. Which sucked so much. Because I still really, really liked her. "I know. I'm late. I'm sorry. But there's something you should know."

The DJ chose that moment to put on some Ed Sheeran, thinking he was doing me a favor.

A girl in a purple ball gown cried, "Oh my god. I didn't know people actually did this!" and clutched her friend's arm.

"No! No!" I waved my arms. "No music! This is not, um, one of those sort of grab the mic and interrupt prom things. Thanks, but . . ." The DJ cut the song. "Thanks."

"Is this a fancy way of apologizing for ditching me tonight?" Kaia asked. "If it is, you'd better hurry up, because we are running low on punch and the dessert table needs refreshing and—"

"Okay. Okay. I know you're busy. Let me just. No. Actually, do you mind if we do this off the stage? I kinda just came up here to look for you. Not to . . ." I gestured weakly at everyone watching us. "Make a big thing."

Kaia crossed her arms. "Time is ticking, Cam. I've pretty much given up on my cheesy romantic prom dream. I'm basically just a caterer in a fancy dress."

I closed my eyes. I guess I was doing this in front of everyone. Squaring my shoulders, I opened my eyes and said, "Kaia, that picture you saw of Steve with that girl wasn't real. I posted it to try to make you think he cheated on you."

"What?" She wasn't even angry. Kaia just looked even more

confused as my betrayal sank in. The rest of the room, however, had already formed an opinion of me.

"You suck!" someone shouted from the back.

I nodded in agreement with this accurate assessment, then continued, "And it's not just that. I have to be honest. I only did the whole Save Steve thing to impress you. It wasn't really about Steve at all. I only did all that stuff because . . . um . . . I hoped you would like me more."

The purple ball gown girl said, "Awwww." But her friend next to her said, "It's kind of creepy."

Kaia just stared at me, baffled. "Cam . . . that's crazy."

I nodded. "I recognize that now. Look, I know I messed up really bad. I know I'm not 'Best Person.' I'm just kind of an average person."

Kaia didn't correct me. There was a beat of awkward silence. The only thing that seemed to move in the whole ballroom were the projected fish slowly circling on the dance floor.

"So Steve didn't cheat on me?"

"No."

"Oh." She blinked a few times. "But then why . . ."

From somewhere above us, someone called, "Hold on. I can answer that."

The entire room strained to locate where the voice was coming from. There was a click, then a quiet hum as an electric motor kicked in, and then, descending from the rafters on the glittering swing, was Steve Stevenson.

The DJ, clearly seeing his moment, leaped back into action,

289

and Ed Sheeran resumed on the PA. With another punch of some buttons, the lights dimmed and a bubble machine kicked in, sending a cascade of iridescent bubbles floating out over the room. They gently popped against Kaia's cheeks as she stood frozen, staring at her ex-boyfriend sitting on a swing eight feet above the stage, clad in a rumpled tuxedo and missing his shoes.

"Steve?"

"Cool, huh? Cardi's people let me try it out." He gave a little rock and almost slipped off. The crowd gasped. "Don't worry. I'm all good. There's a harness, too."

"Steve . . . what are you . . . why . . . ?"

"I'll explain, but . . ." Steve beckoned Kaia forward. "Can you come up here? Cam started talking and I was already strapped into this thing and it's super hard to get out of, so I just went with it, but you're kinda far away."

A dazed look in her eyes, Kaia ascended the steps through a curtain of bubbles. Steve waved to someone offstage and the swing began to lower again.

"I'm sorry I lied to you, Kaia," Steve said as he descended. "I only pretended to cheat on you because—" With a jolt, the swing lurched and then halted. The crowd gasped as Steve was flung forward. He grabbed for the cables holding the swing, but missed and tumbled off. He dangled almost seven feet from the stage floor, spinning gently in a safety harness.

"Steve!" Kaia exclaimed.

I ran forward, but Steve waved me away. "It's cool. Uh, Kaia, I'm just gonna wait a sec until I stop spinning."

She nodded. "Um. Yeah. Okay."

Dangling above her, he waited for the spin to slow. A cloud of bubbles wafted between them. Kaia tried to wave them away. Steve tried to kick at them as he spun. "So many bubbles."

"Comes with the undersea theme," Kaia said through the puffs.

"No, no. I get it," Steve said, still precariously spinning. Finally, the bubble storm passed and they could see each other. "And you did a great job. I love the . . ." He looked around for something specific. "Kelp."

"Thanks," Kaia said, and smiled awkwardly.

Finally, the harness contraption settled into a gentle sway. Steve reached for the bar of the swing dangling nearby but couldn't quite grasp it. He looked to the wings for some guidance. "Are we stuck?" A roadie shrugged. "Okay then. I'll just do it here." He shifted in the straps and looked down at Kaia with big apologetic eyes. "I'm sorry I lied to you this morning. I just went along with Cam's ploy so you wouldn't have to deal with my crap. I know it was stupid and selfish. But I panicked. Because, well . . ." In the pause, I could feel the entire room lean in. Kaia, too. Steve's eyes flicked to mine and I saw a flash of fear, but he continued, "I got some test results back, and . . . the cancer's not going away."

There was a soft inhale from the crowd.

"What?" Kaia asked, shocked.

"Yeah, it looks like I might be getting sicker. A lot sicker, maybe. And it might get ugly."

"Oh god, Steve." Kaia stretched her hand to where Steve dangled above her. Steve extended his. Their fingers brushed. Tears sprang to her eyes. Then, as if feeling the heaviness of the moment, Steve gestured to himself and tried to lighten it. "I mean, you can kiss this hotness goodbye." It lacked his usual confidence, but Kaia still stifled a laugh through her tears. "I was embarrassed," he continued, sincere. "I didn't want you to see me like that. Weak. Maybe even dying. So I pushed you away. Got you to break up with me rather than admit the truth. Because I'm a coward. But even if I am, there's something I want to ask you."

The room stilled. Guys put down their drinks. Girls made hopeful fists. Couples held each other close. Kaia wiped a tear from her cheek as Steve continued, "I'm still afraid, Kaia. But I'm not afraid of you seeing me weak anymore." He smiled, vulnerable and honest. Steve gestured to the harness. "So, if I can ever get out of this thing, I wanted to ask if you would—"

"Steve, stop," Kaia breathed.

There was a murmur of excitement. Everyone could see how desperately she wanted to just pull him down and wrap her arms around him.

"Jump up and kiss him!" yelled the girl in the purple ball gown, and the room tittered.

"Are you sure no one can get me down?" Steve called to the wings again. "Because I feel like I could do the whole making up with my girlfriend thing a lot better standing on two feet."

"Steve . . . ," Kaia repeated.

"What?" Steve asked, his eyes once again on her, his

292

expression open, ready to give her whatever she wanted.

"Steve . . . I don't love you."

What? The? Fuck?

The crowd let out a mix of "Ohhhhhhhhhhhh" and "Whaaaaaaa?"

"Did she say she didn't love him?" I asked out loud. I must have misheard.

"Oh, thank god!" Steve exhaled. He slumped. Then the cables hissed and he fell toward the stage, stopping with a jerk just before he crashed.

"Jesus! Can someone help him?!" Kaia asked, flustered.

"I'm okay," Steve said, and gave a thumbs-up to someone offstage. Shaking, he righted himself, only to discover his feet still hovered a foot off the floor.

I started across the stage. Steve was getting so humiliated. I needed to stop it.

"Please turn off the music!" Kaia said, brushing away another cascade of bubbles while trying to steady Steve. "This is crazy," she said as she tugged the buckle on the harness, trying to free him. A burble of discontent spread through the room. I thought I heard a "boo." Then a couple more. Were people booing at Kaia?

"Wait! No!" I hurried to the center of the stage. "Hear him out, Kaia!" Steve needed to finish. He needed to tell her he loved her. "Steve . . . ," I begged.

"Cam, stop . . . ," Steve said as he waved Kaia off from trying to free him.

"Can someone turn off the bubbles?" Kaia stomped toward the wings.

"But you two— You have to—" I grabbed Steve by the hand and pulled him after Kaia, the wires zuzzing as I tugged him toward her. The crowd cheered. Kaia stopped. I gave Steve a push, but maybe it was a little too hard, because as Steve sped toward her, Kaia jumped out of the way and he sailed past.

The whole room erupted. A senior in a pink tux yelled out, "Are you seriously breaking up with a guy with cancer?" The crowd agreed. I even heard someone shout "bitch."

"It's fine!" Steve said as he coasted to a stop on the edge of the stage. "Really! I'm not sad!" How could he say that? This was Kaia. If Kaia had just rejected me, I'd be devastated. Crushed. Spiraling into a black void of oblivion. But Steve merely shrugged. "Honestly, having cancer is a lot. I'm not sure I have the emotional bandwidth for a relationship right now," he told everyone. "And anyway, we really don't have anything in common."

But no one was listening. The boos were getting louder. Kaia stared at the crowd. She looked like she was staring into her own black void of oblivion. Steve attempted to swing himself in front of her to protect her from the outrage. But she pushed him aside and stepped toward the edge of the stage.

"Are you booing me?" In answer, the crowd redoubled their efforts. She blinked and stepped forward. "You're seriously booing me?" Her body quivered and her face flushed. "Yearbook, really?" And then she caught another offender. "Student council! AND prom committee!" Her eyes darted from group to group, her rage building. And then something in her snapped. "Motherfuckers . . . ," she growled under her breath. She brushed by me as she stalked toward the steps leading off the stage, and I swear I felt heat radiating off her.

Kaia stepped onto the dance floor, waving her arms. "Stop booing, assholes!"

"Language!" Mr. Holmes, our principal, chided, but Kaia gave him a death stare and he shrank.

Out of shock, the booing petered off. "I'm so sick of all of you!" She walked right up to the yearbook table. "What? You want me to do this for you, too?" She jerked her head at them, taunting. "Huh?" They scuttled back, scared. She spun around and carved through the stunned crowd as she addressed them. "Is that it? Date a guy I don't really like?" Promgoers parted in her path. "I was going to break up with him! And then he promposaled me and I tricked myself into thinking I was actually in love with him because I was too embarrassed to say no in front of all of you. Sure, I was pissed that he cheated, but I was also fucking relieved. But okay, let me keep dating a guy I have nothing in common with because he rode in on a swing and has cancer and that makes you feel all swoony! How long do I need to do it? Just for tonight? A few weeks? Forever?" She got in the face of the pink tux kid. "How long will make you happy?" Furious, she slammed her hand on a table, causing the plates to shudder.

Everyone was stone-cold frozen.

"Maybe I should marry him? Why the hell not? I already do everything else for you assholes!" She circled back toward the stage as she counted off, "Student council! Debate! Prom! Feminists for fucking knitting! You think I like doing all that?! Getting texts at midnight?" She switched to a whiny, singsongy voice. "Oh, we need poster board for tomorrow, Kaia. Can you get some for us?" She dropped it and barked, "Fucking get it yourselves!!! Papier-mâché your own damn mermaids! I. Am. Done!" She screamed and thrust all her rage at the life-sized mermaid, toppling it over.

Kids by the stage screamed and scattered. "Go ahead, hate me all you want!" Kaia walked to the other side of the stage. "Guess what?" She kicked the second mermaid in the fin. "I no longer care what a bunch of mediocre high school kids think of me." She punched a hole in its face. "I am through." And then she ripped off its head and threw it at the crowd.

"Fuuuuuccccckkk alllll ooooof yooooooouuuuu!" she finished, and stomped out of the room.

In the new silence, we all absorbed what we'd just seen.

Holy shit, that was hot.

Beside me, I heard Steve laugh, his bare feet still hovering a foot above the stage. "Ahh, Cambone."

I blushed.

I hadn't realized I'd said it out loud.

Steve and I walked out onto the ballroom's wide orange tiled balcony that looked over the ocean below. We'd eventually managed to untangle Steve from the harness with the help of Cardi's people. For our own safety we figured we'd look for Kaia together. We found her on the far side of the balcony, her elbows propped on the ledge, her dress fluttering around her in the night breeze, and scowling at the water like it had something to do with what happened.

"Well, that's a prom to remember," Steve said as we crossed to her. Kaia turned and sniffed, wiping her nose on the back of her hand.

"Are you okay?" I asked.

"Yeah. I still want to murder someone. But, yeah." Her eyes flicked to Steve's and back down again. "I'm sorry."

Steve raised his hands. "Uh, don't be. All I want is for people to treat me exactly like they would if I didn't have cancer. And if that includes dumping my ass publicly, that's fine with me. In fact, it's a bit of a relief. You kind of scare me."

Kaia laughed. "Thanks."

Steve leaned close to me and whispered in my ear. "But there are some people who get off on unhinged displays of rage." He nudged me in the ribs. I widened my eyes and gave a tiny shake of my head. What the hell was he thinking? He couldn't be— "Kaia, can we get you something to soothe those ravaged vocal cords? Some punch, perhaps?" Steve asked smoothly, taking my elbow. I tried to yank it back.

"Sure," Kaia agreed, and turned back to the ocean.

Steve pulled me over to a table that had a half-filled punch bowl and some compostable plastic cups (Kaia) and slopped some sticky pink liquid into a glass. "Dude, this is your chance."

"Are you insane?" I yell-whispered. "I can't ask her out now. She just broke up with you!"

Steve grabbed another glass and filled it. "Cam. Camarindo. Cam-my-man. She kissed you. Twice. That angry one was super hot. And she spent all that time with you. Even while we were dating, she talked about you nonstop. That dance you did. I mean, she would not shut up about it. And, honestly, I didn't want to tell you this that night at mini golf, but . . . you were right. You are better for her."

I stared at Steve, really, really wanting to believe him.

"It doesn't matter. I can't ask her out now. She knows everything I did and she just said she wants to murder someone. You saw what she did to those mermaids!"

"So? You spent months trying to engineer the perfect moment. Look what happened." I wilted a bit. Damn. He was right. Steve gave me a little shake. "Besides, if the shark didn't take you out, you really think this will?" With that, Steve handed me two glasses of punch and gave me a shove.

I walked back toward Kaia, carefully clutching the cups, the pink liquid nearly spilling over with each step, waiting for all the horrible feelings to start boiling up. But there was nothing. No stomach clenching. No legs bracing. No chest collapsing and stealing my breath. Why not?

I reached Kaia. She must have visited the snack table because she'd found a piece of cake and was angrily stabbing it. I tried not to take that as a sign.

"Here." I offered her the cup.

"Thanks." Kaia grabbed the glass from me and set it on the ledge.

I stared at the ocean, nervous. But just a little. It was different from every other time I'd been about to ask her. Before, all I could think of was some endless black void. Complete annihilation. But now . . .

I turned to look over my shoulder. Steve was on the other side of the balcony, feeding bits of cake to a seagull.

And maybe that was the difference.

Steve.

I turned back to Kaia. "Just so we're clear, I fully recognize this is the worst time to do this."

Kaia didn't even look up from her cake. "What?"

"So, you heard everything I said onstage earlier . . ."

"Yep." She stabbed the fork into the cake and ground the crumbs into the plate.

"On a scale of one to ten, how mad are you at me right now?"

"Eleven." A tine broke off the fork as she pressed down.

Okay, actually, maybe I should wait an hour or two. The image of the decapitated mermaid flashed through my mind. "Yeah. I think maybe I didn't make it clear before, but I am super, insanely sorry for everything. Like infinity. And, uh, I'm just gonna—"

"But I'll get over it," she said, and I froze. Kaia put the mutilated cake on the ledge of the balcony. "Even though your motivations were . . . less than pure, you did raise, like, thirty thousand dollars for Steve. And, I don't know, we were a pretty good team for a while, right? I mean, you never made me go on midnight runs for poster board." She sighed and turned to me. "I guess what I'm saying is, there are more sharks to save." Her eyes widened. "Oh my god! Did you hear about the shark? Crazy, right?"

"Oh. Um." I looked over my shoulder to Steve again. He had a flock of seagulls around him now. He looked a little worried about it. "Yeah. Crazy."

"And . . . I . . . I did some stupid shit, too." I turned back to Kaia. She was picking at a rhinestone on her dress. "Not as stupid as your shit. But I shouldn't have kissed you to get back at Steve. That wasn't great."

"Oh, um, well, it was kinda great for me."

She looked away, out toward the ocean, and bit her lip.

This was the moment.

"Kaia, I should have asked you this a long time ago, but I didn't and I just . . ." My voice was all squeaky. Why? I tried to lower it. "I want to know." No, that was worse.

"What?"

I cleared my throat. "After prom, maybe tomorrow, or next week, or, you know, whenever . . . will you go out with me? Not as friends. Or to save anything, but . . . like on a date. A normal date?"

Holy shit. I'd said it. For a moment I didn't know where I was. I was just somewhere in a world where I'd finally said the words and I was flying. And then I realized Kaia was looking at me, a few loose curls brushing her face as the ocean breeze whipped them around, the moonlight making a perfect silver highlight on her shoulder, her eyes soft and warm. She sighed, close enough to me that I felt her breath on my neck. This was better than any dream I'd ever had. This was—

"No."

Behind me, I heard Steve drop his cake plate. "Oh, fuck! Sorry, dude." He rushed over, sending seagulls flapping in every direction. "My fault. I totally misread the sitch."

Kaia was still talking, her eyes wide and earnest, but I couldn't hear anything she said.

The worst had happened.

Kaia Gonzales had rejected me. Just like I'd always been afraid she would.

I waited for the darkness.

The void.

It was coming . . .

21

But then . . . nothing.

No void.

No annihilation. Just Kaia. Still talking. "I mean, Cam, if you had asked me before all this happened, I probably would have said yes, but for the wrong reasons." Where was the darkness? "I would have said yes because I didn't want to hurt your feelings." Where was the destruction? "That's my problem. I've been so worried about everyone's feelings that I didn't think about my own. But I have to stop being everything for everyone else, even if they hate me." Why wasn't I broken into a thousand pieces? "Cam, thank you for asking me out. But I just want to be friends." She looked confused when I didn't react. "Cam?"

"Give him a minute," I heard Steve say. "You just destroyed him."

"I'm not destroyed," I said, more to myself than anyone else. "I'm fine." And this time I actually was.

"I know that wasn't what you wanted to hear," Kaia said.

"No. It wasn't," I admitted. That was an understatement of epic proportions. But I was still glad I'd asked. Not just glad. Relieved. And realistically, I would need at least a week of non-stop moping and a couple of boxes of Strawberry Pop-Tarts to piece myself back together. But still, I held out my hand. "Friends?"

Kaia relaxed, the tension leaving her body. She gave me a small smile and I returned it.

She took my hand. "Good friends."

Steve stuck his hand in and laid it on top of ours. "Friends with benefits?"

We jerked our hands away and shouted "No!" at the same time. Steve threw his head back and laughed.

Then, through the open doors to the ballroom, the DJ announced, "And now what you've all been waiting for! Cardi BBBBBBBBBB!" A huge cheer erupted from inside as bass thumped loud enough to shake the windows.

Steve gestured to the open doors. "They're playing our song."

I made a skeptical noise. "I think it's really your song."

Steve threw his arms over Kaia's and my shoulders and pulled us close. "*Our* song," he insisted.

"Your song."

"Ours."

"Nope." A smile tugged at my lips.

"Whatever," Kaia groaned. "Can we dance now?"

We walked through the doors and into the bright, flashing lights of the ballroom.

"You're a legend," a kid I didn't know said to me as he left the ballroom. The last few hours had been like a crazed super train. The three of us jumping around onstage. Cardi challenging me to a dance-off. Steve taking over the mic to duet on "Drip." And finally, the quinceañera crashing the prom. It was total madness.

And now I was one of the last ones here. I never dreamed I would shut down prom. But I couldn't stand to see the night end. I watched Cardi's people pack up her gear. The ballroom staff cleaned up the disaster that the fifteen-year-olds and promgoers had left. Steve was still here in one corner, having a balloon-popping contest with a couple of his bro buds. After his cancer speech, they had actually been pretty cool to him. I guess that was progress.

A few of the prom committee members packed up the reusable items. Earlier I was glad to see Kaia ditch them without offering to help. But in her rush, she had forgotten to say goodbye to me. I couldn't say I wasn't disappointed, but after all the shit that she had gone through tonight, it was fine. She probably needed to just get to sleep.

My mom texted me: Did you fix everything? 😉

It sounded ridiculous now. But I guess everything was fixed. Just not the way I had imagined. I texted her a thumbs-up and a party favor explosion and that I'd be home soon. When I looked up, Steve was gone. He must have left with his old friends.

I took one last look at the ballroom. If I was honest, I was a little bummed to be leaving alone. But I didn't feel sorry for myself. I was still a legend, apparently.

Suddenly I was grabbed from behind. "What the—?"

I turned to find Kaia with a big, mischievous grin on her face.

"Where's Steve?" she asked.

"I thought you'd left—"

"Where's Steve?" she demanded.

"I . . . I don't know. He was just here."

"Come on," she said, and grabbed my hand. Holding her dress up, she pulled me through the hallway, yelling, "Steve! Steve!"

Her excitement was infectious. I called out with her, "Steve!" even though I had no idea why.

A couple of busboys were pushing a cart and Kaia slowed to ask them, "Have you seen Steve?"

"Steve who?"

"Never mind," she said, and we raced on.

In the lobby, she questioned the woozy prom stragglers. They either hadn't seen him or were too drunk to follow the question. But then one of Steve's balloon-popping bro buds heard us. "You guys looking for Steve?"

"What gave it away?" Kaia snarked. She was flushed and happy in a way I'd never seen.

"Some guy who worked for Cardi told Steve she wanted to give him something. I think he went to her trailer."

"To the trailer!" Kaia ordered, and pointed out to the parking lot.

"What are we doing, Kaia?"

"Just wait."

We ran through the automatic sliding doors and headed to the parking lot. Luckily, Cardi's trailer was parked curbside. Just as we skidded up to the door, it popped open and out stumbled Steve. He was wearing a gold Cardi B hat that she had signed, had a lipstick kiss on his cheek and a big old goofy smile on his face.

"She's soooooo nice!" he gushed. "Cancer was worth it!" He high-fived me and then leaned close. "You should get cancer, Cam."

"I'll pass," I laughed.

Kaia rolled her eyes. "I can't believe I dated you."

"Don't you have some poster board to get?" he teased.

She smacked him on the arm and then smiled. "We have some important business to attend to, gentlemen. To the beach!"

"The beach?" I asked.

But she didn't wait to answer and took off toward it. I looked at Steve, confused. He just shrugged and repeated, "To the beach!" And he ran off after her.

To the beach.

We passed Kaia's shoes, which she had apparently flung off even before we got to the sand. Reaching the beach, I kicked mine off, while shoeless Steve ran ahead. Chuffing after her, I could see her silhouette running with wild abandon toward the crashing waves. Maybe it had something to do with the shark? The sudden release might have shocked his system. But she was too happy for him to be washed up dead onshore. Was he leaping out of the ocean like a dolphin and blowing whalelike spurts? Anything seemed possible tonight.

Kaia finally reached the edge of the soft sand and fell to her knees. Steve plopped down on her right and I took the left. Kaia pulled her bag to her lap and unzipped it.

"Tell me you got some of that Purple Kush!" Steve's eyes lit up.

"Better." Kaia smiled and pulled a jar from her bag.

"What could be—"

"One hundred percent pure grade Acacia Farms Orange Blossom Honey," she exclaimed, and held the jar up like the Holy Grail.

Steve bolted upright. "No way!"

"Where'd you get that?"

"They had it in the lobby store. You guys creamed your jeans so much over it, I had to try it."

"But the lobby store is closed," I added lamely.

"I just batted my eyelashes."

"That a girl," Steve said.

"And when they said no, I gave them a little taste of Angry Prom Girl."

Steve laughed and nudged her. "You are one gangsta bitch!"

"You know I am." Kaia laughed and popped open the jar.

Steve went to shove in his finger, but Kaia blocked him.

"Ladies first, Mr. Eager." She whisked a dollop off the top and we watched as she tasted the gooey glob. Steve and I exchanged an excited look, anticipating the moment. Then, just like we'd hoped— "Holllllyyyy shit, guys. What the fuck is in that?"

Steve shoved his finger in and said, "It's bee vomit."

"Double vomit," I clarified, and plopped my finger next to his.

"You guys are disgusting," Kaia said.

The honey burst in my mouth and I felt a ripple of sugary pleasure explode through my body. It was better than last time. Was it just the brand? Or was it me? I wasn't sure, but I felt it in my legs and my stomach and my chest and they all expanded with the flavor.

We took turns dunking our fingers and savoring the sweet perfection. The moon shimmered on the ocean, which surged and retreated in front of us.

"Hey, Cam, do you think your shark is out there murdering innocent children because you set him free?" Steve asked.

"No. He's a pescatarian," I said, and gave him a sly smile. Kaia high-fived me and Steve laughed.

"You're getting too quick for me, Cambone."

We polished all of it off and then soaked in the aftertaste.

Steve sighed.

Kaia sighed.

I sighed.

Then Kaia tossed the empty jar behind her and, to our surprise, put her arms around us. "Promise me we'll do this next prom, whomever we go with."

"Deal," Steve and I said at the same time.

With all that Steve would have to go through, the thought of next year was comforting. We would still be there for Steve. We would still be there for each other. Even though the ocean was still rising. And the coral reefs were still dying. And the rain forests were still burning.

I knew that today was the day I wasn't going to ask anyone for proof that I was okay.

Acknowledgments

Writing books is a joy and a privilege, so we'd like to thank everyone who makes our lifestyle of sitting in coffeeshops possible.

Brianne Johnson, agent extraordinaire and person-we-very-much-enjoy-getting-a-drink-with (it seriously sucks we live on opposite coasts), thanks for all your continued support, encouragement, and for laughing at our jokes. Alexandra Levick, Cecilia de la Campa, and everyone else at Writers House, thanks for all your work at getting Cam, Steve, and Kaia's story out in the world.

To the unstoppable Mary Pender and everyone at UTA, thank you for your ferocious belief in our story.

Hannah Ozer and Ben Neumann, thank you for all your hard work and support.

Alyson Day, our wonderful, tireless editor, thank you for your guidance and helping us dig deeper into our characters' journeys. Megan Ilnitzki and the rest of our team at HarperTeen, thank you for all the hours you put in and for letting us know exactly how much Cardi and Kelly we can legally get away with. Joel Tippie and Estudio Santa Rita, thank you for your beautiful book design and for bringing our characters to life. It's really hard to get cancer-love-triangle-with-sharks in one image.

Personal thank-you time!

Jenni, here. Thank you so much to Warren, Clark, and Calvin. I love you guys so much. Best family ever. Clark and Calvin, sorry once again I wrote a book without pictures that you aren't allowed to read. Someday, I promise.

Ted, thanks for writing with me and entertaining ideas that start with, "but what if there is a shark?" While having a writing partner doesn't seem to halve the workload, it does make it a lot more fun.

Finally, I'd like to send love to my mom, a breast cancer survivor, to my father-in-law, Keith, a colon cancer survivor, and to my friend Maggie, a Stage 4 Lung Cancer Thriver (seriously; it's on her business cards).

Fuck cancer.

Okay, Ted here now, and I've got a few thank-yous as well. First and foremost to my wife, Kirsten. I couldn't ask for a better partner, and can listen to her yell at the news all night long. Also, my two amazing kids, Andrew and Ione. They are the light of my life and I can't wait until they can read this book and tell me there's too much cursing.

And now a thanks back to Jenni. I'd be disappointed if your ideas didn't start with something like, "what if there's a shark." I can't wait to see what the next crazy idea is!

My mother (Bubby) and father (Pop) also deserve a big shout-out for all the love and support they've showered on me. To be clear, they are in no way like the parents in this book, even though they went through something similar.

When I was twelve, we lost my brother to lymphoma. Watching him go through the illness for two years, it was clear how hard he worked to be strong through the whole awful thing. Acknowledging him seems a little small, and this book is certainly not a fitting tribute. But I know he's watching over me and I'd like to hope that I've made him laugh once or twice and, more important, that he sees that he's remembered always.